Alasdhair. His name—the name she hadn't allowed herself to think, never mind say, for fear of the pain it caused—shimmered into her mind.

Her Alasdhair, he'd been once. Fleetingly.

Somehow, Ailsa found the courage to step through the gate and into his presence. It were better they get this over now, with no one else around. It had to be done. The pain would ease after this, as it did when a wound was lanced.

'Alasdhair?'

Pain, pure and bright as the sharpest needle, pierced him.

Ailsa.

She sounded different. Her voice was older, of course, and lower—husky rather than musical—but he'd recognise her anywhere.

'Ailsa.' Her name felt rusty with disuse. His voice sounded hoarse.

They stared silently at each other. Six long years. They stood as if set in amber, drinking in the changes the years had wrought…

AUTHOR NOTE

Highland Scots have a long and successful history of emigration to North America. Jacobites on the run, impoverished lairds and dispossessed crofters alike sought fame and fortune in the New World in their droves during the eighteenth and early nineteenth centuries in a bid to escape persecution or poverty. Some failed, some returned home, but many, like Alasdhair my hero, carved out a very successful life for themselves.

At the same time entrepreneurial Glaswegian merchants were taking advantage of the favourable Trade Winds to cross the Atlantic quicker than their English counterparts. Their clippers laden with consumer goods difficult to obtain in the New World, these canny Scots willingly granted the plantation owners credit with which to buy their goods—something their English counterparts were reluctant to do. Returning with a cargo of tobacco (and, sadly, in many cases slaves), the Tobacco Lords, as they came to be known, became rich on the proceeds, and by the middle of the eighteenth century completely dominated the trade. It was a logical step for plantation owners such as Alasdhair to enter into a business deal with these distributors, ensuring the best price for his own produce. It was actually the research I did for an article about Glasgow's Merchant City, home of the Tobacco Lords, which planted the seed for Alasdhair's story.

As a historian and writer of historical romances, authenticity matters a lot to me. As a Scot, evoking the true ambience of the Highlands is also something I'm passionate about. Though Errin Mhor, where this story is set, doesn't actually exist, I know exactly where it is: on the west coast, near Oban. All the surrounding places mentioned in Alasdhair and Ailsa's story are real places in my native Argyll. The *Tigh an Truish*, a drovers' inn on the Isle of Seil, so called because it was where Highlanders going any further south swapped their plaids for trews, is still there today, as are many of the little ferry and drovers' inns which would have provided my hero and heroine with shelter on their journey. They visit Inverary at the time the present-day castle was being built. In order to secure the view, the Duke of Argyll really did have the original fishing village 'moved' a few hundred yards along the banks of Loch Fyne, where the town, with its Palladian frontage, remains to this day.

If you visit Argyll you won't find Errin Mhor, but I hope that you'll discover for yourself the essence of it, which is far more beautiful than anything I could ever describe.

THE HIGHLANDER'S RETURN

Marguerite Kaye

First published in Great Britain 2011
by Mills & Boon, an imprint of Harlequin (UK) Limited.
Large Print edition 2012
Harlequin (UK) Limited, Eton House, 18-24 Paradise Road,
Richmond, Surrey TW9 1SR

© Marguerite Kaye 2011

ISBN: 978 0 263 22501 3

Harlequin (UK) policy is to use papers that are natural,
renewable and recyclable products and made from wood grown in
sustainable forests. The logging and manufacturing process conform
to the legal environmental regulations of the country of origin.

Printed and bound in Great Britain
by CPI Antony Rowe, Chippenham, Wiltshire

Born and educated in Scotland, **Marguerite Kaye** originally qualified as a lawyer but chose not to practice. Instead, she carved out a career in IT and studied history part-time, gaining a first-class honours and a master's degree. A few decades after winning a children's national poetry competition, she decided to pursue her lifelong ambition to write, and submitted her first historical romance to Mills & Boon. They accepted it, and she's been writing ever since.

You can contact Marguerite through her website at www.margueritekaye.com

Previous novels by the same author:

THE WICKED LORD RASENBY
THE RAKE AND THE HEIRESS
INNOCENT IN THE SHEIKH'S HAREM
  (part of *Summer Sheikhs* anthology)
THE GOVERNESS AND THE SHEIKH
THE HIGHLANDER'S REDEMPTION*

Highland Brides

and in Mills & Boon® Historical *Undone!* eBooks:

THE CAPTAIN'S WICKED WAGER
THE HIGHLANDER AND THE SEA SIREN
BITTEN BY DESIRE
TEMPTATION IS THE NIGHT
THE SHEIKH'S IMPETUOUS LOVE-SLAVE

For J, my own Highland hero! Again.
And again. And always. Just love.

Prologue

The Highlands, Scotland—Summer 1742

The sun was just beginning to set as they made sail for home and Errin Mhor. They had spent an idyllic day on the largest of the scattered string of islands known locally as the Necklace. The Highland sky was streaked with pink and burnished gold, slowly turning to crimson as the sun made its stately journey towards the horizon. The little skiff, *An Rionnag,* bobbed her way across the silver-tipped waves towards shore, her single sail catching the faint breeze that had risen with the turning of the tide.

Alasdhair sat in the stern, one hand keeping a loose hold on the tiller, the other arm resting along the side of the boat. They'd made this trip so many times he could probably navigate it blindfolded. He was sitting with his usual casual grace, bare-footed and bare-legged, wearing only his plaid and an old shirt, open at the neck. Facing him, from her seat in the prow, Ailsa smiled contentedly. It was her sixteenth birthday, which meant, Alasdhair had reminded her this morning, according to tradition that she was an adult now, free to do anything she wanted. All she had ever wanted was to escape, to get away from the oppressive atmosphere of the castle, released from the autocratic iron rule of her father and the cold indifference of her mother. But Ailsa knew that it wasn't as simple as that. As a laird's daughter, her life wasn't hers to dictate. The clan and duty took precedence over personal desires. But on a day like this, what better place to escape to, albeit temporarily, than the island. *Their* island. On board *The Star.* With Alasdhair.

Her skin felt tight from the salty sea-spray and the heat of the sun. Her hair had escaped its braid as usual, curling wildly down her back, reaching almost to her waist. She felt pleasantly tired; the kind of contented lethargy that comes from a day spent laughing and lazing with no one but themselves to please.

A perfect day. As ever, she and Alasdhair had been in total accord. Despite the five-year gap that separated them, they had always been close. Closer still since Ailsa's older brother Calumn, Alasdhair's boyhood friend, had left Errin Mhor to join the Redcoat army. Now that it was just the two of them at the castle, they spent even more of their free time in each other's company. The laird's much-neglected daughter and his rebellious ward, kindred spirits united by adversity—for neither of them felt wanted, neither was loved.

She had known him all her life, the young man seated opposite her, his dark brown eyes closed as he tilted his face back to catch the last of the sun's rays. His hair, the blue-black of a raven's wing, tangled and unkempt, grew almost to his shoulders—shoulders that strained at the seams of the old shirt he wore. She'd noticed earlier, as they sat fishing from the rocks, how much he seemed to have filled out of late. What had been skin and bone was now sculpted with muscle and sinew. He was no longer all sharp angles, but quite definitely contoured. A sprinkling of silky black hair grew over his chest, his forearms and his muscular legs, that had lost their stork-like appearance. Alasdhair wasn't a laddie any more, but a man. And, Ailsa realised of a sudden, as if looking at him for the first time, an extremely attractive one at that.

Her heart did a funny little skipping movement, a hop and a jump, giving her a fluttery feeling in her stomach, as if there were a shoal of herrings—silver darlings—swimming about in there. *When had all these changes happened? Why hadn't she noticed until now?*

Alasdhair opened his eyes, pushing his hair back from his high brow, and smiled lazily at her. His mouth always curved readily into a smile. It was made for smiling, despite the fact that life had given him little to smile about. Ailsa smiled back.

Her smile was dazzling, Alasdhair thought. There was something about Ailsa, a natural exuberance, that always made him feel as if nothing was quite as bad as it seemed. Despite her mother's indifference and her father's tyranny, Ailsa had a love of life that was infectious. Alasdhair held out his hand. 'Come and sit up here with me and watch the sunset,' he said, making room for her on the narrow bench.

He watched as Ailsa picked her way daintily towards him. Her skirt and petticoat were old, a faded grey that was once the same vibrant blue as her eyes. Her *arisaidh* lay discarded at her feet. She had no jacket or waistcoat, only her sark, the ties at the neck loose. The wide sleeves of the shift billowed out over her arms, that were tanned a light biscuity colour. Her fair hair, streaked almost white in places by the sun, trailed in a cloud down her back, wispy curls haloing her forehead. He saw it then, so clearly he couldn't understand why he hadn't realised it before. She was beautiful.

As she sat down beside him, her skirts brushing his plaid, awareness shot through him. He could feel her thigh, warm and soft through the fabric of her skirts. Her forearm touched his, slim and elegant, the wrist delicate, so tiny he could circle it with his fingers. She smelled of sea and sand and pure Scots air.

Ailsa, the feisty wee lassie he had taught to ride and to fish, and to sail, and even, at her urging, how to use a dirk. It was with that wee Ailsa he had spent the day, but it was a different one who was in the boat now, her scent making it impossible for him not to notice her. This Ailsa, the enticing creature sitting next to him, her arm resting on his, her hair tickling his face, the contours of her breasts outlined by the breeze pressing against her sark, was someone quite different from the girl he'd sailed out with only this morning. This Ailsa was a sensual creature, with distracting curves and a tantalising presence.

Desire lurched at him, sending the blood surging to his groin. Embarrassed, Alasdhair shifted in his seat. Under the pretence of tightening the sail, he looked at her and wondered if he had been blind. The long neck. The tender hollow of her throat. The soft swell of her bosom. The indent of her waist. The elegant line of her calves. Her ankles, the slender high-arched feet that rested on a lobster creel that lay on the bottom of the boat, so delicately beautiful he had an overwhelming urge to press his lips to them.

How had he failed to notice this remarkable transformation?

He swung *An Rionnag* round to catch the wind. The tiller jerked violently as the sail filled and instinctively Ailsa reached out to help try to control it. Her hand met Alasdhair's on the worn wood. Something sparked at the contact, a crackle in the air like the drop in pressure that presages a tide turning or a storm coming. Blue eyes, almost purple, met smoky brown. They looked at each other as if seeing for the first time. As if being for the first time.

Alasdhair's breath caught in his throat. His stomach tightened. 'Ailsa?'

She felt as if she had been waiting for this moment all her life. As if everything in the world, the stars, the sun and moon, had been waiting too for this time and this place and this man. As if they were about to emerge from their chrysalises, transformed, readied for their real purpose. This moment. This perfect, perfect moment.

'Alasdhair.' Even his name seemed different. He hardly dared touch her, but he was hardly able not to. He tenderly stroked the wisps of curls away from her forehead. He kissed the fair brows. She closed her eyes, tilting her face towards him. He kissed the sunburnt tip of her nose. It was lightly scattered with freckles. She sighed. He put his arm around her. She nestled closer. Her bare foot brushed his. It was the most erotic thing that had ever happened to him. The arch of her sole. The tickle of her toes, curling delightfully on his.

Then his lips found hers and he kissed her, and in that second where their lips met, that awkward moment of his inexperience and her untouched lips, he knew. And he knew, from the crackling of the air around them, the stillness of sea, the suspension of *The Star*'s rocking, he knew that she knew, too—how could she not? For their kiss had changed the world for ever.

His kiss was gentle, too gentle to be sufficient, already more than he had ever dreamed of. He was afraid to frighten her with the depths of passion even this almost innocent caress aroused in him. He was horribly conscious of the five-year gap in experience that lay between them, astounded, astonished at the way her untutored, naïve touch set him afire.

It had always been he who protected her when she courted danger. It was always he who came to her rescue when she came to grief—and she often did, for she was fearless. It was always he who was there to pick her up and dust her down and dry her tears and promise not to tell. He who kept her safe.

He did so now, forcing himself to end their embrace, to put her from him, though his body sang and pleaded and begged him not to and Ailsa, too, murmured a soft, breathy protest in a voice he'd never heard before. A voice that whispered over his senses like a siren. He had never felt such a whirlwind of emotions storming through him, yet he had enough, just enough, control left. He would not take advantage. Despite her mother's poor opinion of him, he was an honourable man.

Ailsa struggled for breath. She touched her lips with her fingertips. *So that was what it was like to be kissed!* Heady, as if she'd had too much wine or too much sun. Frothy like the waves. Exciting like a sudden summer storm. *That was a kiss.*

'Ailsa, I didn't mean—I should not have—you know I would never take advantage.'

'Don't be daft, of course I know that.' She smiled at him, daringly taking his hand and pressing it to her cheek. It was a nice hand, though it was callused from the endless menial jobs her father doled out, his way of trying to bring Alasdhair's rebellious spirit under control—teaching him his proper place in the scheme of things. Her father would have a long wait, she thought.

'Are you sure I didn't frighten you?' Alasdhair asked.

She shook her head.

'I don't know what came over me. I felt as if I was seeing you properly for the first time.'

'That's exactly how I felt.'

They laughed. Then they kissed again, and

this time their kiss was more confident. It had the tantalising sweetness of a promise not yet bloomed to full ripeness. Tentative, like all new-born things, and heady, like all things strange and illicit.

The tilt of the boat on the crest of a wave, the scrape of her keel on the first of the rocks that bordered the shore, finally brought them to their senses. They laughed in unison when they realised how far they had travelled without noticing. With the ease of familiarity and long practice, they set about bringing *An Rionnag* into the castle's little private jetty where the laird's own boat, embossed with the Munro coat of arms and with places for sixteen oarsmen, took pride of place. Leaping on to shore, Alasdhair eyed it with a mixture of disdain and trepidation. *Dread God,* was the Munro motto. He doubted the laird did. Lord Munro bowed to no one. He alone owned his world, his fiefdom and all the people in it. A feudal laird in every sense, even his wife and children were there to do his bidding. Looking up, Alasdhair saw the shadow of a figure at the long windows that overlooked the castle's gardens.

'Mother,' Ailsa said anxiously, following his gaze. 'I didn't tell her where I was going.'

'Do you think she'll have had plans?'

'For my birthday?' Ailsa laughed scornfully. 'I doubt she'll even have remembered it's today.'

'Do you want me to come in with you?'

'You'll only make her worse if she's in one of her moods.' The brightness of the day was fading with the sun, that had almost set. Her mother was waiting for her, she could sense her brooding presence. 'I'd better go to her, get whatever it is out of the way.'

'Ailsa?'

'Aye?'

'Today. It was special.'

Ailsa smiled. 'Yes it was, Alasdhair, the most wonderful thing that has ever happened to me.'

'And me.' He wanted to kiss her again. He hated it ending like this, under Lady Munro's watchful gaze. In the gloaming, they should be nothing but shadows, but Alasdhair wasn't convinced she couldn't see in the dark, like some malevolent wildcat. 'One day,' he said, satisfying himself with pressing Ailsa's hand, 'we'll be together for always and then every day will be special like today.'

'One day, and for always,' she agreed.

It was a promise. A solemn vow they both intended to keep.

Chapter One

Spring 1748

The drums had been beating out their grim message for over a week now. Highlanders had gathered from near and far on this most sombre day for the burial of Lord Munro, Laird of Errin Mhor. In the great hall of Errin Mhor castle, the coffin stood on its bier, draped in a black velvet mort-cloth embroidered in gold thread with the Munro motto, *Dread God*. It was the same cloth that had adorned the coffin of Lord Munro's father, and his father before him.

Ailsa Munro leaned precariously out of the tiny window of the small turret room that she had claimed for her own parlour, the better to survey the gathering mourners. Tall as she was, the window was built high into the wall, requiring her to stand on tiptoe. Had any one of the mourners chosen to look up, they'd have caught a charming glimpse of the laird's daughter, her distinctive golden hair piled precariously high on her head, her vibrant blue eyes alight with interest, looking rather more like a princess from a fairy story waiting to be rescued than a grieving daughter about to join a funeral procession.

The mourners, however, were too intent on passing the time of day with each other and speculating upon the likely changes the laird's passing would entail, to bother with looking up. Auld enemies and allies alike mingled in the weak spring sunshine. Kith and kin, and a few—a very few—friends. For it took fortitude and a thick skin not to become for ever estranged from such a dour man, as Lord Munro had been. Downstairs, where Ailsa should be by now, the men of highest status loitered, ready to be granted the honour of bearing her father's colours, his standards, claymore, dirk and targe. Clan chiefs and neighbouring lairds, the cream of the Highland aristocracy, all had come to pay their respects. Even those who had been for the Pretender during the late Rebellion had, with the passing of Lord Munro, a staunch and vociferous supporter of the crown, come to mend fences with his son, Ailsa's brother Calumn.

The funeral of a laird. Such an occasion as this should be filled with lamentation, but for Ailsa, as for the majority of people present, the day was much more about marking the end of an era and looking to the future than mourning an old man's passing. In these fast-changing times, with the Jacobite cause defeated, Bonnie Prince Charlie fled for France, and the Government set on turning the law of the land into the weapon that would destroy the rebellious Highland clans, Lord Munro had become an anachronism, an old-fashioned feudal laird intent on keeping with tradition at any cost. He'd retained the loyalty of his people, if not their respect, but he never knew their love.

Ailsa sighed as she closed the window. Her own relationship with her father had been like the Scottish winter, she thought as she made her way, via the back stairs, to her bedchamber—cold and driech with occasional storms, when her own not inconsiderable will clashed with Lord Munro's consistently unyielding disposition. Fortunately, since the laird had been largely indifferent to his daughter's existence, and on the whole she had been at pains not to remind him of it, these confrontations had been memorable but infrequent.

Images from that worst confrontation of them all crept into her mind like spectres. Six years had passed, long enough for it to be water under the bridge. Cold, dark and icy water. Ailsa shivered and tried to banish the haunting memories from her mind. There were enough ghosts at large today already; no need to conjure up any more from the past.

She stuck a few more precautionary pins into her thick golden hair, in what she already knew was a vain effort to prevent it escaping the constraints of its bun. 'Thrawn old bugger as he was, he was still my sire,' she said aloud to her reflection. 'It would be nice if I could come up with one happy memory on the day we bury him.'

But she couldn't, though it was not for the want of trying. For old Lord Munro had been a long time dying, grimly clinging on to the thread of his existence long after his wife, his children and his doctor had given him up for gone. As in life, so in his exit from it, Lord Munro had been determined not to depart his mortal coil until he was good and ready. 'So we can't really be blamed for being more relieved than sad,' Ailsa said, continuing to speak out loud to herself, a habit developed as a child, when she had invented several friends to keep her company. Being the laird's daughter, she had not been allowed to mix with the village children. 'At least he'll have a grand send off, for this must be the most long-awaited and best-planned funeral there has been in the Highlands for many a year.'

She fixed a pretty gold brooch intricately worked with an ancient Celtic design to her dress, and surveyed her appearance in the long mirror with a critical eye. Almost without exception, everyone acquainted with Lady Munro, an acknowledged beauty, commented on the strong resemblance between mother and daughter, but Ailsa found the comparison wearisome. Frankly, the last thing she wanted to be told was that she was like her mother, but there was no getting away from it. In the last few years her hair had lost its girlish fairness, taking on the same burnished gold shade as her mother and both her brothers. Like herself though, it seemed to have rather too much of a mind of its own, and was never tamed for long. And as to her eyes—yes, they were the same striking colour as her mother's too, though not, as one swain had claimed, royal purple. They reminded Ailsa more of the purpley-blue colour of a bruise. Her face was a nice oval, and her features on the whole seemed to please people, though in her own opinion her mouth was a little too large. Did that amount to beauty? She didn't know. What she did know was that unfortunately there was no escaping the mirror's evidence—she was her mother's daughter.

Ailsa pulled a face. In her opinion, her mother had more reason than most to be relieved by Lord Munro's death, for it had by no means been a happy marriage. How could it have been, with the laird expecting unquestioning obedience, and his lady forced to forsake all others for him? Even her own children. If his death was a welcome relief, Lady Munro was doing her celebrating in private. 'Whatever it is she's feeling, she's keeping to herself as usual,' Ailsa muttered to her reflection. 'I swear it is ice and not blood which runs through Mother's veins.'

She gave the neckline of her dress a final twitch. Like all her clothes, it was an expensive garment, something her mother had insisted on since she had turned sixteen.

'I'm going to have to take you in hand, Ailsa,' Lady Munro had said firmly. 'You're not a child any more. It's time you started dressing, and behaving as befits your position as a Highland laird's daughter.'

Lady Munro had insisted on stays and lacings and stockings and all the other trappings of wealth and status, too. Not that Ailsa had anything against pretty clothes, but she felt constrained in them. Sometimes she yearned for the feel of her bare foot on sand, the sun on her neck, the freedom from corsets and lacing without having to face the recriminations that inevitably followed such minor aberrations.

Today's *toilette* was an open robe made of silk woven in the Munro colours over a dark blue petticoat. As was the fashion, the bodice was tightly laced, showing off the curve of her bosom and the contrasting tiny span of her waist. Voluptuous, is how most men would describe her, but in this one respect Ailsa would have preferred to resemble her mother's slimmer, less curvaceous figure. She was rather self-conscious about her body and despised the way it drew men's attentions. The *arisaidh*, a traditional plaid shawl of blue-striped silk, which today she wore belted and pinned, went some way to disguise it.

Her indifference to the fulsome compliments she attracted and her rejection of all attempts to make love to her seemed, perplexingly, to encourage her admirers to try all the harder. Intimacy of that sort left Ailsa cold. Her handsome dowry and position as the rich laird's only daughter ensured she had no lack of suitors, but despite the sheer volume of them, none had ever come close to touching her heart. Not in the way that…

Automatically, Ailsa put a sharp brake on that strain of thought. What was the saying? Once bitten, twice shy. She was in no need of a second lesson. Not that love entered into the equation, in any case. She existed for the sole purpose of making a good match—her father had made that abundantly clear six years ago.

The slow tolling of the bell in the castle tower began, rousing Ailsa from her reverie, its low peal reverberating out across the flat fertile Munro lands, bouncing off the mountains that bordered Errin Mhor to echo eerily in the still of the morning. The bell warded off the evil spirits that everyone knew lurked at a wake, ready to take advantage when people's defences where down. It also marked the beginnings of the funeral rites.

It was time. Pulling her *arisaidh* up to cover her hair, Ailsa quit her chamber and made her way quickly down the stairs.

* * *

In the great hall her brother Calumn, cutting an imposing figure in full ceremonial Highland dress, readied the chief mourners for his father's last journey. The low drone of the bagpipes being inflated was the signal for all to assemble in good order. The new Laird of Errin Mhor kissed his wife lingeringly on the lips. Madeleine, who was expecting their first child, would stay behind to be Lady Munro's chief comforter—not that the newly-made widow would accept comfort from anyone, but it was the custom. As it was the custom that Ailsa, too, should remain with her mother while others formed the funeral procession, but in this Ailsa had been adamant. She would pay her last respects with the men, not sit meekly at home with Lady Munro's chosen group of gentry women.

The dead laird's piper struck up the mournful lament of the pibroch. Ailsa took the black cushion bearing her father's gauntlets and hat from Calumn and made her way outside. The dead man's champion, Hamish Sinclair, waited, astride a horse with a black-velvet cover, to lead the procession. Lord Munro's own horse, similarly draped in black, was pawing nervously at the ground. Saddle-less, it was a stark symbol of the laird's absence.

Four long poles were inserted under the coffin. By tradition, the first eight bearers were the deceased's closest kin. Calumn and his half-brother Rory Macleod took the lead, a decision that had caused some controversy since Rory was not a blood relation of the dead laird, being the product of Lady Munro's first marriage. Lord Munro had insisted his wife surrender her first born upon their own marriage. Lady Munro and Rory had been estranged ever since, but Calumn had insisted that his brother have his place at the funeral regardless.

The coffin was hoisted up from the bier. The pipes wailed. The bearers walked slowly down the front steps of the castle, keeping their eyes firmly focused ahead and concentrating on the task at hand, for it was a precarious job, balancing the heavy coffin on four thin poles.

Ailsa stood at the head of the mourners.

Behind her, the long winding line of men and women fell in, ranked in order from the clan chiefs and their women to the castle servants, the laird's tenants and serfs, crofters and cotters, drovers and fishermen. She knew most of them, if not personally then by reputation. Almost without exception the men wore the two plaids, the *filleadh beg* and the *filleadh mòr,* in defiance of the law that banned Highland dress for any but the aristocracy. Most of the women wore their best Sabbath blacks. Expressions were suitably sombre. The two horses, one mounted, one riderless, led the way.

The procession wended down the castle's imposing driveway, through the heavy wrought-iron gates emblazoned with the Munro coat of arms, to the village of Errin Mhor where the first change of bearers took place. 'Twas customary for this to happen while the procession continued, so the new bearers stood ahead in formation, two lines of four men performing the transfer of weight in pairs. Since dropping a pole was believed to signify the death of the bearer, each was very careful to effect a perfect handover. Villagers, bairns and even dogs stood silent, heads bowed respectfully as the procession passed on its way. The Munro siblings remained at the front of the mourners, a striking threesome with their golden hair and tall figures, that drew the eye of every onlooker and raised a sigh in the breasts of several.

'Twas also tradition that refreshment in the form of *uisge beathe,* the water of life, otherwise known as whisky, was meted out in generous drams en route, for following a wake was thirsty work. Neither of the Munro brothers partook, but many others did. So much so that two hours later when they finally reached the lonely graveyard in a remote corner of the Munro land that was the traditional burial place of the lairds, the *uisge beathe,* combined with the steepness of the incline, the narrowness of the coffin track, and the suppressed anticipation of a long-awaited event finally coming to pass, a weariness had set in on the procession. The ordered train had become ragged. Red faces, sweaty brows and a general air of relief replaced the solemn expressions with which they had started the journey. The old laird was no light-weight.

Ailsa stepped aside at the gate, the eulogy and interment being strictly a male province. Not even she was brave enough to break that rule. She was joined by the other women. Tired and dusty, glad to have the long hike over without mishap, they stood around in little groups, by and large ignoring the ceremony at the grave-side, occupying themselves with a little light gossip and a little idle speculation, murmuring together in the low, musical lilt of the Gaelic that they continued to favour over the use of English decreed by the new law.

Ailsa roamed from one clique to another, ac-cepting the politely offered platitudes and con-dolences from those ladies she knew her mother would insist be given precedence, before joining a huddle of Errin Mhor tenants, the wives and daughters of local villagers. At the centre of the group was Shona MacBrayne, the fey wife, with whom Ailsa spent some of her days, gathering herbs and mixing potions, assisting her in tending to the sick and helping out at the occasional birth.

'I'll no insult you by saying I'm sorry, Ailsa,' Shona said in a voice too low for the others to hear. 'Your father had his time and plenty more besides. I can only pray that the journey he is taking now is up the way, and not down.'

'Whichever direction it is, you can be in no doubt that it is of my father's choosing,' Ailsa said irreverently. Like everyone else, she was beginning to feel the light-headed relief that so often occurs in the aftermath of a funeral.

Shona chuckled. 'Aye, well, at least now he's out of the way that brother of yours can finally get his hands on the Munro lands. They're in bad heart, no getting away from the fact that the old laird didnae gie them the attention they need.'

'Poor Calumn, he's been champing at the bit to make changes since he returned last year,' Ailsa agreed with a smile.

'Aye, and change is bound to put your mother's nose out of joint. However carefully he goes about things, there's going to be a stramash,'

Shona said astutely. 'You'd be better off out of it. Anyways, 'tis time you were settled in a home of your own. Your father was a long time dying; I'd no be surprised if the McNair was getting impatient to put his ring on your finger.'

Ailsa fiddled with the fastening of her brooch. 'Why should he be? My father settled things between us a while ago. The contracts are signed—what's the rush?'

Shona's brow furrowed. 'It is a good match for the clan, Ailsa. Donald McNair is a rich man, the marriage will secure us a good ally. Don't tell me you're thinking of throwing him o'er?'

'Of course not. I'm perfectly well aware of how good a match it is. My father would not have made it otherwise.'

'And you, lass. What do you think of it all?'

'What does it matter what I think?' Ailsa said dismissively. Seeing the shocked look on old Shona's face, she realised she had been indiscreet. One thing to think such things, quite another to share them with her father's—brother's—tenants. She touched the old woman's arm. 'I like him well enough. As well as he likes me, any road. Donald and I have an understanding, Shona.' Ailsa stooped to give her a quick hug. 'Don't fash yourself over me, for there's no need. I can take care of myself.'

'Aye, that's true enough,' Shona agreed sadly. 'Your mother—'

But at this point they were interrupted by the blacksmith's wife wanting Shona's opinion on the best way to treat her husband's aching joints. Ailsa wandered off, staring abstractedly down at the winding coffin track. Shona was right, it was high time she was wed. She had agreed to the betrothal eventually. Donald, her father's choice, was handsome enough, in a stern way. Why not? she'd thought at the time. What other fate was there in store for her save spinsterhood and dependence? At least this way she would have a home of her own.

Yet, once the papers were signed, she had found herself curiously reluctant to act. She had procrastinated and pleaded the mitigating circumstances of her father's illness. Now his death meant she had run out of excuses and her fate loomed dishearteningly ahead of her. She'd persuaded herself that her father's death would be liberating, but instead of feeling free she felt even more trapped and constrained.

She'd also hoped that his death would be the catalyst for the thawing in her relationship with her mother, but Lady Munro had, if anything, retreated even further behind the invisible barrier that separated her from her daughter. Ailsa had thought herself too inured to her mother's coldness to be hurt by it. She discovered that she was not.

What she needed was a different sort of change, though she had no idea what that could possibly be. Marriage to Donald McNair did not feel like the answer, though deep in her heart she knew it was her fate. There was no avoiding duty, another hard-learned lesson. The carefree lass she had once been was long gone. Her future, which for a few magical hours six years ago had seemed such a glittering place, now loomed, lacking lustre and faintly intimidating.

Ailsa wandered over to the cemetery gate. Calumn was still speaking, the attention of all the men fixed firmly on him. Turning back to rejoin Shona, she was startled by a tall, black-clad figure.

He seemed to appear from nowhere. One minute the coffin track was empty, the next minute there he was. Ailsa jumped out of his way, but he barely seemed to notice her, so intent was he on reaching the ceremony at the graveside. She had an impression of a strikingly handsome face, a fall of black hair, and then he was through the gate, standing at the back of the male mourners with his hat in his hand.

Her curiosity well and truly roused, Ailsa leaned over the crumbling dry-stone dyke that formed the graveyard's boundary. Something about the man's stance seemed familiar. Something about the way he held his head, the way he stood, his hands, holding his hat and gloves, clasped behind his back. He was a tall man, taller even than Calumn. His curtain of hair, which she saw now was not black, but the blue-black of a raven's wing, brushed a pair of exceedingly broad shoulders.

Her heart began to thump heavily. *It could not be!* A passing resemblance merely, that was all.

The stranger wore riding boots, highly polished under the dust of travel. Black breeches clung to his long legs. A black coat of expensive cut with full skirts and heavy cuffs accentuated his well-built frame. White lace ruffles on his shirtsleeves covered tanned hands. In comparison to the other men, he had an air of sophistication, of foreignness even, yet he stood there for all the world as if he belonged. The agility with which he had climbed the hill was impressive, too. His dress might proclaim him the wealthy city gentleman, but his body was that of a Highlander.

It could not possibly be him, yet part of her was absolutely certain it could be no one else.

But Alasdhair Ross was banished!

Six years ago he had left and not a word since. It could not be him, it made no sense. Why would he come back after all this time? And though he looked like him, this stranger was far too self-assured and far too sophisticated to be Alasdhair. If it was him, he had not just changed, he had been transformed.

It could not be him, Ailsa told herself. It couldn't be.

She had just about persuaded herself when he moved, turning fractionally to the side so that she could see his profile. Her heart, encased in ice since the day he left, gave a sickening lurch, like an animal woken too soon from hibernation, and in that instant she knew.

Just a fleeting glance she caught before he turned away again, but it was enough. He was clean shaven. A strong jaw, with a mouth held in an austere line, but it was the same mouth that always used to quirk up in a half-smile. Fine lines around his eyes, grooves running from mouth to nose, his face deeply tanned. But they were the same eyes, dark brown, peat-smoked, under brows heavy and black, almost meeting in the middle. A forbiddingly handsome face, harder and more defined than the good-looking young man she remembered, who had not had this mature man's air of authority. But it was still the same face.

Though she had never in her life fainted, Ailsa thought she was about to do just that. Her vision swam. Her head pounded. Her mouth was dry. She clutched at the mossy top of the cemetery wall, closed her eyes and breathed deeply.

'Tell me my old eyes are deceiving me.'

Ailsa looked up, startled.

'It *is* him, isn't it?' Shona said, nodding at the man in black. 'Alasdhair Ross, a ghost from the past, come to join all the others in the graveyard.' She chuckled. 'He was banished for challenging the laird's authority, but your father never did say why.'

'No,' Ailsa replied shortly. 'The laird was never one to explain himself.'

'You had aye time for him, did you not?' Shona probed. 'I mind now, you used to follow Ross about like a wee puppy.'

'It was a long time ago. I was very young.' Ailsa tried desperately to hold back a tear she could feel welling up. 'But, yes, I was…' She paused. 'I was very fond of him.'

'I can't blame you,' Shona said. 'He was always good looking in his own wild way, but he's turned into a right handsome devil. Made something of himself, too, judging by those clothes. Who'd have thought that Factor Ross's son would do so well? Do you think he's come back to rub our noses in it?'

'How would I know? What has it to do with me?' Ailsa said tersely. *What was he doing here?*

'Whatever he's doing, it's stirring up a few ashes.' The fey wife's low laugh was more like the cackle worthy of the witch she was sometimes called by the village bairns. 'Would you look at him, all in black, hovering over your father's corpse like Auld Clootie himself. I'm surprised we canna hear the laird spinning in his coffin.'

'Shush, Shona,' Ailsa whispered urgently, 'they'll hear us.'

Sure enough, some of the men had turned towards the disturbance, and in turning they began to take notice of the stranger. Ailsa watched as they shuffled away from Alasdhair, as if his very presence would contaminate them. She saw some of the shock she herself was feeling reflected in Calumn's face when he recognised his friend. Her heart felt as if it were being squeezed through a wringer. Her emotions were a maelstrom of anger and hurt and regret and bitterness, so that she could only clutch the stone dyke for support and watch as the man whom she had so foolishly thought the love of her life stood impassively over her father's grave.

When Alasdhair Ross left Errin Mhor six years ago, he swore never to return to the Highlands. He had dreamed of leaving since he was a wee boy, almost from that first time he'd seen the globe Lord Munro kept in his library. He couldn't get over how tiny Scotland looked, or how big the New World was in comparison. His ambition to travel to the other side of the world and make his fortune grew stronger with every passing year, weaving itself into a warm blanket that protected him through the long cold nights after his mother abandoned him and his father departed this mortal coil very shortly afterwards. It protected him, too, from the scorn and derision that his aspirations elicited from the laird, who had taken him in and become his guardian.

'Dinnae be so soft, you and your fanciful notions,' Lord Munro told him contemptuously. 'Your place is here, lad, your bounden duty to serve me. If ye're lucky and you behave yourself, I might just make you factor one day. That should be the height of ambition for the likes of you.'

But as Alasdhair grew older, his ambition to forge a new life in America became the only light at the end of the dark tunnel of subservience that was his lot as the laird's ward. The laird's property. The laird's serf.

America had been everything Alasdhair had ever dreamed of. Hard work, sound judgement and a bit of luck had paid off in spectacular fashion. Having eventually found employment in the Virginian plantation of a fellow Scot, he had, through diligence and determination, worked himself into the position of manager and trusted right-hand man before setting up his own business. It had been a tough life, but it had been worth it. Alasdhair was a very rich man, a respected plantation owner and merchant, known to be fair and honest, two qualities sometimes in shorter supply than they should be in the tobacco business. But Alasdhair's integrity meant more to him even than his wealth. He answered to no one but his own conscience. He relied on no one but himself. His life had turned out just as he'd always dreamed it would. He had proved them wrong, all of them, succeeding on his own terms, without having to pay dues to his laird. He was his own man, in his own place, and no one cared who his kin were or even where he'd come from.

Except, lately, Alasdhair had found that *he* cared, and cared deeply. Now that he had what he had always wanted, he found it was not enough. The past, which he had been too busy and too tired to even think about, was beginning to haunt him. The story of his mother's absconding with another man made less sense, the more he thought about it. Why had she left no word, nor ever tried to contact him? And his father's death. Alasdhair refused to believe that it had been anything but an accident, but he did wonder if Alec Ross had had cause to encourage the tragic fate that left Alasdhair orphaned and uprooted from his family home to become the object of Lady Munro's unrelenting hostility. Despite this, and his guardian's determination to bend his ward to his will, Alasdhair regretted the terms on which they had parted. Though his life was in Virginia now, he wanted the right to return to the home of his heart, even if he did not intend to exercise that right often, or ever.

And then there was Ailsa.

Why? The question buzzed around his head like an angry hornet. And like a hornet, the more he swatted at it, the more persistent it got.

Why? Eventually, he realised he'd have no peace until he found out, and to do that, he must return to Scotland. A clean sheet. A blank page. That is what he wanted to return to Virginia with. Then he could write whatever future he willed on to it.

Circumstances colluded with him. An opportunity to form a new partnership with a merchant in Glasgow arose, and at the same time, one of Alasdhair's own ships was about to depart for that very port.

He had arrived in Glasgow two weeks ago. Travelling north, he had reached Argyll when the tolling of the bells had alerted him to a death. Hearing it was Lord Munro, a long-awaited event after a protracted illness, he had been taken aback by the strength of the feelings that shook him. Regret that he was too late, and sorrow, of course. But anger, too, for the old man must have known his end was coming, yet he had made no attempt at amends nor to lift Alasdhair's banishment.

He was just in time to pay his last respects, having arrived at Errin Mhor on horseback only this morning. Around him, familiar faces anxious to avoid his eye. Across from him, Calumn, the new laird. He had not changed much. Broader, face etched with a few lines, but in essence his childhood friend looked exactly as he had the last time Alasdhair had seen him, setting off to join the King's army. More than ten years past now.

Memories flitted through his head as he listened to Calumn pay tribute to his father. Sharply sweet memories, piercingly painful, and the darker ones, creeping out of the recesses of his mind like whipped curs or, more appropriately, spectres at a wake. Up here, they said that opening the ground to receive fresh bones released the spirits of the old ones. Today, he could believe it.

Rousing himself from these melancholy thoughts, Alasdhair saw that Calumn was finishing the closing prayer. Standing at the head of the grave, the new Lord Munro was now receiving the formal condolences of the other men. They shuffled forwards, each shaking his hand, some pausing to mutter a prayer of their own over the gaping hole. He watched them nudging and whispering amongst themselves as they left the graveyard, casting surreptitious glances, their expressions ranging from astonishment and embarrassment to downright hostility. A few turned their backs upon him.

Alasdhair's temper simmered. What difference did it make to them, these crofters and fishermen? What did they even know of the circumstances of his leaving? Not the truth, he'd be willing to bet. It made him furious, that the corpse that lay in the damp soil could still wield the decrepit hand of influence. He did not merit such treatment. He would force them to see that.

The occasion obliged him to bide his time for the moment, but Alasdhair refused to be intimidated, holding himself rigidly upright, his hands clasped behind his back, as the men filed slowly out. At the gate they were reunited with their womenfolk, and the whispers became an excited buzz. Surveying them scornfully, ruthlessly despatching the shadowy figure on his shoulder, the unloved outcast boy he had once been, Alasdhair saw his old friend coming slowly towards him.

'Alasdhair! It really is you.'

'Calumn!'

The two men clasped each other in a bear hug of an embrace.

'It's so good to see you, old friend,' Calumn said warmly. 'I've thought of you often these past years.'

Alasdhair nodded. 'As I have you. I just wish the circumstances of our reunion were different.'

'Aye, but you're here, and that's the main thing. We have much to catch up on, but I need to get back to the castle and my guests for now, you understand, don't you? We'll talk properly tomorrow.'

'Aye, I would like that,' Alasdhair replied.

'Good. You'll come to the wake?' Calumn asked, but when Alasdhair shook his head he was not surprised. 'Till tomorrow, then.' With that, the new laird made for the gate, where the old laird's horse had been left for him.

Hidden from view by the crowd, Ailsa watched the solitary figure left in the cemetery. Alasdhair. His name, the name she hadn't allowed herself to think, never mind say, for fear of the pain it caused, shimmered into her mind. Alasdhair. A bitter name, acrid with regrets and betrayal, yet it used to be the sweetest of names. *Her* Alasdhair, he'd been once. Fleetingly.

Around her, the mourners were laughing and talking animatedly with all the gaiety that often follows a sombre farewell to the departed. Life was reasserting itself over death, but she hardly noticed them. They'd be making their way back to Errin Mhor castle for the funeral wake soon. The roast meats, the conspicuous consumption of wine, the regular toasts with whisky glasses raised, and the reminiscing, which would continue well into the night, and culminate with the funeral pyre of the laird's bedding and clothes that would be lit by his widow. She would join them. But not yet.

Not yet.

Somehow, Ailsa found the courage to step through the gate and into his presence. It were better they get this over now, with no one else around. It had to be done. The pain would ease after this, as it did when a wound was lanced.

'Alasdhair?'

Pain, pure and bright as the sharpest needle, pierced him.

Ailsa.

She sounded different; her voice was older,

of course, and lower, husky rather than musical, but he'd recognise her anywhere. He had assumed she would be back at the castle, with her mother. He wasn't sure he was ready for this.

'Ailsa.' Her name felt rusty with disuse. His voice sounded hoarse.

They stared silently at each other. Six long years. They stood, as if set in amber, drinking in the changes the years had wrought.

Chapter Two

She was taller, and had become much more statuesque in the intervening period. The soft contours of girlhood were gone; her beauty was more defined, no longer blurred by the immaturity of youth. The hair escaping its pins had darkened slightly from fair to gold. Only the wispy curls that clustered round her brow were the same. And her eyes. That strange purple-blue colour, like a gathering storm, they were exactly the same.

Ailsa.

She didn't look as if she smiled much now. She lacked the exuberance that had once so defined her. 'I hardly recognised you, you've changed so much,' Alasdhair said.

'Not as much as you.'

'That's certainly true. I'm no Munro serf to be used and abused any longer.'

Ailsa flinched. 'I never thought of you that way.'

'Aye, that's what I used to believe, until you proved me wrong.'

'What do you mean?'

'Did you think I'd have forgotten? Or forgiven?'

His face was set in forbidding lines. Everything about him was dark and intense. Had Ailsa not been so overwrought, she'd have found time to be intimidated. 'Forgotten what?' she demanded. 'That you broke your promise? One day, and for always, that's what you said.'

'And I meant it. Unlike you.'

'How dare you! I meant it too, I meant every word of it, you must have known that I would not have said it unless I did.' Ailsa's voice was trembling on the brink of tears. She bit her cheek, an old trick, to staunch the flow.

'What I know is that you played me for a fool,' Alasdhair replied coldly. 'No surprise, really, with that mother of yours as a teacher.'

'I am not anything like my mother.'

'I used to believe that too, but you proved me wrong on that score also.' Alasdhair's face was set, his smoky eyes hard-glazed.

Before she could stop them, tears filled Ailsa's eyes. She brushed them impatiently away. 'I don't know why you're being like this. If anyone has the right to be angry, it is I.'

'*You!*'

She tossed her head back, dislodging a cluster of pins. 'You left without even saying goodbye, without even trying to explain.'

A frown, so fierce his dark brows met, clouded Alasdhair's brow. He felt as if mists were clouding round the facts, obscuring them. 'That's rich coming from you. You're the one that betrayed me that night.'

'I don't understand…' She could still see him, but he was hazy, as if a haar had come down from the hills. Her knees were shaking. There was a booming in her ears. 'I'm sorry, I'm feeling a bit—I need to sit down.' Ailsa staggered over to an ancient gravestone, sinking on to it regardless of the damage the lichen would do to her robe.

'Ailsa.' She was white as a sheet. Stricken. Her eyes glazed with shock. Surely she could not be acting? Alasdhair knelt down before her, tried to take her hands between his. Even through her gloves he could feel how cold they were. Then she snatched them back.

'Please don't touch me.'

Mortified, Alasdhair got to his feet. Big eyes framed by ridiculously long lashes gazed up at him. Silver-tipped lashes. Eyes glistening with tears. He had to remind himself that he was not the cause of them. Rather it was he who was the victim.

'I'm sorry.' Ailsa sniffed and wiped her eyes with her gloves again.

Alasdhair took his handkerchief from his coat pocket and handed it to her. Silence reigned for long, uncomfortable moments. In the background, Lord Munro's final resting place was being filled in by a sexton who glanced over curiously every now and then at the intriguing scene being played out in front of him. The regular thud of sodden earth hitting the coffin lid beat a tattoo in Alasdhair's brain. For a split second they met each other's eyes. Recognition hung between them. Another ghost, almost tangible. The pure bittersweet clarity of the memory twisted his gut, sending him tumbling back to that day. Her birthday. *An Rionnag.* Their kiss. The simple joy of it. Happiness.

He closed his eyes, but it wouldn't go away. It wouldn't ever go away until he exorcised it, though the exorcism would be like ripping out his innards. It was what he had come for, after all. No matter how painful, no matter what it cost him, he would do it. 'I need to know the truth, but I don't want to talk here,' he said. 'There are more than enough ghosts here as it is.'

'We could walk to…'

He instinctively knew what she was going to say. 'The tree. How appropriate.' His sarcastic tone did not wholly disguise the jagging pain.

The old oak, reputed to be more than two hundred years old, was a favourite spot of theirs in the old days. Its branches gave shelter, its trunk formed a comfortable prop to lean against, and the views out over the bay were spectacular. They made their way towards it in silence, settling down out of a habit as they always had, side by side, Ailsa on the right, Alasdhair the left, careful to keep a gap between them that had never been there before.

Alasdhair pulled off his gloves and hat, tossing the expensive items carelessly on to the ground. In front of them, the little chain of islets could clearly be seen. The Necklace provided a natural barrier, which bore the brunt of the vicious winter storms, creating a warmer, calmer stretch of water that could be fished all year round and where, in the summer, porpoises could be seen. None of the islets were inhabited. Grey seals came to pup on the beaches. Errin Mhor's fishermen found occasional harbour waiting on the tide, and Errin Mhor's children played and swam there.

'Have you ever been back to the island?' Alasdhair asked.

Ailsa shook her head. 'No. No, I couldn't.'

Alasdhair sighed heavily. 'Why did you not come to me that last night, to say goodbye?'

'*I!* It was you who did not come to me.'

'But then…' He stopped, looking perplexed. 'I don't understand.'

'Any more than I,' Ailsa replied, 'but it is beginning to look as if neither of us is in possession of the whole story.'

She looked so forlorn that he automatically reached for her hand, drawing back only at the last moment. 'I'm not interested in your excuses, Ailsa, not after all this time,' he said bitterly. 'I just want to know the truth.'

'I'm not lying,' she replied indignantly. 'I really did think you'd left without a word.'

'How could you have thought I would treat you like that?'

'I don't know. I didn't. I mean—I was—I thought—' Ailsa broke off and took a couple of deep breaths. 'Maybe if you could tell me what happened? What you think happened, I mean, then I could tell you what I thought, and…'

'And out of the two halves we might just get a whole, you mean?' He wasn't ready. Ancient history as the tale was, there were parts of it so raw he had barely allowed himself to look too closely at them. But it was what he had come for, wasn't it—to throw the dust covers off the story?

'All right. I'll tell you my truth, but you must swear that you'll tell me your own in turn. I want no lies, Ailsa.'

'I swear.'

He stared at her for a long moment, at the big blue eyes that had never lied to him before, the set look on her face, as if she were girding herself for an ordeal, and that was so like how he felt himself that he believed her. 'Very well.'

Alasdhair closed his eyes, blocking out the beautiful view and the distractingly beautiful face and took a tentative step back into the past, to a time when he was not Alasdhair Ross, the rich and successful tobacco merchant, but Alasdhair Ross, the outcast. He took another step, and another, until he was back where it all began and it all ended, on Ailsa's sixteenth birthday, six years ago, and the past became the present.

Summer 1742

The world had changed irrevocably with that single kiss. The future burned bright and hopeful, a glittering place they would inhabit together.

How? Well that would have to wait until later. For the moment, Alasdhair's burning desire to grasp this new world order held sway, such overwhelming sway that immediately after leaving Ailsa at the castle he went in search of Lord Munro. He needed to declare himself, and he needed to do it as soon as possible.

He had not allowed himself to think of failure, so when it came, as it did almost immediately, it was a shock. It should not have been—he knew perfectly well the laird's views on his position—but love, Alasdhair had naïvely believed, could conquer all. It had given him confidence. Greatly misplaced confidence, as it turned out.

'How dare you! The de'il take you, boy!' Lord Munro rapped his walking stick furiously on the flagstones of the great hall.

The steel tip of the stick made a harsh grating

sound. The deerhound that had been sleeping at the laird's feet rose and let loose a low menacing growl. Alasdhair gritted his teeth.

'Do ye have no sense of your place, boy? No sense of what you owe me? I took ye in when your ain mother abandoned ye and yon weak-willed man you call father upped and died on you as a result. I as good as own ye, and this is how ye repay me?'

Lord Munro got shakily to his feet. He had been a tall man once, but age and gout had taken their toll on his frame—though they could not be blamed for his temper, which had always been foul. Leaning heavily on the stick, he glowered at the upstart in front of him. 'Obviously staying here in the castle has given ye an inflated idea of your own importance, boy.'

Inflated! Between them, the laird and his lady made sure there was no chance of that. Like the deerhound, Alasdhair's hackles were up, but he forced himself to uncurl the fists that had formed in his work-calloused hands and to look the old man firmly in the eye. 'If you mean I'm ambitious, Laird, then you're in the right of it. You know fine that I've no intention of staying here to work as your factor. I've always dreamed of going to the New World and I will one day, but first I want your permission to court Ailsa. We have feelings for each other. I want to marry her and take her with me to America as my wife.'

Lord Munro snorted contemptuously. 'You insolent upstart. Do ye really think I'd allow my daughter to be courted by the likes o' you? You're a serf, and what's more you're my serf. It's high time ye remembered that. You've as much chance of marrying Ailsa as ye have of realising yon pipe dream of yours of making your fame and fortune abroad. Your place is here and your future mapped out. You'll be my factor and a good one, I don't doubt.'

Lord Munro looked at Alasdhair appraisingly. 'I like you well enough, lad, you know that. You've got spirit, but you haven't got the brains you were born with if you think there's any point in pursuing this farcical notion. Now away with you, before I lose my temper.'

Alasdhair's hands formed into two large fists.

He had tried to do the honourable thing. He'd asked permission, and he'd asked on all but bended knee. He deserved better than to be so casually dismissed. 'What about Ailsa?'

'What about her?' Lord Munro snapped. 'I'm her father. I can do what I want with her, just as I can do what I want with you, Alasdhair Ross.'

'She loves me.'

'I've no doubt she's smitten with you,' he snorted. 'She's at that age. But if she's an itch, it's most certainly not for you to scratch. I've plans for Ailsa, and I'll no' have you damaging the goods.'

'What if Ailsa has other plans of her own?'

'She's a Munro born and bred, she kens fine what her duty is and she'll put it before an impetuous cur like you.'

'I don't believe you.'

Lord Munro's tenuous hold on his temper snapped. 'You will keep your filthy hands off her, do you hear me?' he roared. 'Ailsa is the very last wench you should be thinking about in that way. You'll keep away from her, do you hear me now? I'm not having Donald McNair accusing me of allowing someone else to plough his furrow.'

'McNair!'

'The Laird of Ardkinglass. 'Tis a fine match,' Lord Munro said with a satisfied smile.

'Damn the match, fine or otherwise! Ailsa and I love each other and nobody, not even you, can change that. I am sorry to have to disobey you, but you give me no choice. I will court Ailsa and you cannot stop me.'

Lord Munro's stick clattered on the flagstones. 'Am I hearing right? After all I have said to ye, ye still insist on disobeying? Do you think I can't stop you? You can think again about that, laddie, for I can.'

Alasdhair glared at him defiantly. 'You can try, but you won't succeed.'

Lord Munro looked at him in absolute astonishment, then he threw back his head and laughed. It was a deeply unpleasant sound and should have been a warning, but Alasdhair was far too caught up in the heady throes of fighting for his love to notice. 'You think to defy me, do you? I'd think again, if I were you, Alasdhair Ross. This is your last chance.'

'I won't change my mind,' Alasdhair said mutinously.

The Laird of Errin Mhor's mouth formed into a thin line. 'So be it. I see now I've given you too much rope. I won't tolerate defiance, no matter who you are. You will keep away from my daughter, Alasdhair Ross, for now and for ever. And you will keep off all Munro lands, too, until the end of your days.' Lord Munro leant on his stick and drew himself painfully up to his full height. 'You are banished. Do you hear me?' he shouted, pointing a finger straight at Alasdhair. 'From this moment on you are dead to me and dead to all my clan. Hamish Sinclair will escort you off the Munro lands. I want you gone by midnight, and if I find you've made any attempt to see my daughter before then, I'll have you thrashed. Away to hell with you. Or, better still, away to America. From what I hear of that savage land ye'll be hard pushed to tell the difference.'

Lord Munro spat contemptuously on to the

flagstones. 'You disappoint me. I thought you had the makings of a man, Alasdhair Ross. I took you in, I indulged your rebellious nature even though it sore tested my patience, but I see now that you are a naïve, romantic fool. It is your own foolishness that has brought this upon your head. Now get out of my sight.'

Alasdhair strode down the corridor from the great hall, his face like thunder, cursing his own stupidity. He should have known better. If only he had thought it through, or bided his time, instead of rushing in with guns blazing like that. He had ruined everything with this one impetuous act.

He had to see Ailsa. He had to explain. He could not take her with him yet, but if she would wait for him—surely she would wait for him? He would go to America and he would make his fortune and he would come back for her and Lord Munro would eat his words and they would be married. It would take him a year or two, but what were a couple of years with so much at stake? She would understand, surely she would understand. Ignoring the laird's dire warning, Alasdhair strode off in search of her.

'And where do you think you're going?' An icy voice stopped him in his tracks.

'Lady Munro!'

'Alasdhair Ross.' She looked at him with her customary disdain. 'I do most sincerely hope you have no plans to further inflict your company on my daughter.'

'What are you talking about?'

A glint like a flame reflected in a frozen pond came into her eye. 'Your rather inept attempts at love-making have frightened her.'

'You lie! Ailsa said—'

Lady Munro smiled coldly. 'My daughter, Mr Ross, is too tender-hearted for her own good. She did not wish to hurt you with a rejection.'

'That's not true.'

'Ailsa is just sixteen. Much too young to know her own mind, and very much too immature to be the subject of your animal lusts.'

'I took no liberties with your daughter,' Alasdhair growled, 'my intentions were completely honourable. You can check with the laird, if you don't believe me.'

'What has my husband to do with this?' Lady Munro asked sharply.

'I am just come from asking his permission to court your daughter.'

'And what did he say?'

'He said exactly what you would wish him to say,' Alasdhair informed her bitterly. 'That I had ideas above my station. But before you start celebrating, you should know that *I* informed *him* that it wouldn't make any difference. I won't give her up, even though I am banished.'

'The laird has exiled you?'

'Aye. And don't pretend you're anything other than glad, for you've always hated me.'

Lady Munro pursed her lips. 'So you are finally to leave Errin Mhor. What do you intend to do?'

'What I've always intended. I'm going to make a life for myself in America. Then I'll come back for Ailsa. She'll wait for me, I know she will.'

Lady Munro's eyes narrowed. 'I don't think

so, Mr Ross. Lord Munro and I have other plans for my daughter.'

'I know all about your plans, the laird told me. But Ailsa loves me, she won't let you marry her off to Donald McNair, no matter how good a match it is. She'll wait for me, and I'll prove you wrong, all of you. I'll be every bit as good a match.'

'No.' Lady Munro's voice was like cut glass. 'No. My daughter's place is here and she knows it.'

'I don't believe you. I don't have time for this. Let me by, for I must see Ailsa before I go. I must explain to her that—'

'Would you believe her if she told you herself?' Lady Munro interrupted him ruthlessly.

'What?'

'You cannot talk to her here,' Lady Munro continued, looking thoughtful now. 'You have been banished, you should not even be here, and if his lordship finds out—well, we will all suffer, including Ailsa. You would not want that, I am sure.'

'I hadn't thought of that.'

'Hmm.' Lady Munro considered him for a long moment, then finally smiled a very thin smile. 'It goes much against my better judgement, but I will speak to Ailsa. If she tells you herself how she feels, will you promise to do her the honour of believing her and leave her alone?'

'Yes, but—'

Lady Munro raised an imperious hand. 'You have vastly overestimated the strength of Ailsa's feelings for you, Mr Ross, but you need not take my word for it. I will arrange a place and time for later tonight, well away from the castle, but I warn you, there is a limit to my influence. If she cannot bring herself to turn up, she will have spoken more eloquently than words ever could and I will hold you to your promise.'

Spring 1748

Alasdhair opened his eyes. 'I waited for you like a fool, but of course you didn't turn up. I realised then that your parents were both right. I was a naïve fool to think you loved me, and even if you had cared, why should you take a chance on someone with no firm prospects who wanted to uproot you from your family and home to take you halfway round the world? I left that night and I kept my promise to your mother. I never tried to get in touch with you again.'

Beside him, Ailsa's face was pale and streaked with tears. 'Don't tell me you're feeling sorry for me,' Alasdhair said roughly. 'You're six years too late for that.'

She shook her head. 'That's not why I'm crying.' The heartache of those days crashed over her like a breaker on to the shore. Ailsa stripped off her gloves and plucked at the brooch that held her *arisaidh* in place, unfastening the clasp, then trying to fasten it again, but her hands were shaking. The pin pricked her finger and the brooch fell on to the ground.

'Here, let me.'

Alasdhair picked it up. He leaned towards her, holding the plaid in place with one hand, fastening the pin through the cloth with the other. His coat sleeve brushed her chin. His fingers were warm through the layers of her clothing. The nails were neatly trimmed. The hands immaculately clean. Tanned. Capable hands. Alasdhair's hands.

She remembered them on the tiller that day. She remembered the way she'd pressed one of them to her cheek. He'd smelled of salt and sweat. Now he smelled of soap and expensive cloth and clean linen. And Alasdhair. Something she couldn't describe, but it was him.

'There.'

He looked down at her and there it was again, for a split second. Recognition. A calling of like to like. And a yearning. She couldn't breathe. He licked his lips, as if he was about to speak. He moved towards her just a fraction. Then he pulled away, shifted so that there was a defined space between them.

'Your finger's bleeding.'

'It's nothing.' Without thinking, she put it in her mouth, sucking on the tiny cut.

Alasdhair stared, fascinated. He forced himself to look away. 'Why are you crying then, if not out of pity?' he asked roughly.

'You'll understand when you hear my side of the story. Oh, Alasdhair, you will understand only too well, as I do now.' Ailsa blinked back another tear and took a deep breath. 'You remember my mother saw us from the drawing-room window that day on our way back from the island? When I went in she was furious. Said she'd been watching how we behaved together and she was becoming very concerned.'

'Concerned about what?'

'My honour.' Ailsa laced her fingers together nervously, fidgeted with her gloves, pulling at the fingers of the soft leather, stretching them irretrievably out of shape. '"He's making cat's eyes at you." You should have heard the way she said it—she made you sound like some predatory seducer. I told her you would never do anything to harm me.'

'What did she say to that?'

'She laughed at me. She said I would learn soon enough that all men were the same. She told me I needed to keep away from you for my own good. I'm sorry, but you said you wanted the truth.'

'It's all right. I've never been under any illusions about Lady Munro's opinion of me.'

'I'm sorry, all the same. I understood my father's attitude, for you were never one to toe the line, and he was always one to expect it, from you especially for some reason, but my mother—to this day, I don't know what it was about you that made her hate you so.'

'My existence,' Alasdhair said with a flippancy he was far from feeling. There was a part of him that didn't want to hear any more, but there was another part of him that needed the whole unvarnished truth, no matter how unpalatable. 'We have wandered from the subject.'

'When my mother told me you'd been banished, I couldn't believe it. I didn't know you'd gone to my father to ask permission to court me—why would I when you'd said not a word to me? She told me you'd argued because you were set on leaving. She said you'd been banished because you'd defied him, that you'd thrown the offer of the factor's post in his face. I didn't know the real reason and had no reason at all to suspect it.'

'But, Ailsa, you knew how I felt about you— how could you have thought I'd leave without even discussing it?'

She sniffed and looked down at the ground. 'You never said what you felt in so many words.'

Alasdhair jumped to his feet. 'Because I thought we didn't need words to express what we felt for each other. For heaven's sake, Ailsa, I thought you understood that. I thought you knew me. I thought you of all people would know that I would never, ever, do anything to hurt you, never mind dishonour you. I thought you believed in me.'

She couldn't look him in the eye. Though her mother's lies were the catalyst for their separation, she felt she was more to blame. What Alasdhair said was true, she had lacked faith and was too easily persuaded. 'She laughed at me when I said you loved me. What did I know of such things, she said, and you know what she was like, Alasdhair. She made me feel like an idiot. It is not you I didn't believe in,' Ailsa whispered, 'it was myself.' That it was all too late, she knew. There was nothing she could do,

but, oh, how much she wished there was. 'I'm
sorry. I'm so sorry, Alasdhair. Please don't look
at me like that, for I can't bear it.'

He knew from bitter experience how very
practised Lady Munro was in the art of belittle-
ment, how she twisted and turned everything
into a deformed version of itself. With both her
parents assailing her, poor Ailsa would have
stood little chance. If she had only believed…
but in his heart, he knew he had not believed
enough, either. It had been too much to wish
for. Too much to deserve. 'You've no more need
to be sorry than I. I don't blame you for not
coming. I can see how it must have looked.'

'But I did come.'

'What!'

'My mother told me she had arranged for us to
meet to say goodbye. Despite her better judgement, she said, she thought it better that I hear
from you direct. It wasn't much, but it was better
than nothing, the chance to see you just one
more time. I was there at midnight as agreed.
I waited and waited, but you didn't come. I
thought you couldn't face me. You didn't love

me, but you cared enough about me not to be able to tell me that to my face. I thought my mother was right. I thought—but I was wrong. I was wrong. I was so wrong.' Ailsa shuddered as sobs racked her body.

Alasdhair ran his hand distractedly through his hair. 'I don't understand. I stood here, under this very tree—our tree—the whole time. Where were you?'

Ailsa's covered her face with her hands. *'An Rionnag,'* she whispered.

Alasdhair cursed, long and low in the Gaelic, words he thought forgotten, then he stooped down to pull Ailsa to her feet, wrapping his arms around her, unable to resist the habit of comforting her any longer. 'My God, but they made sure of separating us, your parents. Your father thought he had solved the problem by banishing me, but your mother knew different, so she set us up to think each betrayed by the other. And it worked. Between them they destroyed any chance we had of happiness.'

He stroked her hair, the way he had always done before to soothe her, but despite the familiar gesture, he felt like a stranger. She was acutely aware of him, not as the person he'd been, but of the man he had become. A man she didn't know any more. It disconcerted, this not knowing, but having known. She had no idea how to behave.

Ailsa pushed herself back from his embrace and wiped her eyes, attempting a watery smile. 'Sorry, it's not like me to cry.'

Alasdhair shook his head and returned her smile with a crooked one of his own. 'God knows, we both have reason enough.'

The wind ruffled his hair. As he shook it back from his face she noticed it, the faint white line above his left brow, made more visible by his tan. Ailsa reached up to trace the shape of it. 'The oar, do you remember?'

'Of course I remember, you nearly had me drowned.'

They had been swimming, and he was climbing back into the boat. Ailsa, struggling to slot one of the heavy oars into its lock, had slipped and the blade had gashed his brow. 'I was trying to rescue you,' she retorted. 'I thought we'd never get it to stop bleeding. You're lucky it's such a tiny scar.'

'I didn't feel lucky at the time, my head ached for days.' Her nearness was disconcerting. The memory of the girl he had once loved was retreating like a shadow at noon, fading in the bright light of the woman standing next to him. She was more different than the same. The years had not left her untouched.

He felt the softness of her curves pressing into him. Regret and wanting swamped him. It was a potent mix that overrode everything else. He pulled her to him. She did not resist. He slipped his arm around her waist, tilting her face up with his finger. She was trembling. She wanted him, too. In that moment, only for that moment, but it was enough. Without any thought of resisting, Alasdhair leaned into her. Their lips met.

Ailsa hesitated. She felt as she did sometimes, wrestling with the boat in a storm or rushing her horse at a high dyke. Exhilarated and afraid in equal measure. Her skin tugged at her, as if it had needs of its own of a sudden, needs it had never expressed. Save once.

Alasdhair felt so solid against her and so warm, the heat from him seeping into her like a dram of whisky. His lips touched hers. She sighed and the warmth spread, like fingers of sunshine on a rock. His hands on the curve of her spine nestled her closer. He angled his head and his lips seemed to mould themselves to hers.

It was breathtakingly intimate. Her heart hammered in her breast. A capricious mixture of wanting and uncertainty swept over her, a yearning for something lost. Her mouth softened under his caress. His tongue licked along the length of her bottom lip. An adult's kiss. Her first. With a soft sigh she nestled closer, touched the tip of her tongue to his. A shock sparked between them and Alasdhair brought the embrace to an abrupt end.

Taking a hasty step back, he felt a flush striping the sharp planes of his cheekbones. What the devil had he been thinking! 'Forgive me.

I should not have—I don't know what came over me.'

Colour flooded Ailsa's face. She stared up at him, wide-eyed with shock.

What did he think he was doing! He had come here to tie up loose ends, not entangle himself further, and especially not with another man's property—a fact that he had managed to forget all about in the shock of seeing Ailsa again.

'Where is McNair anyway?' Alasdhair asked roughly, furious with the man for his absence. If he had been here to take better care of his wife, this would not have occurred. 'I did not see him at the grave.'

Confused as much by the repressed anger in Alasdhair's voice, which seemed to have come from nowhere, as by the abrupt change of topic, Ailsa struggled to assemble her thoughts. 'He's been ill. A fever of the blood. He has been confined to bed.'

A fever of the blood! Perhaps that is what he had himself. Alasdhair shook his head, as if doing so would clear the mist that had clouded his judgement, that was distracted by the completely irrelevant puzzle of Ailsa's response to him. If he had not known better, he would have thought she had no more experience of kisses than the last time their lips had met. 'I should not have kissed you. It is no excuse, but I forgot that you were married, just for the moment.'

Ailsa flushed a deeper red. 'But I'm not married. Despite what my father told you I was not betrothed to Donald McNair six years ago—or if my father made any promises on my behalf then, it was without my knowledge. I admit, I am betrothed to Donald now, but it is of much more recent standing.'

'Not married!' It had not occurred to him that she would still be single. It was a disturbing notion and not one he wanted to think about. 'Wed or betrothed, long-standing or recent, it makes no difference,' he said, more to himself than Ailsa. 'You are spoken for and I should not have taken such a liberty.'

'Nor I granted it to you,' Ailsa said unhappily. She had never had any difficulty in refusing such liberties to others. Not even Donald had been permitted such intimacy, but kissing

Alasdhair had seemed the most natural thing in the world. And the most delightful. She had forgotten it could be delightful, a kiss. Like a promise. Except this one, like the last one Alasdhair made, would remain for ever unfulfilled. 'What about you, Alasdhair?'

'What about me?'

'Are you married?'

'Of course not,' he snapped. 'Do you think me the sort of man to go about kissing women if I were? Anyway, I have no need of a wife. I have no need of anyone.'

He wasn't married. He didn't want to be married and it was probably her fault that he was set against it. She couldn't blame him. *He wasn't married.* This thought above all buzzed around in her head, as impossible to ignore and as useless as an angry blue bottle, and it was all too much. Far too much. She didn't want to think any more. She wanted nothing so much as to be safe under the covers of her bed. Weariness assaulted her.

Noticing her pallor, Alasdhair felt a twinge of regret. He, too, felt as if he had been pum-

melled relentlessly, reeling from the onslaught
the day had made on his emotions. 'Come,' he
said, picking up her gloves from the ground and
handing them to her, 'I should get you back to
the castle. You look exhausted.'

Ailsa tried valiantly for a smile. 'It's all been
a bit—overwhelming.'

'That's one way of putting it.' Alasdhair took
her hand. 'We belonged to each other once,
before you were pledged to Donald McNair.
We did not get to say our farewells six years
ago. We were long overdue that kiss. I won't
feel guilty about it, and nor should you.'

Through the starkly handsome face of the
man, the boy peered out. She answered him
with the sweet smile of the girl she had been.

He would have kissed her again, seeing that
smile he remembered so well. She would not
refuse him. It was with immense difficulty
that he chose honour over desire. Even as he
tucked her hand into his arm, he was regretting
it. Ailsa stumbled against him as the path grew

rocky. Alasdhair tightened his grip on her arm. He could help her home. That much at least he could do with a clear conscience.

Chapter Three

Errin Mhor castle was built on a promontory. There had been a fortified building of some sort on the site since ancient times. Indeed, the dungeons, now used as cellars for the famed Errin Mhor whisky, were reputed to date from the age when the Norsemen held sway over large tracts of the Highlands. The current castle consisted of a three-storey square tower complete with battlements built in the mid-sixteenth century, a later wing extending from the south of the tower built in baronial style, which included the great hall, and a smaller round tower complete with a laird's lug, the listening room, that had been the whim of the late Lord Munro. The massive oak-beamed portico with the look of a drawbridge that framed the main entrance was also the last Lord Munro's work. Stables, a dairy and the home farm, along with a few tied cottages and the larger house customarily inhabited by the factor, which had been Alasdhair's home until his father died, were situated at the north-eastern end of the grounds. The grey granite used for the majority of the buildings gave the castle a forbidding air, but the view to the west, which faced out to sea, was more mellow, for creepers had been permitted to grow up the square tower. Tall French-style windows from the drawing room at the centre of the main building opened out on to the terraced garden that sloped down to the beach.

As they passed through the gates and headed up the long driveway to the main door of the castle, Alasdhair's mood darkened.

'I won't come in.'

'You haven't got anywhere else to stay.'

'Your mother...'

'Calumn is laird now. He would never forgive me if I let you sleep anywhere save under his roof.'

'I've already told him I won't be attending the

wake. I won't stay in the castle until the banishment is formally lifted.'

She could tell by the stubborn tilt of his chin that he meant it. She recognised it of old, and knew it was pointless arguing. When Alasdhair thought he was in the right there was no convincing him otherwise. But if he went, she feared he would leave without her seeing him again. She was too raw to be at peace with him, but she wanted to be. 'If you leave now, my mother will have won again.'

'I'm not going anywhere yet, you needn't worry. I have other business to attend to.'

'I see.' She waited, but he showed no signs of confiding in her.

'Will Calumn be holding a Rescinding tomorrow?'

It was an old traditional rite, the forgiving and forgetting of wrongs by a new laird. 'Yes. He was talking about it yesterday, telling Madeleine, his wife, to make sure there was plenty of food, for the queue was like to be long. My father was not slow to take offence, as you know, and he was quick to bear a grudge. It's likely most of Errin Mhor will be there, wanting something or other rescinded.'

'All the better, for then the whole of Errin Mhor can witness the end of my banishment.'

'Alasdhair, you're not planning on confronting my mother, are you? She won't apologise for what she did, but she will be forced to welcome you to the castle—is that not enough?'

'No, it's not. Why are you defending her, Ailsa? Don't you at least want her to admit she lied? Or maybe things have changed since I left. Maybe Lady Munro has learned how to play the role of a loving mother and you're afraid of hurting her.'

Ailsa looked scornful. 'Hardly. I have come to the conclusion my mother is incapable of love. Even Calumn she disowned for a while. She only mended those fences when my father became too ill to manage and she needed him back here. I thought then that perhaps she would try to do the same with me, but she did not. And after what I have learned today about her role in our parting, I think the damage between us is beyond any mending.'

'Then surely you have as much cause as I to wish to see her grovel.'

'Don't you see, Alasdhair, by showing her she matters, you're handing her power? Best to do as I do and pretend indifference. Please.' She put her hand on the sleeve of her coat. 'Trust me on this, she will give you no satisfaction.'

Alasdhair frowned. 'I'll think about it.' Through the open door of the castle, muted sounds of laughter and the scraping sound of fiddles being tuned could be heard. 'You'd better go in.'

'I don't know if I can face it.'

She looked exhausted, fragile. Despite her curves, she was very slim. He caught himself wondering about her life in the last six years. For the first time her lack of a husband struck him as odd. She was twenty-two. In the Highlands, that was well past the usual age for one of her kind to marry. Why had she delayed? Was she happy? She didn't look it.

But Ailsa's life and Ailsa's feelings were none of his business. 'They'll be expecting you,' he said brusquely. With a curt nod, he turned his back on her and strode off down the path. He didn't look back, though she lingered for quite a while to see if he would.

From the window of the laird's bedchamber, where she had been supervising the removal of the last of his personal belongings to the funeral pyre, Lady Munro looked down at her daughter and Alasdhair Ross. She hardly recognised him in his fine clothes, but that cocky tilt of the head and the stubborn chin, said it was him all right.

Alasdhair Ross. For years she'd put up with the brat, the spit of his mother, taking the place in the castle that rightfully belonged to another. For years she'd put up with the way her lord favoured him, too. Though outsiders might think Lord Munro dealt harshly with his ward, Lady Munro knew different. It was the only way the Munro knew how to show affection, with a stick or the back of a hand. She knew that better than most.

When Alec Ross died only a short while after his wife Morna had left, Lady Munro had felt a little guilty—for a little while. It had passed quickly enough though, subsumed by the resentment that made her loathe his so-called son's upstart presence in the castle. The relief of finally being rid of Alasdhair Ross had been immense, especially when it had become obvious how things were between him and Ailsa. Fortunately, the fool had played into her hands. As if she would ever allow her daughter to go off to the other side of the world with a man of *such* bastard origins! No, she had made sure that wouldn't happen. Ever, she had thought. Though now, here was Ross, back again like a bad penny, and with uncannily inconvenient timing.

For years Lady Munro had sacrificed her own happiness and her relationship with her children to do her laird's bidding. It had cost her, more than even she was prepared to admit, but with the Munro finally gone the path was clear for her to start to make amends. Beginning with Ailsa.

Lady Munro looked down at her daughter, her heart tight with the love she had never been able to express. She had waited a long time for this chance. Too long. She wasn't going to let anyone get in the way now. Especially not Alasdhair Ross.

Below her, on the steps of the castle, Ailsa watched Alasdhair striding off into the distance before she straightened her shoulders and adjusted her *arisaidh*. Looking up, she saw her mother at the window. For long seconds, two pairs of violet-blue eyes gazed at each other. Then Ailsa turned away and made for the great hall to join in her father's wake.

After a night spent in one of his old childhood haunts, a secret hiding place where he had often slept under the stars, Alasdhair reluctantly concluded that Ailsa was right. Lady Munro would not apologise, any more than she would admit to a wrong. It would be a pointless and humiliating exercise to try, and he had more important things to confront her with. Like the mystery of his mother's absconding, and her own determined antipathy towards himself. He would confront her in private.

Having resolved to do so as soon as convenient, Alasdhair found his mind returning once again to Ailsa. It was a pointless and frustrating exercise, but he could not prevent himself from replaying their story over and over in his mind. No matter how many different permutations of the truth he construed, though, it changed nothing, a fact that he tried very hard to be glad of and assured himself he would be, just as soon as he had accepted it. Ailsa had loved him with girlish intensity, as he had loved her with the fierce heat of a first passion, but she cared for him no more than he cared for her now. She was betrothed to McNair. She was of age, too, and did not have to wed, so it was obviously her own choice, arranged or no. And he had his own life, too. A life carved from the virgin lands of the New World, a life that he was determined not to share with any other human being, a harmonious, ordered life that he would not allow to be disrupted by the capricious vagaries of love. A missed opportunity it might have been, but more than likely that was for the best. They were clearly not meant to be.

Except.

Except there was the passion that had flared between them yesterday. But it was an old flame, merely, fuelled by loss and memory. Ailsa was a beautiful woman. Of course he desired her. Any man would.

It signified nothing. Nothing at all. So Alasdhair reminded himself as he strode out towards Errin Mhor castle on that dull grey morning to attend the Rescinding.

The ceremony was to take place in the great hall, a huge room, stone-flagged, with a hammer-beam ceiling and a massive stairway at the far end that ran up towards a gallery. The long table, set in front of the fireplace that took up most of one wall, was piled high with food and drink. As he took in the scene, Alasdhair felt slightly nauseous. It was not just the memory of that last confrontation with the laird, but the memories of all the other times. He could see the ghosts of himself, the lost boy, the rebellious one, the callow youth, and the angry young man, all of them hauntingly present, tauntingly real. The ghosts he'd come to exorcise. He hadn't realised there were so many of them.

Calumn was sitting on the high carved chair that was only used for formal occasions. Beside him, on the right, and much more comfortably seated, banked by cushions, was a petite blonde female, heavily pregnant and with the exotic look of a sea nymph. This must be Madeleine, his wife and, judging by the way she was looking at his friend, clearly very much in love with him. Lady Munro stood at Calumn's left-hand side. Ailsa presided over the table. She stood as he entered the room, made as if to come forwards to greet him, caught her brother's eye and sat back down again.

Various tenants formed a line in front of Calumn. Alasdhair recognised some, including Hamish Sinclair, the smiddy and the old laird's champion. It had been Hamish who had been forced to see him off the lands. Poor Hamish, it was a duty he would rather not have been forced to carry out, especially when Alasdhair had insisted they wait until the last possible moment in the vain hope that Ailsa might still show up.

'Please Alasdhair, we must go, lad,' Hamish

had entreated him not once, but several times. 'The laird will have my guts for garters if we tarry any more.'

'Just five minutes more, Hamish,' Alasdhair remembered replying each time, little knowing that five years more wouldn't have made any difference.

Proceedings for the Rescinding had not yet begun. As the villagers took note of Alasdhair's tall form standing like an avenging angel on the edge of the room, the low hum of conversation ceased, silence fell and all eyes turned towards him. There was not a soul who did not know his identity, for his presence at the graveyard the day before had been much discussed in his subsequent absence from the wake. As he strode across the room, the villagers fell back from the laird's chair to give him precedence.

'My Lord Munro.' Alasdhair took off his hat and made a low, elegant bow.

Calumn, in a mark of respect, rose from the chair to return the bow. 'Mr Ross.'

'I am come to demand the lifting of my banishment.'

A shocked murmur came from the onlookers. Tradition for the Rescinding was for the petitioner to beg forgiveness and the laird to grant absolution, but Alasdhair, now standing straight and proud, meeting the new laird's eyes boldly, showed no signs at all of penitence.

Calumn pushed his hair from his brow, and approached his friend, looking slightly discomfited. 'Alasdhair, there is a form to this,' he said quietly. 'You must apologise first before I can perform the act of rescinding.'

'It was your father who gave offence,' Alasdhair replied. 'Your father and one other,' he said, eyeing Lady Munro balefully.

Calumn sighed heavily. 'If you would say a few token words, you don't have to mean them, then maybe...'

Alasdhair shook his head stubbornly. 'I don't want your forgiveness. The only thing I want from you is a formal lifting of my banishment and an acknowledgement that it was a mistake.'

'Alasdhair, you must realise I need to uphold tradition. I must be seen to respect the ancient ways.'

'Calumn, we were friends once, good friends. Do you trust me?'

'You know I do.'

'I did defy your father, I admit it, but the punishment far outweighed the crime. I give you my word of honour that it was completely undeserved.'

'You don't make it easy for me, you know. You're as stubborn as you ever were.' Calumn ran his fingers through his hair, frowning hard, but eventually he nodded. 'Very well, we'll do it your way. I hope you mean to stay with us for a few days—you owe me that much for making me break all the rules on this, my first day as laird.'

Alasdhair grinned. 'It's the least I can do.'

Calumn put his arm round Alasdhair's shoulder and turned to face the audience. He raised his hand for silence, but he had no need. The two made a striking pair, the one so dark, the other so fair. 'Yesterday we mourned the passing of my father. He is buried now, and with him, as is the custom, all of his past grievances. As most of you are aware, this is

Alasdhair Ross, son of Alec, who has been wrongly exiled, unjustly banished, and from whom, on behalf of my family, I beg pardon.'

Hearing his friend's words, the generous terms of his acceptance and the whole-hearted acceptance of his integrity, only then did Alasdhair realise how much it meant to him. A weight he hadn't realised he'd been carrying rolled off his shoulders. He bowed before Calumn and, as was the custom, kissed the ring that bore the Munro seal. 'Thank you. With all my heart, I accept your apology, Laird.'

'Alasdhair Ross, I now proclaim your exile at an end. Welcome back to Errin Mhor.'

There was a spontaneous burst of applause from the onlookers. In the months since his return, Calumn had made an excellent impression on his people and his neighbours. If the new laird wished to break tradition, they were only too happy to concur.

As Calumn made his way back to the laird's chair to resume the formal Rescinding, Alasdhair was surrounded. The welcome was repeated and questions were flung at Alasdhair from all sides, most concerning his absence and obvious success, some—which he ignored—more persistent about the circumstances of his departure. Astonishment and admiration, envy and respect, pleasure and a little skepticism—all were expressed. That the son of a factor from Errin Mhor could now be a rich merchant, with land that outstripped the laird's and his own fleet of ships, too—no one could really believe it. And though some, such as Hamish Sinclair, claimed they had always believed Alasdhair would go far, and others minded well that he was never shy of hard work, still it was difficult to believe that this sophisticated man of the world in his velvet suit and polished boots and feathered hat was Alasdhair Ross, son of Factor Ross and his runaway wife. Not that anyone dared remind Alasdhair of that. Not to his face, at any road.

In the centre of it all, Alasdhair felt strangely detached. It was a good feeling, right enough, to be vindicated. It meant something, but not as much as he'd thought it would. Though he continued to nod and smile and talk and joke, what he really wanted was to escape.

As soon as the Rescinding was over, Calumn pushed his way through the crowd. 'Alasdhair, if you've had enough of catching up for the moment, I'd like to introduce you to my wife.' He led the way over to the table, where the pretty blond woman was now seated. 'This is Madeleine, who has given up her native Brittany in the name of cementing the auld alliance we Scots have with the French,' Calumn said with a tender smile at his wife.

Unexpectedly touched by his friend's obvious love for the charming Frenchwoman, Alasdhair bowed with a flourish of his hat. '*Enchanté, madame.* Calumn is a lucky man.'

Madeleine beamed, showing a pair of dimples. '*Bienvenue,* Monsieur Ross, it is a pleasure to meet such an old friend of my husband's. He tells me you are one of the few men as able as he with a broadsword.'

'I think your husband has been misleading you,' Alasdhair replied, raising a quizzical eyebrow at his friend, 'I don't recall a single occasion when Calumn bested me in a challenge with the claymore.'

Madeleine cast her husband an impish look. 'You must forgive him, Monsieur Ross, it is in the nature of a husband to boast to his wife.'

'Aye, and it's supposed to be in the nature of a wife to accept what he says without question,' Calumn said with a grin.

'Oh, but I do, *mon chère,* only it would be rude to say to our guest that I don't believe him,' Madeleine replied contritely, making both men laugh.

Seeing them together, Alasdhair had no difficulty at all understanding why Calumn was so contented. A starker contrast between Lady Munro's austere beauty and the frankly sensual bundle who was her successor could not be found. At the head of the table, having taken over from Ailsa to preside regally over the meats and cheeses, bread and wine, the new dowager sat with a face set in an expression of frozen disapproval.

'Where is your brother, Rory?' Alasdhair

asked Calumn, 'I saw him at the graveside yesterday, I think. I assume it was him since I almost took him for you, the resemblance was so striking. I am anxious to finally make his acquaintance.'

'He left immediately after the funeral to return to Heronsay.'

'He and your mother are not reconciled, then?'

'When he's here she can hardly bring herself to look at him. I sometimes wonder if it is guilt that makes her so.'

'In order to feel guilt she would need to have a conscience and a heart. I have seen little evidence of either.'

'Nor are you like to, I'm afraid. Come, we might as well get the formalities over.'

Lady Munro's expression seemed to gain an extra layer of ice as she watched her son ushering his guest towards her chair.

'Mother, you remember Alasdhair Ross.'

'I do, though I would rather not.' Lady Munro did not rise.

'Mother, you will be hospitable and welcome him into our home.'

'I will not,' Lady Munro said in a low voice. 'Your father banished him. Alasdhair Ross is dead to me.'

'No, Mother,' Calumn continued implacably, his arm on hers, forcing her to her feet, 'it is my father who is dead. You will do well to remember that I am the laird now. It is I who dictate who is, and who is not, welcome in my home or upon my lands.'

Calumn's mother cast him a bitter look, but after a tense moment she deigned to give Alasdhair a nod. 'Mr Ross.' As if her contempt was not clear enough, Lady Munro made no curtsy.

Alasdhair, on the other hand, swept the widow a deep bow. 'Lady Munro. As warm and welcoming as ever, I see.'

Lady Munro looked through him. Her very determined indifference made him furious, equally determined to raise some sort of reaction from her, but even as the taunt formed in his mind, he caught Ailsa's frowning look and remembered her warning. She was right. Much as it went against the grain, she was right. He would not afford Lady Munro another opportunity to anger him again, nor would he allow her to see he was angered. 'A toast is in order, I think,' he said, turning to Calumn.

'One of Errin Mhor's finest vintages.' Calumn filled the glasses from a dusty whisky bottle that had obviously lain many years in the dungeons.

'To old friendships and new,' Alasdhair said to Calumn and Madeleine, 'and to old enemies, too,' he said, turning to Lady Munro, 'may they find a suitable resting place.'

'To the return of the prodigal,' Calumn said with a smile.

'The return of the prodigal,' they all said in unison, raising their glasses. With the exception of Lady Munro, that is, who said nothing. Her hands remained clasped tight together on her lap. The pain from her nails, digging into her palms, was a sweet relief.

Later that day, in search of solitude after the drama of the morning, Alasdhair made his way to the churchyard, where his father was buried in the small cemetery that adjoined the kirk.

Kneeling on the ground, he traced the fading name on the large stone with his fingertips and lost himself in the meagre memories of the gentle man whom loss had destroyed.

'I thought I'd find you here.'

He had been kneeling there for so long his knees were stiff, so deep in thought that he hadn't noticed Ailsa approaching. Alasdhair got to his feet, brushing the dirt from his breeches. 'I was paying my respects.'

'Am I interrupting?'

'No, I was done.'

'You were very young when he died.'

'Old enough to know he'd gone.'

'Only a few weeks after your mother—left,' Ailsa said awkwardly, 'you must have felt as if they'd abandoned you.'

'She did.'

'And he?' she asked after some hesitation, for she had heard the rumours.

'I don't believe he took his own life, if that's what you mean,' Alasdhair said harshly. 'It would be more accurate to say he died of a broken heart, for that is what happened. It was my mother's fault—if anyone's to blame for his death, it is she. Her, and the man she ran off with.'

'Who was he?'

Alasdhair shrugged. 'No one seems to know. She kept her sordid little affair secret.'

'Do you ever wonder about what became of her?'

'Why do you ask? You never have before.'

'I don't know. Thinking about my own mother after what you told me yesterday, I suppose. Why did she lie to me like that? I can't think of any reason except that she must really hate me.'

'I felt my mother must hate me too, the way she just disappeared. Not one word to anyone, not even to Mhairi Sinclair, Hamish's wife, and they were old friends. I asked her, several times, but she always claimed to be as much in the dark as me.'

'Are you thinking of trying to trace her? Is that why you've come home?'

'No, I've no wish to see her. She made her choice and has never made any attempt to contact me, so, no, I have no wish to see her, she is not part of my life now.'

'But?'

Alasdhair laughed bitterly. 'Like you, I want to know why.' He shook out his coat skirts and started to make his way back to the cemetery gate. 'What are you doing here, anyway?'

'I came looking for you. I couldn't get near you this morning, with everyone so keen to hear all about your life across the sea.'

'The return of the prodigal,' Alasdhair said with a wry smile. 'I hope Calumn knows there's no need to slay the fatted calf. I'm glad you're here. Will you walk with me and we can catch up properly? We might not get the chance again.'

'Yes,' Ailsa said gratefully, 'that's exactly what I'd like.'

Errin Mhor village was a cluster of white-washed thatched cottages facing out to the long strand of golden sands that bordered the sea, each with a strip of cultivated land at the back, reaching towards the hills. The kirk where they stood was at one end, at the other the inn, the smiddy and the harbour that formed a secure arm in which a number of little fishing boats lolled drunkenly on their sides, for it was low tide. They made their way across the tough grass that formed the border with the beach and walked along the hard sands at the water's edge.

'Tell me about Virginia,' Ailsa said.

'You must have heard more than enough from the interrogation I was subjected to this morning.'

She laughed. 'Enough to know that you're as rich as the king and have three, twenty, a hundred times more land than Calumn, depending on who you talk to. I want to know what it's like, not what you own. I want to be able to picture you there. Tell me what's different about it from Errin Mhor.'

'Well, in the summer the light is often hazy. It's hot, but it's damp, as if the sun is raining, and everything looks as if the colour is bleeding out of it. The earth smells rich, a sweet smell, like a clootie dumpling, and it gets sweeter as the tobacco ripens.'

'What does Virginia look like?'

He described it to her, and when she pressed him for more information he gave her that too, allowing her enthusiasm, and the wry sense of humour she'd always had, to lead him into talking far more about himself than he ever usually did. Eventually, he turned the conversation to the recent Rebellion.

Ailsa cared not for the cause, but having had a brother on each side, felt its effects deeply. 'I think our life here is going to change for ever because of Charles Edward,' she said sadly. From what she had not said, Alasdhair was forced to agree.

They walked on. They talked, they laughed, then grew sombre, then laughed again, at ease in one another's company for the most part, as they had always been. At times they grew silent: tense, awkward moments when they threw each other sideways glances. As she walked at his side, Ailsa's skirts brushed against Alasdhair's legs. Their hands touched. Awareness flickered like the stars in the dusk, there and then gone, then there again.

Eventually, they sat down in the dunes, taking shelter from the wind. In front of them the sea glittered turquoise and green. Above, the sun glinted, peeking in and out of the puffy clouds. The air was cold and fresh, sharp with the snow which held to the peaks higher up, smelling of peat smoke and mud, of salt and pine. The breeze whipped the waves on to the shore with a soothing slap, slap, slap. A cormorant dived for a fish, emerging triumphantly an impossibly long time later, a flash of silver in its beak signalling success.

Ailsa dug her hands into the sand, allowing the grains to trickle through her fingers. 'Why did you approach my father without even consulting me?' she asked abruptly.

'I've asked myself that a thousand times. I suppose it was partly out of a sense of honour—I didn't want to do anything behind your father's back, but also because I didn't want to wait a second longer than necessary before we could be together. But I bitterly regret going about it so impulsively. It was a stupid thing to do.'

'Yes, it *was* a stupid thing to do. If you hadn't, things might have turned out differently.'

'Come, Ailsa—you don't really believe that, do you? Neither of us was thinking straight. We were too wrapped up in the excitement of our feelings for each other to think properly about the future at all, or any of the problems we'd have to manage. You were only sixteen, I had nothing but a vague dream to cling to.'

'I know,' Ailsa said regretfully, 'looking back now I can't believe how unrealistic we were. One kiss and we just assumed everything would fall into place. I could not have come to the New World with you straight away. I would have been a burden to you until you had established yourself. That could have taken years.'

'Would you have agreed to come out and join me later, if I had asked you?'

'Would you have not gone in the first place, if I had said no?'

The question hung between them like a vast chasm, deep and unknowable.

'Your parents were right about one thing. We were naïve, hopelessly naïve,' Alasdhair said sadly. 'It was our innocence that was our real undoing. Much as I'm sure we'd both like to lay all the blame at your parents' door, we were the architects of our own downfall, for we thought love would change everything, but in the real world it changes nothing.'

Out at sea, the cormorant emerged with another fish, tipping back its elegant neck and swallowing it down in one long gulp.

'I know you're right,' Ailsa said, 'but I just wish...'

Alasdhair got to his feet and shook the sand from his clothes. 'You know what they say. If wishes were horses...'

'...then beggars would ride,' Ailsa finished. 'You mean it's pointless.'

He held out his hand. 'What's done is done. Come on, we should get back. It's getting cold.'

She allowed him to help her to her feet, stumbling as her boot caught in the sand into which she had burrowed it. She fell against Alasdhair's chest and, in trying to right herself, braced herself with her hands. The connection was instant, as was the sudden surge of longing.

They stared at each other unmoving, barely breathing. Smoky brown eyes filled with the promise of something she hadn't known she wanted until then met hers.

Yesterday had been tantalising. She had tried to put if from her mind, tried not to think of what would have happened if the kiss had gone on, tried not to think of how it would feel, tried not to think about the way that it had made her feel. She had tried. But standing so close to him, her senses filled with the feel and smell and almost-taste of him, she knew she had failed. She wanted him to kiss her. She couldn't bear it if he didn't.

Alasdhair's fingers curled into her hair. He had been unable to forget it. The honey-sweetness of her mouth on his. The perfect fit of her lips. The touch of her tongue. He knew he should not, but he also knew if he did not he would regret it. He had had enough of 'what ifs'. Yesterday's kiss had been too tentative a goodbye. She had been his before she was promised to anyone else. It was wrong to have this still between them.

His lips touched hers. The tiniest, faintest touch. She was still his until it was over. This was the only way to make it be over. His tongue licked its way into her mouth. She tasted intoxicating. He pulled her closer, wrapping his arms around her slender back, wrapping a long tress of her hair around his hand. Ailsa gave a soft sigh and her tongue touched his.

One minute they were suspended in time, the next they were lost in it. Their kiss had none of the uncertainty of the previous one, nor any trace of wistfulness. It was a sensual kiss, lips scraping lips, and as it deepened, it became a raw kiss, the kiss of a man and a woman who desire each other. Their mouths tasted, then drank thirstily. Their hands clutched and tugged and pulled, closer and closer and closer, until their bodies were pressed tight, Alasdhair's hardness against Ailsa's softness. Their mouths hungrily sought each other, more and more and more, as if to make up for all they had lost, and all they would never have, the seeking igniting a hot searing passion that took them both by surprise.

Ailsa had no idea how it happened. She had no idea of what was happening to her, for nothing, nothing she had ever known, had prepared her for the raw sensuality, the shivering excitement, the rising crescendo of feeling caused by lip on lip, mouth on mouth, tongue on tongue. Alasdhair's hands stroked her arms, her waist, her back. Her breasts were crushed against his chest, her nipples aching, though she didn't think it was pain, and all the time he was kissing her in a way she had not known it was possible to kiss. She felt urgent, as if she was seeking something, or had lost something, and only he could help her find it. She felt dizzy and restless and heavy and slumberous. She reached up to stroke his hair, the blue-black of a raven's wing. Silky soft. She could feel his heart hammering against her, just like hers, so maybe it was hers after all.

Reluctantly, Alasdhair ended it. Ailsa put a finger tentatively to her lips. They felt swollen.

'A proper goodbye kiss, this time,' he said, for both of them. 'Before I leave to go south with

Calumn tomorrow.' Though he felt so unlike saying goodbye that it frightened him.

'Yes,' Ailsa said. Leaving? He was leaving? *But it didn't feel like goodbye.* Weren't goodbyes supposed to be endings? This felt like a beginning.

'Yes,' Alasdhair affirmed. If he said it out loud, it would make it true.

And it was true. He intended seeing Lady Munro today. Armed with the answers he was certain she would give him, he had arranged to leave Errin Mhor tomorrow, taking part of the journey with Calumn and his wife, who were journeying to Edinburgh on some urgent business to do with the settling of the old laird's will. But the kiss had made his certainty drain away. He could tell no one else had ever kissed her in that way. It thrilled him and yet disturbed him. *He* should not have kissed her. How could he leave with this—this—this whatever it was, hanging over him? There had to be a way of ending it.

Chapter Four

'A clean slate,' he muttered, staring down at the lovely face that had the dazed look of a sleeper just awake.

'A clean slate?' Ailsa frowned. 'Do you mean a fresh start?' She was trying to tidy her hair, just for the sake of having something to do. *Was it passion she'd just experienced—or something else?* Was he as surprised by it as she was? Slanting a look up at him, she thought he probably was. She wished he hadn't kissed her. She wished he hadn't stopped. She felt as if she'd been trusted with half a secret she'd rather have remained ignorant of. 'I don't understand,' she said despairingly, not meaning to say the words out loud.

Her words drew a reluctant laugh from Alasdhair. 'Nor do I.'

'What are we to do?'

Violet eyes, pleading with him, and he had no answer. It wasn't supposed to be like this, his homecoming. Answers, not questions, were what he sought. Other people's soul baring, not his own. 'Nothing.'

'Pretend it never happened?'

'We can't do that, but we can make sure it never happens again. Why are you not married, Ailsa?'

She blinked at what felt like a sudden change of subject. 'I beg your pardon?'

'How long have you actually been betrothed to McNair?'

'A year or so. Maybe nearer two.'

'So why aren't you married?'

'My father has been ill.'

'All the more reason, I'd have thought, to have you safely wed.'

'Calumn's wedding took precedence.'

'Judging from the condition of your sister-in-law, that must have been a good few months ago now. You're a beautiful woman. You've a good dowry and kin whose connections are a huge advantage to McNair. I'd have thought he'd be eager to take you to his bed.'

Ailsa flushed. 'Stop it. It is none of your business.'

'I thought you were married. For the past six years I've had to live with the knowledge that you were another man's wife. And now it turns out you've been single all along.' *And it's too late now!*

She had been hanging on to her self-control by a thread. Now it broke. 'Why are you bringing this up now? You're the one that just said it was pointless to speculate. You're being completely unfair, Alasdhair. It's not my fault, this mess; it's not my fault any more than it's yours. I'm sorry things haven't turned out as you wished. I'm sorry to disappoint you by being unwed, and I'm sorry my being unwed made you kiss me again. I'm sorry you enjoyed kissing me so much. I'm sorry I enjoyed it, too—believe me, I'd rather not have. In fact, I'm sorry you came back, because I was just about getting accustomed to my life and now you've turned it all on its head.' Ailsa covered her face with her hands. She was shaking. She never lost her temper like this, but it felt as if she'd been holding it in for years, and it would not now be easily contained. 'Just go away, Alasdhair, go back to Virginia and leave me alone.'

'Oh God, Ailsa, I didn't mean to—here, come here.'

Strong arms engulfed her. As he held her close, making inarticulate shushing noises and stroking her hair, Ailsa released a torrent of pent-up tears that left her limp and feeling hollow, empty. She must look a fright. She had soaked his shirt. She had no idea what he thought of her, and right now, she didn't care. As her sobs gave way to hiccups, Ailsa pushed herself away.

'Better?'

At least he wasn't angry any more. More likely he was appalled. Ailsa nodded. She tried to wipe her face with the ends of her *arisaidh*.

'Here. Let me.' Alasdhair tilted her face up, mopping it with his large kerchief, carefully untangling her hair from her lashes and cheeks, where it had become plastered down with her tears. 'You're right, I was being completely unfair,' he said softly, tucking her hair behind her ear and straightening her *arisaidh*. 'It's not your fault, it's just that I've grown so accustomed to thinking that it was easy to blame you. I shouldn't have kissed you. Maybe it's to do with wanting what we never had. Maybe it's just that you're a very beautiful woman and for a moment there I forgot that you are spoken for. I don't know. I really don't have an excuse or a proper explanation, and that made me angry, too—with myself. I am not accustomed to acting recklessly. Forgive me.'

She managed a watery smile. 'If you will forgive me.'

'There's nothing to forgive. What you said was true.'

They began to make their way slowly back along the beach to the castle. 'Are you really set on marrying McNair?' Alasdhair asked.

Ailsa shrugged. 'It's a good match. There's no getting away from that.'

'For your family and for Errin Mhor, but what about you?'

'What is good for my family and Errin Mhor is good for me.'

'Why marry at all if it is not what you wish?'

'It is my duty—anyway, what else would I do? You have wealth and independence, I have neither. I will be a burden if I do not marry. At twenty-two I am still an asset to the clan, a prime piece to barter, but I will not have so much value at twenty-five, and almost none at thirty.'

'That's a horrible way to talk about yourself.'

'Horrible, but realistic. It's how things are.'

'So speaks Lady Munro. You sound as if you are set upon following in her footsteps.'

Ailsa flinched. 'On the contrary, I am quite determined not to. The circumstances are quite different.'

They had reached the main entrance to the castle. 'Are you sure about that?'

He did not wait for an answer. Alasdhair strode off down the corridor in search of Calumn. Raking over old times and catching up on new with the simple, uncomplicated camaraderie of two old friends would be a welcome diversion.

She could not put it off any longer. Ailsa knew that she owed it to herself to at least attempt to find out why Lady Munro had felt it so necessary to destroy her first love. She was, however, far from confident that she would succeed.

As she knocked on the door of her mother's parlour, her fingers were trembling. Even after all these years, Lady Munro's hold over her could not be ignored. Try as she might to pretend indifference, Ailsa knew in her heart of hearts that what she wanted was some sign— any sign—that her mother felt something for her. Love was too much to hope for. Lady Munro was incapable of such an emotion, and in any case, Ailsa had decided she was unlovable. Well, didn't all the evidence point to that? No, her relationship with her mother would never be a loving one, but approbation would have been nice, perhaps an occasional seeking out of her company for its own sake.

She thought herself inured to the situation, but

since her father's death, and the little flicker of hope that things would be different had been quashed, she had been forced to accept that she was not. The forthcoming interview was bound to turn up yet more unpleasant truths, but how could she face the future mapped out for her, with all those questions hanging unanswered over her head? In that respect she and Alasdhair were similar, she realised. She could appreciate what drove him. The need to know.

Her mother's voice bid her enter. The resemblance between Lady Munro and her daughter was striking. Both women had the same colour of hair, the same violet-blue eyes, and perfectly symmetrical features, though on Ailsa the mouth was softer, the expression warmer. Ailsa's beauty was vibrant, where her mother's was that of a marble statue. In their carriage, too, they differed, for Ailsa's step was quick and graceful, her mother's was more measured.

They eyed each other across the parlour, a room that had been furnished back in the days when furniture was made for durability rather than comfort. The heavy chairs, made of solid black oak, were about as welcoming as a tombstone and less comfortable. Lady Munro sat by the fire and fixed her daughter with one of her piercing stares.

Ailsa willed herself to meet her gaze. 'Mother, I am come to ask you—'

'I know what you are come to ask, I have been expecting you. You will oblige me, Ailsa, by curbing your enthusiasm for that man's company,' Lady Munro said firmly. 'It has not escaped my notice that your childish penchant for him has not entirely burned itself out.'

'If by *that man* you mean Alasdhair, then you must know that I have ample reason to seek him out and it has been a most enlightening experience. Oh, Mother, how could you? How could you tell us both so many lies?'

If Ailsa had been expecting an admission of guilt, she was to be disappointed. Lady Munro pursed her lips. 'I had my reasons.'

'What reasons?'

'I have no doubt that you and he have swapped stories and concluded that you were star-crossed lovers. I have no intention of explaining myself or justifying my actions. It should be enough for you that I thought—and continue to think— them justifiable.'

'You lied to me!'

Lady Munro's lip curled. 'I think you'll find, Ailsa, that you lied to yourself. Do you honestly think you would have been happy, living with that son of a whore among a bunch of savages halfway across the world?'

'We'll never know, will we? You didn't give me the choice.'

'I stopped you making an appalling choice. I did what I thought best, and time has confirmed the wisdom of that. I wish he had never come back here.'

'Alasdhair has made an enormous success of his life.'

'He may have money, I'll grant him that, but it doesn't compensate for a lack of breeding. Underneath that veneer of wealth Alasdhair Ross is still a peasant with ideas above his station.'

Ailsa looked at her mother in despair. There seemed to be no way of breaking through the barrier of her certainty. 'Why do you hate him so much? I don't understand—what has he ever done to deserve your enmity, for it goes back way beyond his daring to court me?'

Way back before Ailsa was even born, truth be told. Lady Munro pulled the shutter over the flash of pain to which the memory gave rise. 'What I cannot understand,' she said slowly, 'is what he has ever done to merit your rather childish adoration?'

'You would not understand that, Mother, would you,' Ailsa replied swiftly, 'never having made any attempt to earn it for yourself.' If she had not known better, she would have believed her mother hurt. But she did know better.

'Ailsa, what is the point in us digging over the past like this? It is far better that we concentrate on the future.'

Ailsa wandered over to the window. It was dark outside. She turned back into the room, where her mother was lighting a branch of candles with a spill. She was as intractable as ever. Pushing her for reasons would only make her further entrenched. And really, what did it matter now, why she had done it? The point was that it was done and could not be undone.

Her mother was once again seated by the fire, her implacable gaze fixed on Ailsa's face. 'I have written to Donald,' Lady Munro said carefully, 'and asked him to call here at his earliest convenience.'

'Why?'

Lady Munro raised a delicate brow. 'Your nuptials have been too long postponed.'

'My father is not yet cold in his grave.'

'His passing allows for new beginnings at Errin Mhor. A wedding will be an excellent start.'

'It wouldn't be seemly.'

'I do most sincerely trust you are not having second thoughts because of that barbarian's most untimely arrival,' Lady Munro said, throwing her daughter an assessing look.

Ailsa looked at her feet. There were times when she felt as if her mother could read her mind as easily as flicking through the pages of a book, and this was one of them. She could feel Lady Munro's sharp gaze sinking into her thoughts as easily as a dirk into butter. She didn't even know her own thoughts, and whatever they were, she didn't want her mother having access to them first. 'Alasdhair's arrival has nothing to do with it.'

'So you *are* having second thoughts! Ailsa, you cannot seriously be thinking of abandoning such an advantageous match,' Lady Munro persisted. 'It was the dearest wish of the laird...'

'My father's dearest wish was that I had been a boy.'

'He was very much in favour of this alliance.'

'And the hand that gives is the hand that gets, isn't it? Even from his grave he hasn't loosened his hold on you. You know, I was half-expecting you to hurl yourself on to his funeral pyre. I'm sure if he'd asked you, you would have.'

'He was my husband.'

'Whom you loved to the detriment of all others.'

'That is not true.'

'No?' Ailsa jumped to her feet. 'No, you're right, it isn't true, for you don't know how to love, do you, Mother?' Her eyes were smarting, but she kept the tears from falling by an act of sheer will. The strength of her reaction dismayed her.

'Listen to yourself, you sound like a spoilt child,' Lady Munro said, getting to her feet and handing Ailsa one of her own delicately embroidered handkerchiefs. 'Ailsa, it was not just the laird's wish, it is mine too. Just think, if you were to be wed to Donald and settled, then we would be neighbours. We could visit and, in due course, when you had children we could—'

'Play at happy families?' Ailsa said witheringly. 'It's a bit late for that.' Lady Munro's handkerchiefs were works of art, the *petit point* was exquisite, though Ailsa doubted the flimsy lace had ever absorbed a tear. She made a show of folding it into her lap without using it. 'I want you to write to Donald. Tell him the time is not convenient. I have no wish to see him at present, until my mind is clearer.'

'His presence will clarify your mind far better than his absence. I trust by the time he arrives that you will have recovered your temper and your common sense.'

Ailsa gazed at her mother helplessly. 'Does not my happiness mean anything to you?' she asked, wishing the words unspoken almost before they were out, yet still unable to stop herself from hoping for an affirmative.

'I happen to think your happiness is best served by doing your duty. When you reflect upon that, I feel confident you will agree with me. You are, after all, my daughter.'

Ailsa stood up. Lady Munro's handkerchief fluttered unnoticed on to the floor at her feet. 'I may be your daughter, but I am of age, and I have a mind of my own. If I decide I don't want to marry Donald, I won't do so.'

'Ailsa,' Lady Munro said urgently, 'please stay away from Alasdhair. I don't want him to come between us again. Ailsa!' she cried more urgently as her daughter made for the door. 'There are things—he is not the man you think he is.' But her words fell on deaf ears. The door closed.

Lady Munro picked up the discarded handkerchief. She pressed the lace to her eyes. They stung, but they remained obstinately dry. Only let Donald McNair answer her summons swiftly.

Let McNair be the instrument of her child's deliverance from that bastard. She was beginning to wonder if Alasdhair Ross had been sent by his father's command from the grave expressly to haunt her.

Sitting at dinner—a meal that, thank God, the Widow Munro took in her own room—trying to make polite conversation, Alasdhair was wishing he had kept his vow never to return to Errin Mhor again. He longed for the tranquillity of his plantation where he could be alone. His own land, his own house, where he had found contentment. Except, of course, if he had really been contented he wouldn't have come here. And coming here had forced him to realise just how unfulfilled his life actually was.

As if things were not difficult enough, Madeleine had placed him next to Ailsa at the table. Her hand brushed his when she passed him a serving dish and they both drew back as if scalded. He caught her watching him, her eyes troubled, and knew he looked at her the same way. In her evening gown of green velvet she was exquisite, though she brushed off Madeleine's compliments with an embarrassed shrug. She was not comfortable with her looks, though most women would kill for them. As would most men, to be near her.

He should not have kissed her. God help him, he wished he had not, for he could not stop thinking of it. In the old days, when he felt this edgy, Alasdhair would have vented his spleen by picking a fight with Calumn, or he would have sought out Hamish for a bout with the claymore. Or gone for a sail. Of course! 'What happened to *An Rionnag?*'

Calumn looked up in surprise, for Alasdhair had been silent these past twenty minutes. '*The Star?* Alasdhair's boat in the old days,' he explained to Madeleine. 'I have no idea what happened to her.'

'She's at Errin Bheag,' Ailsa volunteered quietly. 'One of the fishermen there keeps her watertight for me; his boy takes her out from time to time.'

'I thought your father would have had her scuppered,' Alasdhair said.

Ailsa met his eyes for the first time that evening. 'He thought she was.'

He smiled. 'You saved her.'

She blushed. 'It just seemed wrong to allow such a beautiful thing to be destroyed out of spite.'

'I couldn't agree more.'

'I didn't know you sailed, Ailsa,' Madeleine said, intrigued by the undercurrents simmering between her sister-in-law and Calumn's forbidding friend.

'I don't, not any more. Alasdhair and I used to go sailing all the time, but my mother doesn't approve of me going out on my own.'

'Ah, oui, je comprends,' Madeleine said in the tone of voice she reserved exclusively for her mother-in-law, whom she secretly called the dragon lady.

'That's easily solved,' Alasdhair said. 'Why don't I take you out in *An Rionnag* tomorrow?'

Ailsa looked at him in surprise. 'But surely there isn't time for that? You're travelling south with Calumn and Maddie tomorrow, remember?'

'Actually, I've changed my mind, I've decided to stay on for a few more days. What do you say? For old times' sake?'

Ailsa looked anxiously at her brother.

'I think it's an excellent idea,' Calumn said. 'I can't understand why you're so anxious to get away from Errin Mhor anyway, Alasdhair, having made such a long and arduous journey to get here. Stay for as long as you want, my home is yours. Anyway, I'm sure Ailsa will be glad of the company while we're gone.'

Madeleine clapped her hands together. '*Excellent!* It will do you good, Ailsa, to get away from all the upset of the funeral. Have a little fun.'

A glance sideways at Alasdhair told Ailsa that he was thinking the same as she was. She longed to sail with him just once more, and maybe put an end once and for all to the fantasy of the past. Perhaps in this ending there could be a new beginning with Donald—though frankly, she doubted it. More likely it would be two endings. What she didn't doubt was that her mother would be outraged by her wilful defiance of her instructions, but after today's confrontation that thought gave Ailsa an almost childish pleasure. 'I could—I would like to, if you wanted…'

Did he? Did he really want to subject himself to such poignant memories? But would not such a thing be the perfect antidote to the attraction which was in danger of proving a distraction? To recreate that day with the real Ailsa would surely eradicate the dream one? To replace illusion with reality, was surely the perfect solution? 'Aye. Yes. I'd like that.'

Sitting beside him, Ailsa's hand was clenched tight around the stem of her claret glass. That she was just as edgy as he made him feel just a tiny bit better.

Helping herself to a bowl of porridge and sprinkling salt over it the next morning, Ailsa took her place at the table just as Alasdhair entered the room, having waved Calumn and Madeleine off on their journey to Edinburgh. He brought with him the scent of fresh air and soap. His hair glistened, slicked back on his head where he had thrown water over it, and he was freshly shaven. He was clad in his breeches and boots, shirt and waistcoat, but without either coat or neckcloth, he looked much younger. Much less forbidding. Much more attractive. Ailsa felt a little skip of her heart and realised she was staring. 'Help yourself to breakfast,' she said.

Alasdhair loaded his plate from the hot dishes before sitting down opposite her. 'Are you sure about today?'

'Are you?'

He laughed. 'If I say yes, will you?'

'Yes.'

'Does your mother know?'

'Not yet, but you can be sure she will find out.'

Alasdhair poured himself a cup of coffee as Ailsa stirred her breakfast with a bone porridge spoon. 'Your clothes aren't ideal for sailing. I could find you a plaid, if you preferred,' she said.

'I thought the wearing of it was banned.'

'Aye, like they've tried to ban the Gaelic, but

you'll not notice too many speaking English up here,' Ailsa said scornfully. 'No one heeds it, unless they go south of Oban. There's even a howff on the Isle of Seil known now as the *Tigh an Truish* where the men change into trews before visiting the mainland.'

'The House of Trousers. Most apt.' Alasdhair's smile faded. 'Calumn told me how it was for him and his brother during the Rebellion.'

'And for many others. We have been through some hard times. It's a shame Rory couldn't tarry, you'd like him. Now, do you want a plaid or not?'

'Have you a plan to turn me back into a Highlander, Ailsa?'

'It's what you are, at heart. Don't tell me that you think of yourself as an American?'

'Not when I'm here. Fetch me a plaid, Miss Munro, and I will endeavour to transform myself.'

Ailsa hummed softly as she dressed. Discarding her morning gown, she pulled on a striped petticoat and a calf-length woollen skirt in her favourite peacock blue—only widows on Errin Mhor were obliged to wear black. A dark blue waistcoat was fastened over her sark and her stays, and a woollen *arisaidh* was belted at her waist over it all, held at her breast with a pretty pewter pin. Her hair she brushed loose so that it lay down her back in long waves, tied back in a simple knot with a length of ribbon. Sturdy boots over her stockings, and she was ready. 'You'll do,' she said to her reflection with a satisfied nod.

Alasdhair was waiting in the great hall, standing with his back to her. Ailsa paused on the landing, taking the opportunity to look at him unobserved. He was certainly worth looking at. In his black clothes he had been striking. Dressed as a Highlander he was breathtaking.

The *filleadh beg,* fashioned from the length of plaid she had found for him, was held in place by a wide belt. The plaid fell in neat pleats that hugged the slight curve of his buttocks stopping just above his knee, giving her a tantalising glimpse of muscled leg above his hose, that were tightly tied around equally muscled calves.

He did not wear the *filleadh mòr*, the large plaid that was the male version of her own *arisaidh*, but instead had on a long leather waistcoat, over his shirt, from which he had removed the ruffles. The whole ensemble somehow emphasised Alasdhair's height and the well-defined planes of his body—broad shoulders, muscled chest, flat abdomen, long legs. But there was something about Alasdhair himself that had changed, too. The fine-looking man at the peak of physical perfection had indeed transformed himself into a noble-looking Highlander with subtle undertones of the savage. Gone was the veneer of sophistication, and in its place was something more primitive. He looked much more like the pioneer she knew him to be. It was blood-stirring.

Ailsa gave herself a shake. *Enough of this, he is just a man in a plaid. You see his like every day.*

It was almost true. She almost believed it.

Perhaps sensing her scrutiny, Alasdhair turned round, and Ailsa made her way hurriedly down the stairs to join him. 'Well, do I pass muster?' he asked her, holding his hands wide.

'I've seen you in a plaid before, Alasdhair Ross,' she replied, thankful that her private preview allowed her to sound satisfyingly dismissive. Refusing to indulge her intemperate thoughts any further, she tried to focus on practicalities and not on the large buckle of Alasdhair's belt, or on the vee of his shirt where she could see the tan of his throat, or on his sinewy forearms, or on the swing of his plaid when he walked.

She led the way through a door in the panelling at the end of the great hall. 'Calumn had *An Rionnag* brought round this morning; she's moored at our own jetty now, we'll go out through the front gardens.' The door led, via a spiralled stone staircase, down to the kitchens and stillrooms. They went out through a side door into the kitchen gardens, then down a pathway that wended its way under a canopy of Caledonian pines to the shoreline.

It was one of those spring days when all four seasons seem to contend for supremacy at once.

The morning had started bright and blustery, but now there were heavy grey clouds rolling down from the north. A couple of months previously they would have brought snow, but in April they heralded either sleet or hail. Behind them, however, and directly in front to the west, the sky was a benign blue and the sea, though choppy, was showing no signs of the ominous kind of heaving that portended rough weather.

'What do you think?' Ailsa asked, anxiously eyeing the sky.

'I think we should take our chances.'

'With the weather, you mean?'

Alasdhair looked at her enigmatically. 'What else?'

They emerged from the pines at the top of a small cliff. A set of stairs had been roughly hewn into the rock face, with a rope attached to heavy iron links forming a rail. The beach below shelved steeply down to the water's edge where a small stone jetty had been cleverly fashioned from an existing formation of rocks. There were three boats moored there. *An Rionnag* was the smallest, no more than a skiff with a set of oars and one sail. Beside her was another boat similar in style, but slightly bigger and obviously new, with the name, *Madeleine,* picked out in gold. At the far end in the deepest of water was Lord Munro's bulky official craft.

The tide was high. The boats bobbed and bumped on the waves that crested on to the beach, making boarding a business that required excellent balance. Alasdhair sprang lithely from the jetty into *An Rionnag,* his plaid swinging out behind him. The glimpse of thigh Ailsa caught was covered in a smattering of hair, underneath that was some more nicely defined muscle, but the skin was pale. She wondered where his tan stopped.

'Ailsa?'

Alasdhair was holding out his hand, smiling up at her in a way that made her stomach lurch. He had tied his hair back with a piece of leather, but it was escaping, tendrils black as a raven's wing whipping over his face. Ailsa perched on the edge of the pier, trying to synchronise the short jump into the boat with the waves that tossed it about, ignoring Alasdhair's offer of help. She had leapt times without number into the boat without even thinking about it, yet now she hovered and hesitated, so inevitably, when she finally jumped, she stumbled. Alasdhair was waiting to catch her, as he always used to. She found she liked that he caught her, and it had naught to do with the old days, but was something more primal, the sensation of being soft and female caught in a pair of strong male arms.

Ailsa stood five foot eight in her stocking soles, yet beside Alasdhair she felt as petite as either of her sisters-in-law. He held her effortlessly. Another wave rolled under the bow of the boat, but Alasdhair merely braced himself, pulling her a little more securely against him.

The wind tugged playfully at his hair. A long strand escaped the leather thong that tied it back, falling into his eyes. Without thinking, Ailsa reached up to smooth it away. It was silky soft, tangled in lashes that were equally soft, thick and jet black. Her palm brushed across his cheek. He turned his head so that his lips brushed the skin on the pad of her thumb. A kiss, warm and soft. A frozen moment when she could have jerked away, but did not. A sharp intake of breath that must have been hers, though she didn't think she was actually breathing. Then a sigh—also hers—as she turned in his arms. Her hand trailed over the line of his jaw and her other arm went around his neck to steady herself against him.

Alasdhair shifted his feet further apart on the rocking boards of the boat as Ailsa sheltered in the lee of his arms. Her body was all soft curves, moulding itself to his in the most arousing way. She smelled delightful. He could feel her heart beating, fast like his own, yet still he hesitated. There was spray on his face. The taste of salt. The rise and fall of the boat, the rise and fall of his chest. The beat, beat, flutter, beat of her heart. A wave, bigger than the others, tilted the boat. *An Rionnag* rocked and the spell was broken.

'We should make sail or we'll miss the tide,' he said, releasing his hold on her reluctantly. Desire, hot and heady, had him in its clutch. If he was honest, he wanted to do a lot more than kiss her. *Perhaps this was a mistake?* What he felt here was no ghostly memory, but something vital and very much of the present. He wanted her, as he had never wanted a woman before.

All too aware of his eyes upon her, Ailsa fumbled with the knot that held *An Rionnag* to the jetty while Alasdhair secured the sail and took the tiller. *Was this a foolish mistake?* She used an oar to push them away from the pier, then she retreated to the space in the prow, sitting among the lobster creels and the fishing lines, as Alasdhair guided the little boat out into the choppy sea. The same stretch of water where she had first noticed him as a man.

Looking at him now, handling the tiller with the ease of one as at home on the sea as the land, she tried to conjure up the spirit of that day, reminding herself that this was what she had come for, to exorcise the ghosts. But the Alasdhair opposite her refused to be replaced by his youthful self. Unfortunately for her peace of mind, this Alasdhair, the real Alasdhair, was likely to prove more persistent still. Though she hadn't known it until yesterday, she recognised the desire that knotted her stomach as she looked at him. Desire that made her mouth dry and her skin shivery. She wanted him.

Ashamed and at the same time more than a little excited with the realisation that she wasn't, as she had thought herself, immune to such needs, Ailsa dragged her eyes away, but her thoughts continued to race. She wanted him.

Just him? Did his awakening of such feelings mean that she would want Donald? With the cold crystal clarity of a melting mountain stream, she knew then that she never would. This revelation would have to be dealt with, and dealing with it would be painful, but right now it felt like a release. Ailsa smiled and tipped back her head to the bright rays of the April sunshine. Today anything could happen. Anything. Tomorrow was another day, as Shona MacBrayne was always saying.

Alasdhair sailed *An Rionnag* around the Necklace, weaving the little boat amongst the islets as if he were making a chain in the waters, enjoying the strain and pull on his muscles as he steered their winding course, taking pleasure in the occasional dexterity required to manipulate both rudder and sail at the same time as the wind direction changed. The tiller felt smooth and worn in his hand. The seat was hard underneath him. Sea and sky needed constant watching, for the weather could change in moments. He enjoyed it all with the relish of a home-comer.

Ailsa sat in the prow like one of those figureheads that adorned the fancier vessels that plied their trade in the bustling harbour back in Jamestown. As the boat dipped in and out of the swell, the spray caught her face and the wind whipped her hair, making her laugh. She looked more carefree than he had seen her in the last two days, as if she had shed her woes into the sea, and like the sea she sparkled.

He wondered what she was thinking. Remembering. It was strange, despite his coming out on the boat today being about exorcising the past, he had barely thought of it. Here she was, sitting where she had sat before, and here he was. But though the past flickered on the edges of his vision, it was ephemeral. It was now that was real. This day. This woman. This heady, harsh desire for her. *Was he making a huge mistake?* But Alasdhair, having set himself upon a course of action, now clung to it stubbornly. It would work. It had to work, because this was what he had come for. A clean slate. A sloughing off of the old.

The middle of the little chain of islands was also the biggest, almost five hundred yards long and half as wide. It was as if *An Rionnag* remembered the way, so easily did he manage the tricky manoeuvre that brought her into the natural harbour formed by two craggy outcrops of rock. As the boat reached the shallows, Alasdhair dropped the sail, discarded his shoes and hose, and leapt into the freezing cold of the water to haul the little craft on to the beach.

Ailsa jumped ashore, and of one accord they headed off to the far side of the island, their own special hideaway. Here there were pools filled with enormous crabs and colourful sea anemones. They sat on the flat rocks together, sharing the simple picnic Ailsa had brought.

They were at ease and on edge by turns, inhabiting some shadowy land between who they had been and who they were now. After they had eaten, they wandered round the perimeter of the island, and the undercurrent of awareness that had never quite left them began to slowly twine itself around and between them, weaving a seductive insistent magic that threatened to cast them under its hypnotic spell.

Chapter Five

'**W**hy did you decide to come here with me today?' Alasdhair asked as they stood in the shelter of the stunted pine trees that fringed the shore, watching a seal diving for fish.

'Because I wanted to go out on *An Rionnag*.'

'And because you knew it would annoy your mother.'

Ailsa laughed. 'A wee bit.' She worried at the shale on the beach with the toe of her boot, conscious of his watching her and the answering blush rising on her cheek. 'You'll think I'm silly,' she said looking up at him, 'but what I really wanted was to lay my—our—ghosts to rest.'

'I don't think you're silly. I came here for the same reason myself.'

'Is it working?'

'Not really,' he surprised them both by saying.

She reached for his hand. 'I didn't want to hear it when you said yesterday that it wouldn't have worked, but it was the truth. We were too young and too unsure of ourselves. You had a future to make, I would have been a distraction.' She rubbed her cheek on the back of his hand. 'It's hard, admitting it, and it's very sad, but maybe if we both accept it's the truth, then the ghosts will be laid.'

Her honesty, and the effort it had obviously cost her to say the words, touched him to the core. 'Another thing that hasn't changed about you,' Alasdhair said with a catch in his voice, 'is that you never lacked courage.'

Ailsa shook her head sadly, thinking that it was precisely this she had lacked over the last few years. It had been eroded, along with her self-confidence, as she surrendered herself to the life her father had decreed for her and her mother had prepared her for.

She was still holding his hand against her cheek. He remembered her doing the same thing all those years ago. He touched the corner of her mouth with his thumb. A tear trembled on the silver tip of her lash. He leaned down to kiss it away before it fell. An aching tenderness filled him, and a regret that was for the first time bereft of anger and hurt. He brushed his fingers through the little halo of curls that clustered on her brow, as if he would free her from the lingering ghosts, free them to float off on the breeze, and in doing so free himself, too.

She smiled up at him shakily and something inside him melted. He took it for the release he had sought, that they both wished for. It seemed like the most natural thing in the world to kiss her then, a kiss to free them both. With no thought other than that, he did. He felt her lips trembling on his. He wrapped one arm around her back to draw her just the tiniest bit closer.

Ailsa sighed. The tension that had tightened across her shoulders, around her neck, giving her a permanently lurking headache, eased as she nestled into the shelter of Alasdhair's body. A letting go, that was what they needed, and this was it. A true farewell, with no regrets nor recriminations. Coming to their island had been right after all. She sighed again as his lips met hers, as he put his arm around her, and he kissed her, softly, regretfully.

Except the kiss did not stop. Alasdhair licked her bottom lip, his tongue seeking out the soft flesh on the inside, and little bubbles of desire began to rise in her blood. She would stop in a minute. Or he would. She did not want the moment to be broken. He licked into her mouth, easing it open, deepening the kiss and she softened for him. The bubbles inside her increased. A different kind of tension began to build, lower down. She stood on tiptoe to put her arms around his neck, to pull his head down towards her, to stroke the silken raven's-wing hair, and stopped thinking.

How did it happen? Just as before, he had no idea. One minute their kiss was tender, the next desire flared between them and it was something infinitely more dangerous, much more difficult to control. One minute their kiss was a finale, the next it was a prelude, a vital, vibrant prelude, fired hot with a passion that seemed to come crashing down on them from the sky.

He kissed her deeply, plundering like the Norsemen who had taken Errin Mhor from the Highlanders many centuries before. She surrendered willingly, her little moaning cries urging him to take more. They sank together on to the ground, kissing, licking, kissing, touching, stroking. Ailsa was so soft beneath him. Her mouth so sweet. Her kisses set him on fire. Her fluttering hands trailed a tortuous path, her touch so light as to be not enough, yet somehow more than enough, too much. He kissed her mouth, her eyelids, her nose, her cheeks, her chin. Her mouth again. Her lips, pink and full and tender.

Ailsa felt as if she had been lifted clean into the middle of a maelstrom, held helpless, suspended, mindless. He was on top of her now. So solid and big and overwhelmingly male. She did not feel safe, yet she did not feel afraid. She was out of her depth. She would drown, but it would be a drowning so darkly enticing that she craved it. His mouth on hers incited her. His hands, too, hinted at dark pleasures.

Skin. Hot skin and cold air. Her waistcoat flapping open, her sark undone to expose the mounds of her breasts above her stays. Goosebumps. A stillness and a sharp intake of breath. Not hers. His eyes smoky with the secrets she would have him tell, looking at her in a way that made her feel exposed, raw and vulnerable.

She was hot and then cold, and chilled enough to shiver. Unnerved. Ambivalent. It could not really be her lying here like this. She could feel the weight of his arousal. She thought it must be that. Heavy. She hadn't expected that.

His kisses slowed. She thought they would end and pulled him to her, but instead they became languorous, lingering on her mouth, then down, tracing over her neck, her throat. The outline of her breasts through her sark. Her nipples hardened against the constraints of her stays. She wanted him to touch them. The brazen wanting shocked her.

Ailsa closed her eyes. If she could not see, this could not be her, this fairy-like creature all sensations and nerve-ends, moaning and writhing and squirming and panting. Behind her lids was a world of new colours. Illicit colours. Pulsing colours of crimson and rose-petal pink, glistening moistly and glittering dangerously. A world of icy heat that made her shiver and tremble, a dangerous country for which she had no guide, where someone forbidding and forbidden demanded things from her she should not give.

Alasdhair opened his eyes. The carefully pleated folds of his *filleadh beg* fell loosely about him. His erection pressed urgently against Ailsa's thigh. Beneath him she lay, her eyes fast shut, her face flushed, her hair tangled and spread like a river of gold on the bare earth. Her lips were swollen. Her skirts were rucked up. One of her garters had come undone, her stocking slipped down to show him the sweet curve of her calf. She never used to wear stockings. He had not seen her without them since his return.

It hit him then, with a force that made him flinch, that it really was over. No matter how much things seemed as they had been, they were not. The world had turned and turned and turned, and they were both irrevocably changed by the passage of time. It was over.

'Ailsa.' Gently, he kissed her lips one final time, pulling her into his arms, holding her close, tight, stroking her hair as if soothing her after a bad dream. 'Ailsa.'

She opened her eyes. Such beautiful eyes. She looked dazed. 'I…'

'Shush.' The tenderness was back again, desire fading, though he knew the memory of that would haunt him, a new ghost for him to take back to Virginia.

Did he regret it? No. He would not hurt her. He cared. It would never be anything else, but it was something, something else new. *Part of the healing?* The thought gave him courage.

Reluctantly, he let her go, setting her down on the ground beside him, pulling down her skirts, straightening her stocking, retying her garter, every movement, such intimate movements, another little ending.

'Listen to me for a moment, Ailsa.' Alasdhair shook his hair out of his eyes, rubbing his hand over his brow. 'I want to explain.' And he did. He did want to explain, and that surprised him. He wanted her to know, and to understand, and it would be nice, for a change, to have that. No one had ever understood him. 'You asked me why I came back here, not just to the island, but to Errin Mhor. I came because I wanted answers. At least I thought it was what I wanted.'

'But?'

'But, I've realised what I really wanted was to be at peace with myself and who I am. I've been...' He searched for the right word, and it came to him with simple clarity. He could admit it now, now that he was well on his way to the solution. 'I've been unhappy,' he said, surprised at how easy it felt, here on the island with Ailsa, to say it. 'At least, not really unhappy, but not happy either.'

Ailsa pressed his hand. 'I know about that.'

'I know you do. Today has helped a lot. What you said to me has helped a lot; I think the ghosts have been laid to rest after all. So thank you.'

His words should have reassured her, but they made her feel unutterably sad, and she could see by the way he was fidgeting with the pleated folds of his plaid that he had not finished yet.

'You know I care about you, Ailsa.'

For one tiny fraction of a second, the time it took for a wave from the incoming tide to roll over one of the flat red rocks on the shore, she thought he was about to declare himself. She hadn't expected it, hadn't allowed herself even to imagine it, but just for that moment, she did and her heart did a little flip of excitement. Then she saw, from the way he was watching her, anxiously, that she had got it all wrong. Again. She forced her mouth into a smile. 'But?'

'But that is all it is. I am not capable of anything else and I'm not looking for it, either.'

'Don't you ever get lonely, living such a solitary life with no one to share it with?'

'You can't miss what you don't have. I am accustomed to being alone. It is safer to be so. My independence is hard won. In my time growing up here I gave, or tried to give, my love to three women—my mother, your mother and you. In each case, for different reasons, it brought me nothing but heartbreak. I vowed then never to put myself in that position again.'

She managed a wan smile, fearing he would see the remnants of her foolish hopes in her eyes. 'You need have no fears, you are safe from me, if that is what you are worried about.'

'I am worried about you. You deserve more from life than an arranged marriage to a man you are, at best, indifferent to.'

'I agree with you.'

'I beg your pardon?'

'I've decided I'm not going to marry Donald. And before you start loading yourself up with guilt, it has nothing to do with you. Well, only a little bit. You were right, about my procrastinating. I was fooling myself, thinking I could go through with it. I hadn't thought what it would mean to—to—to be his wife—properly, I mean. Until now.' She could feel the blush staining her cheeks, but forced herself to finish what she had to say. It was not so much the confession to Alasdhair, as to herself, that mattered. Saying it out loud would mean she couldn't ignore it any more, and hopefully that would give her the courage she needed to say it to her mother. 'It wouldn't be fair on Donald, to land him with a wife who found the sharing of his bed an ordeal.'

'Not fair, but not unusual,' Alasdhair said.

'Aye, I don't have to look too far from home to know that,' Ailsa said sarcastically, 'but I refuse to be like my mother, I told you that yesterday. I have not the tendencies towards martyrdom she has.'

'Nor her cold blood.'

'No.' She blushed more fiercely, digging her fingers into the pine needles that carpeted the ground on which they sat. 'Though I had grown to believe that I had.'

She looked so lovely and so confused and vulnerable that he wanted to take her in his arms again, to soothe away the raw pain of her confession. Though it was none of his business, his relief that she wasn't marrying McNair was immense. He told himself it was because he wanted her to be happy and he knew that

McNair would never make her so. 'This is quite a turnaround from yesterday.'

'It was having to defend myself to you yesterday that made me realise what a foolish stance I had been taking. You were right. If I'd really meant to go through with it, I would have done so by now.'

'What will you do?'

Ailsa shrugged. 'I haven't thought that far ahead. I don't know—maybe being an aunt is not such a bad thing.'

'A waste. I think you would make an excellent mother.'

'With my own as a role model?'

'Rather as a warning.'

'Don't you ever want children, Alasdhair?'

'My own memories of childhood do not tempt me down that track. I am content as I am.'

'As am I.' Recognising from his voice that the subject was closed, Ailsa got to her feet and shook out her skirts. While they had been talking, the sun had disappeared; the clouds that had been threatening had now gathered overhead with some purpose. 'We should go back, before the wind picks up.'

They made their way quickly through the canopy of trees on to the beach where the boat was sitting on the shale. Rain began to fall in a fine mist, the breeze making a froth of the waves like a cream on a pudding. 'Get in, keep dry, I'll push her off,' Alasdhair said, throwing his boots and hose into the boat.

Ailsa did as she was bid. Alasdhair pushed *An Rionnag* back into the water and jumped in. As she lowered the rudder, he unfurled the sail, but when she went to take up her seat at the prow, he stayed her with his hand on her arm. 'You do not regret that you came today?'

She shook her head.

'Sit with me here.'

For the last time. The words hung between them.

So she sat with him. Her thigh pressing into his. Her booted foot beside his. Her arm on the tiller beside his. The little boat scudded along, back to Errin Mhor. Behind them on the island that was once their island, the ghosts settled with a mournful sigh into their last resting place.

But there was one ghost that had not been laid. As they made their way from the jetty back up through the gardens of the castle, the shadow of a lone figure could be seen outlined against one of the long windows. Ailsa's heart sank. 'Mother. Standing sentinel, just like six years ago.'

Alasdhair halted in front of her, protecting her from Lady Munro's vision. 'I'm glad she's there, for it saves me the bother of seeking her out.'

'What do you mean?'

'Lady Munro and I need to have a conversation which is long overdue.'

'I hope you have better luck than I did in getting answers.'

'It is not a question of luck, but will.'

Ailsa chuckled. 'In that case, my mother may be about to meet her match, for I would not like to set myself against you, Alasdhair Ross. Do you really think she'll be able to tell you anything about your mother?'

'I don't know why, but I'm sure of it.' Over Ailsa's shoulder he could see that the shadow had gone from the window. He would seek her out and get the answers he needed. 'Go on in now. I am to sup with Hamish and Mhairi Sinclair tonight, but I will see you in the morning.'

'Before you leave, you mean?'

He didn't feel ready to leave. 'It depends on what I get out of your mother,' he said, relieved—though he wouldn't admit it—to have that excuse. 'Go on in, it's getting cold. I'm going round the long way, it will give me time to marshal my thoughts.'

She left him, winding her way through the gardens to where the long drawing-room window that opened on to the terrace was still partly open. Her mother had no doubt been chastising the gardener for being insufficiently ruthless when pruning the roses, as she did every year. Wearily, Ailsa headed for the sanctuary of her bedchamber. Her skin tingled, tight with salt and sun. It had been a long time since she had spent so much time outdoors like that. It felt good. She resolved not to let such a long time pass again. She would claim *An Rionnag* for her own, when Alasdhair was gone.

When Alasdhair was gone. If she let herself, it would be easy to fall for him again. Too easy. And too painful. He cared for her. That should be enough. He would not care for another. That should be a comfort. It wasn't, though the idea of another woman at his side was no comfort either.

'So contrary,' she chastised herself in the mirror as she unpinned her *arisaidh*, 'you cannot expect to have it all ways.' Her reflection looked back at her, wind-burnished, her hair in a tangle, the soft line of her lips blurred. She touched her finger to them. Well-kissed lips. The feel of his hands, his mouth, his body hard on hers, was so vivid she closed her eyes, the sudden rush of wanting that flooded her with such a poignancy making her feel as if it were happening again. Any doubts she had about her own sensuality were put to flight. She could desire. She could need. She could feel.

All the more reason for being on guard. Her feelings would not be returned. Much better not to have them exposed. Safer. She knew that. Why then was caution, her watchword, now such an unattractive proposition?

A short while later, Alasdhair entered the castle by the front door, heading through the great hall and up the main staircase two steps at a time. Striding along the complex series of corridors that connected the various parts of the castle, he had no difficulty at all in recalling the way.

The large room on the top floor of the oldest part of Errin Mhor castle commanded a view out over the front of the grounds towards the village. It was Lady Munro's book room, from whence she was wont to oversee her domain, and in which Alasdhair had on many occasions been on the receiving end of her icy reproaches. Not doubting she would be there, he rapped loudly on the door and went in without awaiting her response.

The room had not changed at all. Shelves of

leather-bound household accounts going back decades. The unpadded wooden visitor's chair placed where the light streamed in from the window into the face of any occupant. The imposing desk, behind which Lady Munro sat, her expression disdainful, her laird's expression in the portrait that hung behind it equally so. Such unwelcome memories it all brought back. Alasdhair straightened his shoulders and strode in. 'Lady Munro. What a pleasure it is to return to this cosy nook. It evokes so many happy times.' He declined to sit, instead leaning his shoulder against the mantel in a pose of studied casualness that he knew would irk her.

Age had left little trace on her countenance, that seemed to have hardened rather than become lined. She looked to him almost exactly as she had always done, the shadows under her eyes the only sign of her recent loss.

'Mr Ross. I do not recall requesting your company.'

Lady Munro's tone was positively glacial. Alasdhair managed a smile with some difficulty, surprised to find that he was tense, bracing himself for the onslaught as if by habit. But she could not hurt him. She was nothing to him, not any more. 'Come, my lady, do you not wish to chat over the old days?'

'What do you want?' Lady Munro demanded uncompromisingly.

Abruptly abandoning all pretence of politesse, Alasdhair took the seat in front of the desk, turning the chair around to sit astride it. 'I want some answers.'

'I see your manners have not improved. No doubt you find yourself quite at home with the savages in America.' She said the word in the same tone as she would say Sassenach.

'None so savage as your tongue, my lady. I see your manners have not changed, either.'

'You are not welcome here, Mr Ross.'

'Oh, but I am, Lady Munro. As your son's guest. Calumn is the laird now, had you forgot, and my name is no longer blackened.'

Her eyes blazed.

'Your whore of a mother blackened the Ross name long before you got yourself banished by setting your sights on my daughter.'

Alasdhair pushed back his chair so violently that it clattered to the ground. He leaned menacingly over the desk, forcing Lady Munro to shrink back in her chair, though she held his fierce gaze unrepentantly. 'If my mother was a whore, as you call her, she had you as her example, my lady. Did not you do as she did, abandoning your son for the sake of a man?'

Lady Munro got to her feet. 'How dare you! How *dare* you compare my actions to your mother's? You know nothing of the weight of duty a laird's wife has to endure, the sacrifices she has to make, the pain she has to bear. All for the sake of her sire and the clan. My motives were honourable, however unpalatable the actions required of me.'

For the first time in his life his blow had pierced her armour and it surprised him. 'Did that include tormenting me? I was an upstart in your eyes, I know, but I was just a bairn, and an orphaned one, to all intents and purposes. You made my life a misery and I think it was deliberate. I want to know why.'

'I made *your* life miserable,' Lady Munro hissed. 'You have no idea what suffering is.'

'Aye, but I do, and it was you who taught me much of it. It would have cost you nothing to be kind to me or even just to let me be, but instead you took pleasure in my pain.'

'I would have taken greater pleasure still had you never been foisted upon me in the first place.'

'That was your husband's decision.'

'Oh, I know that only too well. He would not have my cuckoo in his nest, but he was perfectly happy to—' Lady Munro took a quick breath. 'He came to regret it, though. Aye, I must remember that. He regretted it. You betrayed him. The laird did not forgive you for that, even though—no, he did not forgive you.'

'I did not betray him!' Realising he was in danger of allowing her the upper hand simply by losing his temper, Alasdhair stood back from the desk and resumed his seat. 'Was it Rory?' he asked in a calmer tone.

'Rory? What about him?'

'Your first born. The child of your first marriage. Is it that simple? You resented me, a factor's son, living here when he could not? It must have been hard, seeing me take his rightful place.'

'Nothing is that simple. You're not capable of taking Rory's place. He is a laird, of noble blood, you are a bastard.'

'But it must have felt as if I was doing so,' Alasdhair insisted. 'I can see that now. All the harder a blow to bear since it was Lord Munro's decision in both cases. Guilt is a terrible thing too, is it not, my lady? No wonder you can't look Rory in the eye. No wonder you don't feel entitled to see your grandchild.' She had paled, though she still did not speak. He had clearly hit upon the truth. Or part of it. 'Is that the only reason?'

For long moments, Lady Munro made no reply, gazing off into the space over his shoulder. Indeed, she seemed to have forgotten his presence all together, for her eyes were blank, her thoughts turned inwards, her hands clasped so tight together that the knuckles showed white. It was a chilling sight. The clock on the mantel chimed the hour. Lady Munro glanced behind her at the portrait of her husband. *Why not? The shame of it would be worth it, if it rid them all of Ross. Why not?* She turned her gaze back to Alasdhair, curling her lip. 'You're right, there is another reason, Alasdhair Ross, but I don't see why I should have the bother of telling you. That honour should go to the root cause of it all.'

'Who?'

'Your mother.'

'My mother!' Alasdhair's brows snapped together. 'She's still alive, then? You know where she is?'

'I have always made it my business to know.' Lady Munro's eyes narrowed. 'When you've seen her, when you've heard what she has to say, there will be nothing to keep you here. You'll be going back to Virginia?'

'That is my plan.'

'Then make sure you stick to it.' Lady Munro's mouth curled. 'When you've heard what she has to say, I don't doubt you will.'

'What do you mean? What has my mother to do with you? Why—?'

'Ask her, Alasdhair Ross. Ask her why I hate you. Tell her I gave my permission for it to be the truth.'

'What are you talking about?'

Lady Munro shook her head. 'She's in Inveraray. Ask her. And then get the hell out of Scotland and leave my daughter alone.'

Realising there was no more to be had from her, and determined not to allow her to see how much her hints had stirred his curiosity, Alasdhair got to his feet. He had what he needed. He was anxious to be gone.

'You need not seek Ailsa out to say your goodbyes,' Lady Munro said sweetly, 'she will be otherwise engaged tonight. Her husband-to-be has just arrived.'

'McNair is here?'

'She told you about the betrothal?'

'Of course. Unlike you, Ailsa has no liking for deceit.'

'I will bid you goodbye then, for I am informed that you plan to spend the night at the smiddy,' Lady Munro said. 'An excellent idea. Hamish Sinclair and his wife are much more your sort of company than the more exalted ambiance of the castle.'

It surprised him, how petty her spite sounded. He wondered if it had always been so. 'You are quite right, Hamish and Mhairi are much more my sort of company, and I hope it is ever so,' Alasdhair said. 'There is, however, no need to say your farewell to me just yet. I shall be back in the morning to see Ailsa. I do not intend to leave a second time without saying goodbye to her. Through your duplicity and treachery you succeeded the last time. I do not intend to let you succeed again, so it is merely adieu.' He bowed. 'I will take my leave now. I find the air in here too fetid to breathe.'

Pulling the door closed behind him, he leaned against the wall panelling. Thank God he was not obliged to face dinner here. Ailsa would have more than enough to cope with tonight without the additional angst which his presence would cause.

Back in the book room, Lady Munro picked

up the letter opener that sat on her blotter. Made of chased silver with an ivory handle, it had belonged to her first husband. Rory's father, one of the very few things of his she had in her possession, for Lord Munro had preferred to believe that Rory and his father and indeed her first marriage had never existed. Taking a deep breath, she lifted the little knife high above her head and hesitated for a moment before plunging it deep into the oak desk.

Ailsa was dressing for dinner, donning a dark green silk half-robe. It had long sleeves, fitted tight to her elbows, where the lacy ruffles of her clean sark billowed out. She wore it over a cream petticoat patterned with sprigs of yellow flowers. She looped a long strand of milky pearls around her neck, and was fastening her hair up, securing it with a good many painful pins, when Lady Munro let herself into the bed-chamber.

'I am glad to see you looking so well,' she said, eyeing Ailsa's *toilette* with approval. 'Donald is here.'

The pin Ailsa was holding dropped to the floor. 'Donald? I thought—I assumed you had postponed his visit, after our last conversation.'

'After our last conversation, I thought his visit was all the more urgent.' Dressed in a close-fitting dress of black silk, Lady Munro looked like a beautiful and lethal serpent. There was a brittleness about her, too, that was rather frightening. Ailsa wondered if it was the result of her interview with Alasdhair. Only the knowledge that her mother would tell her nothing, unless it suited her, prevented her from asking.

'You do not rate my advice, I know,' Lady Munro said, picking up the fallen hairpin and placing it carefully into Ailsa's coiffure, 'but you would do well to heed it, none the less. You would be very foolish indeed to give way to this flight of fancy and end your betrothal.'

'Which flight of fancy would that be?'

'Don't play the innocent with me. It is no coincidence that your sudden change of heart has come hot on the heels of Alasdhair Ross's return. I have seen the way you look at him, like a besotted schoolgirl.'

Did she? 'Indeed I do not,' Ailsa said defiantly. 'Alasdhair and I are friends. We were always close, until you put an end to it.'

'Well, I have no need to put an end to it this time,' Lady Munro said with a glacial smile, 'he is quite capable of doing that himself.'

'What do you mean?'

'He is off tomorrow, seeking tears and reconciliation with that mother of his.'

Ailsa swallowed. She had suspected, despite his protestations, that Alasdhair would be unable to resist seeking his mother out once he knew her whereabouts. She had not expected he would discover them so quickly, though. 'So you knew all along where she was?'

'Of course I knew. Everything that happens on Errin Mhor is my business.'

Ailsa bit her cheek. This time she would not lose faith. 'Alasdhair wouldn't leave without saying goodbye. If you say otherwise, I won't believe you. You lied the last time, but it won't work again.'

'No, you're right, he wouldn't. He said as much.' Lady Munro twisted her jet bracelet round her wrist. 'He may say his sentimental goodbye if he wishes. That is of no real consequence to me. The important point, daughter of mine, is that he will be gone and gone for ever,' she said with a triumphant smile.

Chapter Six

Ailsa gazed at her mother in despair. 'Why do you detest him so? Why are you so desperate to see the back of him?'

'I know you and I have—there have been—in short, you think I do not care, but…' Lady Munro faltered under her daughter's look of disbelief. 'Now your father is gone, I had hoped we would have a chance to put our relationship on a better footing.'

'Now my father is gone! My father had been ill for a long time, yet you showed no sign of any such wish. In fact, you have never given me any sign at any time that you care for me. We do not have a relationship to rebuild.'

'That is not true. I may not have shown you outward affection, but—

'Please, don't tell me that you have always cared for me in your heart, for you do not possess one. This has nothing to do with my father dying. You are like a dog with a bone, Mother, only interested in it if someone tries to take it from you. You want me to marry Donald so you can keep me close, under your control. Alasdhair is a threat to that, that is why you are so desperate to see him gone. It is not out of love for me, but to protect your own selfish wishes.'

Lady Munro, who had momentarily seemed to be on the point of some softer emotion, now paled, and stiffened into something more nearly resembling a marble effigy. 'Listen to me, Ailsa, and listen well. Whatever it is you think you feel for Ross, it is wrong. It cannot be. I won't—I can't—it would be wrong.' She took a quick breath. 'Ross feels nothing for you. You cannot be so foolish as to end such an advantageous marriage as has been arranged for you for the remnants of an adolescent fancy.'

'I'm not.'

Lady Munro relaxed a fraction. 'I knew you would see sense.'

'I'm not ending my betrothal because I think I'm still in love with Alasdhair. Mother, you must listen to me for a change. Just this once, you must take me seriously.' Ailsa took a swift turn about the room. 'I cannot marry Donald. I will not marry Donald. I am sorry if it upsets your plans, but I will not sacrifice myself to duty as you did. Whether you believe me or not, my change of heart has nothing to do with Alasdhair, and everything to do with my finally coming to know my own mind. We would not be suited.'

'There is no one who would suit you better. If not Ross, then tell me, Ailsa, what is it that has changed your mind so suddenly? It is not as if this betrothal is a new thing, nor, I am sure you do not need me to remind you, has it been undertaken without your consent.'

'I know that, of course I know that, but I was wrong. I cannot, Mother. I don't care enough for him.'

'*Care?* You will learn to care, once you are wed.'

'No. I don't love him.'

'I wonder where you get these fancies from! A good marriage comes about from shared interests, an investment in the next generation and a common desire to make it work. It takes commitment and unquestioning loyalty and hard work. It has nothing to do with affection.'

'Yours certainly did not.'

'My marriage was a success. As yours will be.'

'I don't want that kind of success—it comes at too high a cost.' Ailsa clasped her hands tightly together to stop them shaking. 'You said you cared for me. Don't you want me to be happy?'

'Marriage to Donald will make you happy, if for no other reason than it is what everyone else wants. There is much to be said for doing one's duty, Ailsa. I cannot commend it to you highly enough.'

'Even if it makes me miserable.'

'You are wilfully misunderstanding me. The doing of one's duty cannot make one miserable. If I cannot persuade you, perhaps Donald will. I will ensure that you and he have some privacy later.'

'Mother! Please, I beg of you do not. I don't

want to be left alone with him. I am not going to marry him, you must accept that,' Ailsa said despairingly.

'Nonsense. You owe it to him and to me and to the memory of the laird, and to Calumn, too, for that matter, to honour this betrothal.' Lady Munro nodded with satisfaction, 'I wonder why I didn't think of this before. Sometimes the old ways are best.'

'What do you mean the old ways?' Ailsa asked suspiciously.

'In times gone past problems were often solved by taking what you might call a more direct approach. There is a lot to be said for pre-emptive action.'

'Mother, what on earth are you suggesting?'

'There is no need to be so dramatic, Ailsa,' Lady Munro said ruthlessly. 'I am talking about granting Donald a few liberties as a token of your willingness, that is all. I am hardly suggesting you surrender your maidenhead to him.'

'I won't. I *can't*. You are under the impression I have taken this decision lightly, but I have not,

I assure you. For a while now, since before my father's death, I have been unhappy about it.'

'My mistake has been in allowing the betrothal to go on so long. We will remedy that urgently, and when you are married I will prove to you that I can be the loving mother you deserve. You will thank me for this later,' Lady Munro said implacably. 'I will leave you to complete your *toilette*. Dinner is in fifteen minutes, do not be late.'

She closed the door of her daughter's chamber behind her and leant against it for support, for she was shaken by Ailsa's strength of will. Shielding her eyes with her hands for just a moment, Lady Munro's sharp mind sifted through the possibilities. She could not take the chance on Ross's leaving, even after he heard what Morna had to say. She could not take the chance on Ailsa being here waiting for him. She could not take the chance on her plans, her long-coveted plans, for keeping Ailsa close, for coming out of the laird's shadow, failing now, at this last moment. She could not take the chance of another of the laird's shadows hanging over her for ever. Ross must go. Ailsa must marry McNair.

The solution, obvious as it was, was also repugnant. But Ailsa would forgive her. And if she did not—Lady Munro took a shaky breath. The truth about Ross. If needs must, she would tell her. Then she would understand.

Standing up straight, Lady Munro set off down the corridor with a determined step. The truth was a last resort. Donald McNair was a first.

The Laird of Ardkinglass was drinking a glass of claret when Ailsa made her way downstairs to the great hall, but he put it down at once to press a kiss on his betrothed's hand.

Ailsa had always thought him a tall man, as indeed he was compared to most Highlanders, but tonight he appeared diminished. It was not just that he was shorter and of slighter build than Alasdhair, but he lacked his presence. She had always thought Donald McNair a good-looking man, too. At thirty-two years old, with dark brown hair, a strong nose and a decided chin, he passed for handsome in most company. She could not decide what colour were his eyes— brown or hazel or a sort of grey-green?

'Here is Donald, come to pay his condolences,' Lady Munro said. Her smile was that of a witch who has completed a particularly taxing spell.

Ailsa curtsied. 'I trust you are fully recovered, Laird,' she said.

'Aye, I'm well enough. All the better for seeing you.' Donald patted her arm.

They made their way through to the small dining room for dinner. Lady Munro presided over the dinner table like a death's head. Donald sat at her right hand, Ailsa at her left, in a state of nervous anticipation bordering on panic. She could not believe her mother really meant what she had said. She could not eat for wondering if she did. She felt sick, and wished fervently that Calumn had not gone to Edinburgh.

The conversation focused largely on the threat of incomers. Lady Munro took little part but sat, sphinx-like and inscrutably threatening, as Ailsa and Donald debated the issue. In the aftermath of the Rebellion, many Jacobite lands had been sequestered by the Crown, and were now being sold off cheaply to farmers from the south of Scotland and the north of England. Intent only on lining their pockets, these men were clearing the land of the crofters and cotters who had lived there for generations, leaving them homeless and starving.

'Fraser of Straad shipped those of his tenants that wanted to go off to a new life in America before the new landowners arrived,' Donald said. ''Tis a sorry sight, seeing men so proud come to this. Fraser has only his name left to him.'

'If we are not careful, it will be the same for us all,' Ailsa replied. Like both of her brothers, she could see the necessity for change. 'Calumn says the trick is to stay ahead of the pack.'

'What can a bunch of Sassenachs teach us Highlanders about farming our own land?' Donald said scornfully. 'We've been working this land the same way for centuries.'

'Precisely. There is no point in sticking to tradition just for the sake of it.'

'Your brother is in danger of throwing away

his heritage. Lord Munro would be turning in his grave to hear you, Ailsa.'

'He's like to be spinning in it by the time Calumn is finished,' Ailsa said, ignoring her mother's warning frown. 'He has no intention of allowing his tenants to follow those of Fraser of Straad across the ocean. If enclosure is what is needed, so be it. The good heart of Munro lands and Munro people is what matters. What use is pride to you, when you have an empty stomach? There is no such thing as a traditional way to starve.'

Donald looked scandalised. 'I hope you're not thinking of bringing this radical talk with you to Ardkinglass.'

Lady Munro pushed back her chair abruptly. 'Ailsa listens too much to her brother's modern ideas. She likes to tease, Donald, I am sure she has no such intentions.'

'It is not just Calumn who says these things,' Ailsa said defensively.

Lady Munro closed her eyes. 'I am aware, Ailsa, that your other brother is even more revolutionary. You would do well not to heed him.'

'My brother's name is Rory, Mother. Can't you even bring yourself to say it?'

'Don't imagine you have the monopoly on feelings, Ailsa,' Lady Munro snapped.

For a split second her mask slipped. There was pain in her eyes, dark pools of it, but by the time Ailsa had opened her mouth to apologise it was gone and Lady Munro was turning a bright smile on Donald. 'You will forgive me if I retire early tonight. I have the headache.'

'I'm sure Ailsa will keep me entertained,' Donald replied.

The meaningful look they exchanged left Ailsa in no doubt that her mother had made good on her threats. She watched incredulously as Lady Munro made her stately way out of the door without even looking back.

The sound of the latch clicking to made Ailsa jump to her feet. 'I must bid you goodnight, too,' she said, backing away from the table. 'I find I am tired.'

Donald drained the contents of his claret glass in one swallow. 'Has not your mother spoken to you?'

'Yes, yes she has.'

'Lady Munro is minded to keep to tradition.'

'Donald, there has been a misunderstanding. You must know that I have…'

He smiled. 'There now, you're nervous. Of course ye are.' He took her hand between his. He had strong hands, calloused and scarred. The hands of a man who worked hard for a living. The hands of a warrior, too. Donald's skills with the broadsword were legendary. It was something she had liked about him before.

She tried to pull away, but his grip on her tightened. 'Donald, you mistake the situation.'

'There's nothing to mistake. We are betrothed. It is high time you showed willing.'

She did not like being in the room alone with him in this way. Though the table had not been cleared, she had no doubt that her mother had left instructions with the servants not to disturb them. The room was in the square tower, in the oldest part of the building, where the walls were almost a foot thick. No one would hear her. With Alasdhair away at the smiddy, there was no one to rescue her.

'I am very tired, Donald, it's been an exhausting few days,' Ailsa said a little desperately.

'Is it wooing ye want? I didnae think you were one for pretty speeches and the like, but if that's what it takes, you must know that I think you a fine-looking woman.'

'Donald, I can't...'

He gave an exasperated sigh. 'And were you not such a fine-looking woman with such a big dowry, I don't doubt I'd be looking elsewhere for a wife.'

'Donald, I'm sorry, but that's exactly what you are going to have to do. We have made a mistake. *I* have made a mistake. It is all my fault. I'm sorry, I'm really sorry, but we are not suited.'

'I wouldn't say that. I've brought more spirited fillies to heel than you. Come now, lass, don't be shy,' Donald said with a smile that was meant to be reassuring. 'A strong hand on the rein and a sure seat in the saddle is what it takes, and I have both.'

'Donald, you must listen to me. I don't want to marry you. I can't marry you.'

'That is not what your mother tells me.'

'She is wrong. She doesn't understand.'

'I think she understands you very well. What you need is taking in hand.' He edged her back against the wall. 'You are to be my wife, Ailsa, best you learn now that I will brook no refusals.'

'Donald, please don't do this.'

But the Laird of Ardkinglass was deaf to her protests. 'Haud your wheesht, 'tis not words I'm wanting from that mouth of yours.' He kissed her, his mouth hard and hot on hers. His tongue and his hands were like an invasion. She tried to push him away, but her flailing blows were no match for Donald's superior strength. He held her easily, though she fought him with all her strength. His hand on her breast was like a vice. Her mouth was suffocated by his. He yanked painfully at her hair to angle her head. She tried to kick his shins, but she was pressed hard against the wall. She managed to free one hand and ripped her nails into his face.

Donald gave a cry of fury and cursed viciously. Touching his finger to his cheek, he stared in astonishment at the blood she had drawn.

Ailsa began to edge away from him, heading for the door. Donald took a step towards her, then stopped. 'A wild cat. Who'd have thought it, with that frigid mother of yours?'

Ailsa grabbed the door and ran, crying and panting with relief and fright, back to the sanctuary of her bedchamber. In the dining room, Donald mopped his face with a discarded napkin. There would be time enough to tame her, but tame her he would, and soon. It would be a challenge he would enjoy, he thought with relish. With a grim smile, he tossed back a fortifying glass of claret, before ringing the bell.

'Tell Lady Munro that I am of a mind to do as she suggested,' Donald told the servant. 'Tonight.' Then he headed out to the stables in search of his groom.

Pacing backwards and forwards between the window and the fireplace as the dawn light crept across the ocean, Ailsa watched the fishing fleet make its way out to sea. Her head felt as if Hamish Sinclair was pounding her brain with the smiddy hammer.

Until today, she had not disliked Donald. On the contrary, she had genuinely believed he had all the attributes of a good husband. Seeing him again, she was taken aback at the degree to which her feelings for him had changed. The very idea of being intimate with him appalled her. He looked at her without really seeing her, he heard her conversation without listening. Save for their heritage, they had nothing in common.

Yet it was their heritage that, according to her mother, would guarantee the success of their marriage. That, and Ailsa's recognising that entering into such a marriage was her duty. She had not realised, until she started to question it, how strongly entrenched her own acceptance of such a rationale had been. She had not realised until tonight just how successful her mother had been in moulding her in her own image, playing on Ailsa's insecurities in order to do so. How successful, too, in making her subdue her own wants and inclinations—in making her feel guilty for having them in the first place!

Tonight had been a revelation in more ways than one. She was not made like her mother, no matter how much she resembled her. The relief of that was so intense that for sometime it obscured the pain of the consequences. She was not made like her mother; she could not be like her. The reservations she had been unable to express, which had been fluttering on the periphery of her consciousness ever since she had finally agreed to marry Donald, now coalesced into tangible objections.

She did not love him and would not bring children into the world that were the product of a loveless marriage. She would not immolate herself on the altar of duty, either. Respect and loyalty to her kin and to her clan she owed, but without integrity, they were meaningless.

She did not love, but she was capable of it. That was the thing her mother couldn't understand. She could, if she let herself, and knowing that she could glimpse happiness. And it made the notion of casting the hope of it aside an outrage. She would not sacrifice herself. Her mother could not understand that, but finally, with a clarity that was dazzling, Ailsa did.

Which begged the question. *Why?*

Ailsa curled up on the window seat, hugging her nightgown around her knees. She knew why. And so, frighteningly, did Lady Munro.

Alasdhair.

Alasdhair, whose kisses she could not help but compare to Donald's. Whose touch made her want to beg for more, not scream for release. Whose honourable restraint she could not but contrast with Donald's ignoble compulsion.

Lady Munro had noticed. Had Alasdhair? Was that why he had so tactfully warned her off? He cared, but he would never care enough, that's what he'd said. He did not want her for a wife. He did not want anyone for a wife. On that point, her mother was right to caution her. She would do well not to build her happiness around a dream that would never become a reality.

But her feelings for Alasdhair had already set her upon the road to happiness—or away from the road to unhappiness, perhaps. His return had forced her to look closely at her life. He it was who had made her realise just how fully she had shut her emotions down. He had roused her from her cocoon. She would not return to it. It was that that she must cling to, to give her the courage to stick to her decision not to marry Donald.

The final lonely star faded from the night sky as the last of the fishing boats turned into a dot on the horizon. Ailsa returned to her bed, curling up under the covers, shivering with the cold. She had been right after all, thinking Alasdhair portended change. The thought made her smile. She had no idea what the future held, but at the moment it was enough to know that a loveless marriage was one of the things it did not.

Tomorrow he would say goodbye and be off in search of his mother. She wouldn't think of that right now. Too painful. Strange, that her own mother had hinted at reconciliation, too. If she was not careful, she would start to feel sorry for her. It was obvious, despite all her claims, that Lady Munro was a deeply unhappy person. Why had she not seen that either, until now?

Perhaps she had been too hard on her mother tonight? Perhaps this time she really meant it. It didn't matter, after all, what put it in her mind. It was a risk worth taking. Tomorrow—today— Ailsa thought sleepily, she would ask her if she meant it. And she would enlist Calumn's help in the matter of her betrothal. Calumn would support her.

Tomorrow Alasdhair would be gone. *Don't think about that.* Ailsa fell into a troubled sleep.

A short while later, a noise outside in the corridor roused her. Even as she struggled to full consciousness, the door was flung open and Donald stood on the threshold of her chamber. He was dressed for a journey, in trews and a short jacket over which was pinned his *filleadh mòr.* His dirk, the long thin knife that no Highlander would travel without, was sheathed in his belt, and his broadsword dangled at his side.

Ailsa sat up in bed. 'What on earth do you want? Don't you dare come in here or I'll scream.'

Donald ignored her and marched into the

room. Ailsa clutched the bedcovers to her. 'Get out,' she said, her voice rising with panic, 'get out of my bedchamber this instant.'

'Be quiet and get dressed. We've not much time,' Donald said, standing at the foot of her bed.

In the grey light she could not see his expression clearly, but she did not need to do so to be afraid. 'Get out,' she said again. Realising how vulnerable she was, she scrabbled out of her bed and tried to edge towards the bell pull by the fireplace. If she could just summon one of the servants...

Donald cut her off. She shrank away from him. 'What do you want?' she asked, backing towards the window.

He smiled. She could see the glint of his teeth. He had very white teeth. 'Get dressed, Ailsa.'

He made no attempt to touch her. She was backed up against the window seat. Her bedchamber was on the second floor. She would not survive the jump. 'Why?'

'Because we're going on a little journey, you and I.'

'Now? It's the middle of the night.'

'It's past dawn. The horses are waiting.'

'Where—where are you taking me?'

'Questions, questions. I warn you, Ailsa, I expect my wife to be a little more compliant.'

'Your—I am not going to be your wife, Donald.' Cold. It was cold. Fear clawed its horny fingers around her heart, squeezing the breath slowly from her.

'By the time I'm finished with you, you'll think yourself lucky to call yourself my wife. You think I'm likely to forget the way you behaved last night? I am McNair of Ardkinglass—no one says me nay. I shall have you, Ailsa Munro, and if you please me, I'll gie you my wedding ring. But if you do not...' He unsheathed his dirk so quickly she realised what he had done only when the sharp point touched the exposed skin under her chin. 'So, you would do well to please me, my dear. Now put your clothes on or I will take you as you are.'

She did not doubt for a moment that he would make good his threats. It was obvious now that her mother was intent on a wedding at all costs.

That Lady Munro was at the very least aware of Donald's plan to abduct her daughter, Ailsa did not question. He would have bound and gagged her by now if he was not certain that no one would come to her rescue.

Shaking, Ailsa pushed the dirk away from her throat. The blade was so sharp that it sliced open her finger. Blood dripped on to the polished floorboards. She put her finger in her mouth. The metallic taste of her own life force trickled on to her tongue. She saw Donald watching her. Saw he found her action arousing and hastily withdrew her finger. 'Turn your back.'

He laughed, a low bristling growl that made her flesh crawl. 'Aye, and have you clatter me o'er the head with something. I'll be seeing it all soon enough, so you may as well drop the modest-maid act.'

As with all things that were once feral, the laird's civil veneer peeled away easily under duress. His accent coarsened. Knowing he was not a man to make empty threats, Ailsa pulled a petticoat and a woollen skirt over her night-gown. She did not bother with stays, lacing herself into a heavy woollen waistcoat and belting and pinning her *arisaidh* over the top. Rummaging in a drawer for stockings, she closed her hand around the jewelled *sgian dubh* she kept there. It had belonged to her maternal grandmother. She had come across it at Heronsay, and Rory had made her a gift of it, on the promise that she would not actually carry it. The little dagger was no more than six inches from hilt to the tip of the blade, but it was sharp. Under cover of donning her stockings and boots, Ailsa tied the *sgian dubh* to her calf with her garter. Tying her hair back with a ribbon, she pulled her *arisaidh* up over her head, and turned back to Donald. Though it cost her dear, she must be all compliance. If he thought her resigned, he would be less careful. At some point in their journey she would stage her attack. She would not let him take her. Rather, she would surrender her life first.

They made their way down the central staircase, confirming Ailsa in her surmise that Lady Munro was well aware of what was afoot. Donald threw back the heavy bolts of the castle's front door without a care for the noise they made. At the bottom of the steps, his groom held three horses. Without protest, Ailsa allowed the man to throw her into the saddle. In the fading light of the night, they made their way through the gates and took the track that headed south. Donald led. Ailsa was in the middle. The groom took up the rear, neatly hemming her in. A pine martin scuttled across the path, making Donald's horse rear up. He cursed.

The very notion of submitting to Donald's touch filled her with repugnance. The strength of her will to survive this ordeal unscathed took her aback. She would fight to her last breath to escape. Ailsa sat up straighter in the saddle. As the morning sun began to rise, so, too, did her spirits. The fog of misery that had encompassed her mind cleared. Ailsa began to plan.

The scent of peat smoke and the tang of salt and the fishy smell of nets drying on washing lines filled the air as Alasdhair left the smiddy in the early morning. Back in the old days, Hamish used to allow him to work off his frustration by taking the hammer to the anvil. Hamish it was who had taught him how to fight with the claymore and how to shoot, too. The smiddy fire was already burning bright when Alasdhair made his farewells. Hamish's beard was as fiery red as the furnace he tended. His welcoming grin burned even brighter. It had been a good night. Old friends, old stories, simple food and good humour. But now he must return to the castle to say his farewells.

The night, spent on a straw mattress in the tiny room that was more of a hayloft reached by a rickety ladder from the main chamber of Hamish's cottage, had brought certainty on one subject. He needed to see his mother, to speak to her face to face, and hear her story from her own lips. It wasn't just the knowing, it was the understanding. Ailsa had made him see that.

Ailsa.

Walking through the wispy morning mist that gave the village a hazy appearance, as if it were on the verge of disappearing, Alasdhair wrestled with the plethora of feelings that one word roused.

Ailsa. Just a name, but it conjured her up so clearly. It could never belong to any other.

He was glad she had decided not to marry Donald. He abhorred the idea of her being unhappy and knew for a certainty that is what such a marriage would make her. She deserved affection. She deserved to be cared for. She deserved to be loved. He wouldn't have entertained such a notion a few days ago. Had it really been such a short time since he arrived on Errin Mhor? A few days? It seemed like weeks, so much had changed.

It was knowing that Ailsa had not rejected him that made him question his mother's rejection. Though he had had to force it from her, the insight Lady Munro had given him into her own mind had helped, too. His mother was the final piece of the picture. Once he had that, he could go home, be finally at peace.

Except there was Ailsa.

He didn't want to leave her. He didn't understand what it was he felt for her. Caring, yes, but he was fooling himself if he thought it was just that, and he was done with fooling himself.

He wanted her. He wanted to imprint himself on that delectable body, to sink into the delightful, sensual essence of her. He wanted to drown in her, and to drink of her, and to teach her pleasure, and to take pleasure with her. He wanted her with a passion he had never felt before, and he wanted her all the more because he knew she felt it too, and never had before. Not even six years ago. Not like this. As well to compare the cheap spirit made from a ferryman's illicit still to an aged whisky, the one a poor pale shadow of the other, lacking depth, quick to effect, short of duration.

Maybe so, but he could choose not to drink the heavenly elixir, Alasdhair reminded himself. He did not need Ailsa Munro, no matter how much he might want her. No fire, however brightly it burned, could flame without fuel. He would not see her again after today. Or maybe after he had seen his mother. She would want to know the outcome of that visit. Since she had been instrumental in persuading him of the need to find his mother, she deserved to know. After that, he would say goodbye. With the distance of the ocean between them, it would be easier not to think of her.

A pang of homesickness for Virginia washed over him. Coming back to Errin Mhor had not been the simple journey of discovery he had thought. He paused at the fork in the road that led to the castle and closed his eyes, picturing the spreading acres of his vast plantation, conjuring up the earthy smell of the summer heat, the sweet, almost rotten smell of the tobacco plants drying in the outbuildings.

Home. He did not doubt it now. For that much alone, this journey had been worth it.

But when he arrived at the castle in search of Ailsa, Alasdhair was informed curtly by Lady Munro that her daughter was not available. 'Where is she?'

'Helping the fey wife with a birth. A difficult one. Twins—she is like to be gone all day.'

Since Alasdhair had passed Shona MacBrayne at the home farm, he knew this for a lie. A cold premonition gripped him. 'I don't believe you. Where is she?'

'If you must have it, she is gone.'

'Gone where?'

'Away from your influence. She is gone to be married to Donald McNair. He came to claim her last night.'

'She has no wish to marry McNair.'

'That may be what she told you.'

Alasdhair shook his head in disgust. 'Your tricks don't work a second time around, my lady. If she is with McNair, it is not of her own free will.'

Lady Munro paled. 'She will not be unwilling, not when she realises it is for her own good.'

'*Not when she realises....* Dear God, do you mean you had her abducted?'

'No! No, of course not. Donald is her affianced husband, he…'

'So, she packed her bags and went off with him of her own accord?'

'She…'

'No, of course she didn't,' Alasdhair thundered. 'She is your own daughter. Your *only* daughter. Are you so set on having your own way that you have had her kidnapped?'

Faced with the large, solid bulk of a furious Highlander, his face drawn tight with anger, Lady Munro quailed. She did not know how it came about that Alasdhair Ross had transformed himself into this forbidding male, who even yesterday had not wholly intimidated her, but he did now. She was afraid.

'I thought that once she saw Donald she would change her mind.' Lady Munro's voice said shakily.

'And did she? No, obviously not, or you would not have resorted to abduction.'

Alasdhair sank on to a chair and dropped his head into his hands. 'When? When did he take her?'

'This morning. Early. I don't know, I…'

'Then it might not be too late.' Alasdhair jumped to his feet. 'Where? Do not tell me he was taking her to Ardkinglass, I won't believe you. He will have Calumn to contend with, and will want to keep her well away from here until enough time has passed to make sure of her shame should her brother try to have her returned. Where? The devil take you, woman, unless you want to see your daughter's life blighted by marriage to a man with all the makings of the tyrant that her father was, you will tell me where he took her!'

'Donald is not—she would not be...'

'He is a laird of the old school, as your laird was. All the men know that. Why do you think the Munro was so keen on the alliance? Do you really want Ailsa to have the life you've had? There's still time to prevent it, if you tell me now.'

Lady Munro staggered against the back of a chair. 'South. They have gone south. What will you do if you find them?'

'I have no idea, save that I will not be bringing her back here until I can be assured of her safety.'

'Despite what you think, I did this because I love my daughter.'

'You have a strange way of showing it.'

As Alasdhair turned to go, Lady Munro clutched at his sleeve. 'Bring her back. Please don't take her with you.'

'I have no intentions of taking her to Virginia,

if that is what you're worried about,' Alasdhair said contemptuously. 'I have wasted enough time already.' Shaking himself free, he strode out of the great hall.

Whey-faced, Lady Munro tottered over to the cabinet and unlocked the decanter that was kept there. Pouring a generous measure of whisky into a single glass, she drank it down in one gulp. Then she collapsed slowly on to the floor, her head in her hands. Despair pierced her heart like a cruel, sharp diamond.

Alasdhair ran all the way to the smiddy. He ignored the startled blacksmith and strode into the cottage. His black suit was discarded in an instant in favour of the *filleadh beg.* Into his belt he slotted his unsheathed dirk. His *sgian dubh* was tucked into the same belt at the back, under his leather waistcoat. The claymore that Hamish had kept meticulously sharpened and polished was lifted carefully from its box.

It had been a present from Lord Munro on Alasdhair's sixteenth birthday. The same birthday on which he had made his son the recipient of a similar weapon. The two-handed claymore of the old days had given way to a smaller, lighter weapon, with a blade measuring some three feet, a good eighteen inches shorter than the one that Robert the Bruce had made his own. Alasdhair's broadsword had a basket hilt made of steel that had been fashioned by Hamish himself. It was worked with the Munro emblems, decorated with semi-precious jewels and lined with velvet. The blade Lord Munro had had specially imported from Germany. Double-edged, it bore the legend *Andrea Ferara,* the sixteenth-century Italian whose name the Germans used as a mark of quality.

Alasdhair buckled the sheath to his belt and placed the claymore reverently inside. Only the other day, he and Hamish had had a practice bout. It had been surprising, how easily the moves flowed back through his sword arm, how well he remembered the need to balance on the balls of his feet, to counter the swing of the sword with his outstretched left arm. He had not thought to use the weapon in anger. Now, he had no doubt at all that that was exactly what he was about to do.

Hamish was waiting worriedly at the stable with Alasdhair's horse saddled and ready. 'Do you need me with you, lad?' he asked.

Alasdhair was touched. Hamish must be nigh on fifty, but he had no doubt that the black-smith's offer was sincere. 'I must do this for myself, Hamish.' Nodding a curt farewell, Alasdhair sprang into the saddle and was gone from Errin Mhor, galloping down the road south in a cloud of dust.

Chapter Seven

Three horses, making no attempt to cover their trail, so sure was Donald of Lady Munro's support, were not difficult to follow. With murder in his mind, urged on by a terror of being too late, Alasdhair had ridden hard in pursuit, abandoning his blown horse at an inn and throwing gold coins at the astonished landlord in return for a fresh mount.

He found them in the late afternoon, on the outskirts of Stronmilchan at the head of Loch Awe where they had stopped to water the horses. Though it was dry now, it had been a showery day. Bringing his horse to a halt out of sight of McNair's party, Alasdhair leapt out of the saddle and tethered it to a tree. Both he and his mount were spattered with mud. As he moved stealthily through the gorse and bracken that gave him sparse cover, Alasdhair's plaids became soaked through. Underfoot, the ground was boggy.

The horses were drinking from the loch. McNair and his henchman were conferring together, standing almost directly in front of Alasdhair. While the laird had his broadsword, his servant was armed only with a dirk. Behind them, Ailsa was sitting on the wet ground. Her hands were bound at the wrists in front of her. A bruise was purpling across her cheek. *Bastard*!

Even as he watched, the mists of rage reddening in his brain, Alasdhair saw the glint of metal as Ailsa tugged a *sgian dubh* from under her skirts and, holding the handle between her knees, began to saw through the leather ties at her wrists. He wondered what the hell she thought she could do with one knife against two men, but he silently applauded her pluck for trying.

He forced himself to wait, keeping an anxious eye on the men, but they took no notice of her. Crouching back on his heels, Alasdhair carefully unsheathed his claymore and pulled his dirk free from his belt. His heart was beating like a drum. Rage coursed through him, thickening to bloodlust as he eyed Donald McNair. He deserved to die for this day's work. He would allow no man to treat Ailsa so badly or to harm a hair on her head. Something primal and vicious snarled in his gut. He wanted more than anything to see Donald McNair slain at his feet.

In the course of the long day, despite her best intentions, Ailsa had several times been unable to stop herself from responding waspishly to Donald's jibes, making her disgust of him too obvious for him to ignore. As a consequence he had slapped her once on the face, a sharp crack that she thought at first had broken her cheekbone. Her head still thumped with the pain. At the last water stop, she had made a break for it, but they had easily caught her and, as a precaution against further attempts, bound her wrists tightly together, making the simple act of staying in the saddle fraught with difficulty.

Knowing that this was her last chance before they stopped for the night and knowing full well what ordeal the night would bring, Ailsa was set upon escape. Though with only herself and what was really no more than a fancy toy matched against two grown men, she knew her chances were slim. Donald had made sure to keep them away from villages where she might raise the alarm. She had only herself to rely on. If she could not escape, she could surely wound him enough to make him come to his senses. She did not want to think about what would happen otherwise. She would not surrender if she could avoid it. If Donald truly was set upon taking her, she would not make it easy for him.

Sawing through the leather that bound her wrists was more arduous than she expected, but finally Ailsa was free. She flexed her fingers, which were numb from the ties, and clenched her *sgian dubh* in her right hand. Then she got to her feet, and, with a scream that seemed to come from the depths of her being, ran at Donald.

Though she had the advantage of surprise,

Ailsa was simply no match for the Laird of Ardkinglass. With a growl that was more annoyance than fear, he dealt her a blow to the stomach that winded her. As she dropped to her knees, Donald grabbed her knife arm and twisted it ruthlessly behind her back. Her vision clouded. She tried desperately to struggle, but Donald's strength was vastly superior. She was clinging on to consciousness by a thread when a wild warrior, a blur of plaid and flowing hair and muscle and grim-faced fury, launched himself like a fiend from out of the undergrowth.

Ailsa's vision cleared as she summoned up the last remnants of her strength. Alasdhair! She had no idea how he had found her, but it was definitely him. He went for Donald's servant first. The man barely had time to draw his dirk before Alasdhair was upon him and thrust his own dirk, clean and easily, high into the servant's right shoulder, severing the muscles and disabling him instantly. The man dropped his knife and howled in pain. Alasdhair dealt him a swift uppercut under the chin with the basket hilt of his broadsword and the servant dropped unconscious to the ground.

Cursing, Donald threw Ailsa to the ground, drawing his broadsword as Alasdhair advanced upon him, his own broadsword in hand. The two men faced each other across the small clearing, the lethal glint of polished steel separating them. Crawling on hands and knees over to the edge of the makeshift arena where the servant lay comatose, Ailsa fought for breath. Terror froze the blood in her veins.

The two men circled each other warily. Donald's face was fiery with rage, his eyes wild with primal lust. In comparison, Alasdhair's was a grim mask, pale and hard, his eyes glittering like the blades he held in his hands. She could hardly bear to look. Though Alasdhair had been a fine swordsman in his youth, he had not the recent experience of Donald. She could not quite believe he was here. How had he known where to find her? That he had come after her at all astonished her. But then he must have known she would not go willingly with Donald, and he was an honourable man. In Calumn's absence, Alasdhair would naturally see himself in the role of her champion. And thank God. Thank God, he did.

Without taking her eyes off the two men, Ailsa scrabbled in the grass for the dirk that Donald's servant had let fall. Her hands closed around the leather-clad hilt with relief. She held the knife secure, clasped with both hands, and struggled to her feet just as the first clang of steel on steel rang out, echoing over the loch like a bell toll.

Ailsa knew that the single-armed claymore was a weapon that requires balance. Though of the sword family, it was not to be mistaken for the épée or the foil, that require the fighter to lunge. Like the sabre, the broadsword, with its double-edged, narrow blade, was designed to cut and to sever. An experienced warrior aims at his opponent's legs and his head. Donald was a very experienced warrior. His first swipe was low, a wide sweep of his arm aimed at Alasdhair's thighs. Alasdhair leapt back, countering with a downward swing that caught Donald's blade, following through with a swipe back in the opposite direction that rent a tear in Donald's jacket.

The men arced the blades through the air with all the force they could muster. Through his rain-soaked shirt, Ailsa could see Alasdhair's biceps bulging. His *filleadh beg* swung out behind him as his sword arm travelled its treacherous path, his upper body following gracefully through, his legs and left arm braced to counter the movement. Forward, sweep, clang. Backward, arch, clang. The sound rang out, echoing back across the loch from the hills on the far shore.

Donald sliced the edge of his blade into Alasdhair's abdomen, but his thick leather waistcoat saved him. As he leapt back, he lost his footing on the slick grass and slid, righting himself at the last moment, taking Donald by surprise with a rare lunge straight at the heart. If it had struck home, it would have been fatal, but Donald leant back, away from the blade, stumbled and fell. Desperately, he tried to swipe with his own blade while prone on the ground, but he had not the strength. Alasdhair stood over him, the point of his claymore pressed against his heart. Donald's eyes widened as he confronted death. Then the blade was withdrawn. *'Bastard,'* Donald cursed under his breath. He knew it was not a reprieve. Alasdhair Ross wanted him maimed, but more importantly he wanted him alive. He wanted him shamed.

Donald fought with renewed ferocity. Both men dripped sweat, their breath forming little clouds of steam in the damp air. The scent of wet plaid and leather and churned-up grass mingled with the unmistakable smell of battle. A hot red smell, raw and visceral.

Alasdhair was exhausted. His sword arm and his shoulder burned. His thighs ached. Sweat seared into his eyes, obscuring his vision, but he clenched his teeth and resolutely closed his mind to everything but the contest. He had wanted to kill, but from the moment their swords met, he had known that death in a fair fight was too honourable an end for Donald McNair. Living with defeat would be far harder for him to bear. Alasdhair shook the sweat from his eyes and concentrated anew.

The end came quickly. Alasdhair slashed high at Donald's neck. Donald's blade met his, and forced it downwards. Summoning all his strength, Alasdhair leapt forwards as Donald leapt back, and the blade sliced through Donald's left thigh to the bone. A crimson flower blossomed instantly through Donald's trews. He fell with one long scream to the ground, dropping his dirk and his claymore.

Alasdhair threw his broadsword aside and rushed over to Ailsa's side, his chest heaving from his exertions. 'Are you hurt? Did he harm you?' He pulled her to her feet, his eyes searching her face anxiously. 'Dear God, Ailsa, please tell me I got here in time.'

She nodded, unable to speak, for now it was over, the shock of her ordeal was making her tremble.

'What is this?' Alasdhair gently touched the bruise on her cheek.

'It's nothing.'

'The bastard hit you.'

'He did, but I took no other harm, I promise.'

'Thank God.' Alasdhair crushed her against

his chest. 'Thank God. I thought—I kept thinking, the whole time it took me to get here, that I'd be too late, that he'd—thank God you are safe.'

He smelled of sweat and blood. She could feel his heart thumping like a hammer on an anvil inside his chest. 'Thanks to you,' Ailsa murmured, closing her eyes just to relish the feeling of being alive and being safe, of being saved from a terrible fate. 'I thought I was seeing things when you emerged from nowhere like that,' she said, with a shaky laugh. She reached for his hand and rubbed the back of it against her cheek. 'I don't know how you found me, but I am eternally, deeply, truly grateful that you did. Thank you, Alasdhair.'

'It is thanks enough that I got here in time,' Alasdhair replied gruffly. Now that he had her safe, the horror of what would have happened had he not found her in time was taking root in his mind. He had not allowed himself to think of anything other than success throughout his frantic race south. Only now that he had succeeded was he beginning to realise how very much it mattered. He could not bear the thought of her coming to harm. Just imagining it was making him nauseous. His arms tightened around her.

Struggling to sit up, Donald McNair let out a low howling moan of agony. 'I should help him,' Ailsa said reluctantly, disentangling herself from Alasdhair's reassuring embrace. 'I would not like you to have his murder stain your hands.'

'Let me take a look at him first.'

The Laird of Ardkinglass lay on the muddy grass, silent now, though the bulging of his neck muscles were testament to the effort he was putting into remaining so. When Alasdhair knelt down beside him, Donald made a desperate attempt to push him away, but his wrists were taken in a ruthless grip and held above his head. 'I'm sorry to disappoint you, McNair, but I'm not going to allow you to extract your revenge on me by bleeding to death,' Alasdhair said grimly. 'Ailsa, come here, take that little dagger of yours and cut his trews as high up as you can, so we can see the wound.'

Ailsa shakily did as she was told. The claymore had cleanly sliced a long diagonal cut across the front of the leg. The bone was not broken. She realised belatedly that Alasdhair must have exercised incredible control not to have done more damage. Blood oozed sluggishly from the wound.

'The blood does not spurt. You did not sever anything vital,' she said to Alasdhair, glad for the training at Shona MacBrayne's side that would allow her to repay a little of what she owed Alasdhair by saving Donald's life. Much as she wished Donald dead at this moment, she knew it would sit very ill with her conscience later. She had never loved him, but she had intended spending her life with him, and she had given promises to that effect. It was not wholly his fault that he lay here with his lifeblood staining the grass. She forced herself to inspect the wound more closely. 'We will need bandages, and something to stitch it with.'

Alasdhair was already hurriedly discarding his waistcoat and hauling his shirt over his head, using his dirk and his teeth to rip the cotton into long strips. 'I'll take a look in his saddlebag, there might be some whisky there, and he is likely in sore need of it, though he doesn't deserve it.'

'If there is whisky, I can find a better use for it than to pour it down his throat.' Ailsa took the pin that held her *arisaidh* in place at her breast and fashioned it into a needle, then rose to pluck some horsehair from the tail of Donald's own steed. 'Hold him,' she said tersely to Alasdhair as she took the bottle Alasdhair proffered and returned to Donald's side, pouring the neat spirit over the wound, causing Donald to scream in agony. Her face set, she then concentrated on the grim task of stitching the two flaps of skin together.

Alasdhair watched her closely, anxious about the toll such a stomach-churning task would take on her already stretched-to-breaking-point nerves. As soon as she was done, he edged her out of the way and competently bound Donald's leg himself, using the bandages that were once his shirt. At some point in the process the Laird of Ardkinglass lost consciousness.

'You've obviously done this before,' Ailsa said, watching as Alasdhair tested the tightness of the binding.

He wiped his hand across his brow, leaving a smear of blood. 'You're not the only one who has benefited from the knowledge of a fey wife. My first job in the New World was on a plantation where they used slave labour. An old woman there, one of the slaves who had been brought originally from Africa, taught me the basics. Of course, she was mostly employed tending the wounds made by the whip,' he said bitterly. 'There, I think that will do.'

As Alasdhair turned his attentions to Donald's henchman, who was only now getting groggily up from the ground, Ailsa sat back on her heels to watch him. His back glistened with a sheen of sweat. His hair clung to his neck. He was a beautiful shape, broad shoulders tapering down to a narrow waist. Even though he was exhausted, he walked with an animal grace that sent his plaid swinging from side to side. He paused to stretch his arms high above his head, rolling his shoulders to ease his aching muscles. They flexed and rippled under his skin. His back was lightly tanned. Except... Alisa could see long thin stripes of paler flesh snaking across his tan. Only three of them were deep enough to ridge. The scars were very old, or very well healed.

She made her way over to where Alasdhair was kneeling on the grass, cutting the sleeve from the servant's jacket in order to expose the wound. Alasdhair got to his feet. 'I'll need something else for a bandage,' he said, frowning.

Without demur, Ailsa cut strips of cotton from her sark, allowing Alasdhair to deal efficiently with his second patient. 'Could you go and fetch my horse for me? It's tethered in the trees over there. I'll just check on McNair,' Alasdhair said. 'Can you manage?'

She nodded, relieved to be spared any further contact with Donald, picking her way through the bracken as Alasdhair turned his attentions back to his adversary.

Donald was lying on the ground, unable to move and sweating profusely. With luck,

Alasdhair thought, he was in for a long and painful recuperation. 'You will regret this day's work.' Alasdhair stood over Donald in a deliberate mockery of the stance of a victorious gladiator. 'If you ever walk again, the limp you'll have will remind you of the wrongs you did.'

'Bastard,' Donald snarled. 'You had not the guts to kill me when ye could have.'

Alasdhair swooped down to grab him by the throat, yanking him painfully upwards, so that Donald howled in pain. 'Killing is too good for the likes of you,' he said contemptuously. 'I would not have you on my conscience.' He leased his hold abruptly. McNair fell back on to the grass with a scream. Alasdhair turned on his heel and walked away. He did not look back.

'We must stop by the inn at Stronmilchan and organise a cart to come and pick those two up,' Alasdhair said to Ailsa when she returned. 'Are you fit to travel? You look all in.'

Ailsa smiled wanly. 'I am just a bit shaken, it is nothing to what I would have been if you had not rescued me.'

'Don't even think of it.'

'I'm trying not to.'

She was pale, her eyes huge, almost black with fright. She looked barely able to clamber on to the horse, but once there she made a valiant effort to sit straight in the saddle, to smile through her frozen face, and his heart contracted again with the fear of what might have been. Alasdhair rode close to her all the short distance to Stronmilchan where the inn was a basic hostelry consisting of a stillroom where whisky was both distilled and consumed, and a stable yard with an enclosed barn in which passing drovers could sleep. Bidding Ailsa to wait for him, he went inside to make arrangements for a dray to be sent for the two injured men. He returned and glanced up at the sky, noting that dusk was just beginning to fall.

'The nearest inn with proper accommodation is about ten miles away. I'm assuming you don't want to stay here?'

Ailsa shuddered and shook her head. 'I'll manage,' she said and turned her horse resolutely on to the road again. Too tired now to do any more than stay upright in the saddle, she followed Alasdhair back out of the village, barely noticing that he headed south rather than north.

The ferry tavern on Loch Awe was somewhat better equipped than the one they had just left. Ailsa was shown to a small bedchamber with a simple pallet bed. As was the custom for ferry inns, the landlord had his own still. As she stood forlornly in the middle of the room, unable to work up enough energy even to sit down, Alasdhair entered the room, carrying a glass containing a generous dram.

'I don't drink whisky,' she demurred.

'Take a little. It will help with the shock,' Alasdhair replied, steering her over to sit on the edge of the bed.

'I'm all right,' she said, though she plainly was not. She was icy cold, and she couldn't stop shivering, not just constant trembling, but sudden violent shakes that gripped her whole body. A tiny sip of the spirit made her cough, but it warmed a path down to her stomach.

A second sip and she felt the tremors subside slightly. She put the glass aside.

'Better?' Alasdhair asked, looking at her anxiously.

'A bit. Thank you.'

'The landlady is sending up some hot water for you.'

'Thank you,' Ailsa said again. 'That's really thoughtful, Alasdhair.'

'It's nothing.'

'It's not nothing. What you did today, it's everything.' Ailsa swallowed the lump in her throat and dashed her hand over her eyes. 'If you had not come...'

'But I did.'

'How? How did you know where I was, what had happened to me?'

Alasdhair frowned. 'Later, we'll talk later. You're too upset just now, you need to rest, calm down.'

'Because what you have to say will upset me more?'

'Later, Ailsa,' Alasdhair said firmly, closing the door behind him before she could object.

She would have to be told of the part her mother had played in her abduction. She was clever enough, any road, to work it out for herself, but he did not relish having to confirm it. She had been through enough for one day.

More than enough. If he had not…Alasdhair ran a hand through his hair and rolled his tense shoulders before taking the stairs two at a time, in search of the tap room. Ailsa wasn't the only one who would benefit from a medicinal dram of the landlord's whisky.

It was not just a jug of hot water, but a tub almost large enough to constitute a bath that arrived, courtesy of the landlady and two sturdy dairy maids. Gratefully, Ailsa stripped off her clothes and stepped in. She soaped herself all over, rinsed with the aid of a pewter jug, then soaped again, letting the trickle of water soothe away the horrors of the last twenty-four hours.

If ever she had doubted her own mind, Donald's abduction had set it straight. The very idea of being bedded by him—how could she ever have thought she could bear it? Sinking down into the hot water, it came to her, a simple fact, pure and clear as a mountain stream, sweeping over her with the same piercing clarity. Alasdhair. It was Alasdhair who had changed everything.

She loved him. It seemed so obvious. It felt so right.

She loved him. 'I am in love with Alasdhair Ross,' she said cautiously, as if trying the words on for size. They fitted perfectly, like a hand-made glove. A glow that had nothing to do with the bath water suffused her body, lighting her from inside. 'I am in love with Alasdhair Ross.' Of course she was.

How long? How? When? Had it always been there, lying dormant these last six years? But, no, what she felt now was different. Very different. She felt this love with the essence of her being, as if it were a part of her that could not ever be rooted out. It was elemental, this love. It was here to stay.

She loved him. She was born to love him. She would die loving him. Strange that her mother had recognised it before she did, ironic that it was her mother's attempt to separate her from Alasdhair that had brought her feelings for him to the fore.

She loved him. She wanted him passionately. She had never desired anything so much in her life as to make love to him; she longed to tend to him and to keep him safe as he had done for her today. He had ridden all this way to rescue her. He cared for her. Her heart grasped at this fact as a starving deer will rush to the first patch of green to emerge from the melting snow, but even as the fresh shoots of hope rose Ailsa saw them wither. He cared, but he would not, could not, love. He had told her that in no uncertain terms. Being an honourable man, he would feel guilty if he knew how she felt. She could not bear that.

Ailsa's inner glow faded somewhat as the reality of the situation began to dawn, but the newness of her feelings and the scale of them would not permit such melancholy thoughts to dominate. Not yet. She loved him so much. Ailsa closed her eyes, and allowed herself to dream.

* * *

When there was a tap on the door sometime later, she was almost asleep. Assuming
it was the landlady come to remove the water,
Ailsa got to her feet, grabbing the drying cloth
that had been placed on the nightstand, and
called out for the woman to enter. In the act
of stepping out of the tub, she froze. It was not
the landlady who stood in the doorway, but
Alasdhair.

'Oh!' Ailsa lifted her other foot free of the
water, but it caught on the edge of the tub.

Somehow Alasdhair made it from the door in
time to catch her just before she fell. The drying
cloth pooled at her feet. He found himself holding a damp, naked goddess. His arousal was
instantaneous.

Hurriedly stooping down to retrieve the cloth
from the floor, he attempted to drape it around
her without looking. It clung to her skin. Her
hair curled in tendrils over her back and her
breasts. She glowed from the warmth of the
water. He released her immediately, turning his
back to the room. 'There's a mutton stew for

dinner. The landlord assures me it is passable.' His voice sounded strangled. He tried to clear his throat. 'If you don't want to eat down in the tap room, I'll have them send some up.'

Clutching the cloth around her, flushing wildly, Ailsa grabbed her sark and pulled it over her head. 'You can turn around now, I'm decent.'

She didn't look decent, she looked delectable, the more so for being completely unaware of the fact. 'Do you want some dinner?' Alasdhair asked, keeping his eyes firmly on her face.

'I'm not really hungry, to be honest.' There was a smear of blood on his chest. Donald's blood. More spots of it on his hands, too. Hands that had fought for her. She wanted to tend to him. She wanted to soothe him. She could feel herself blushing, but hoped he would put it down to her skin being flushed by the hot bath water. 'I don't like you having Donald's blood on you,' she said. 'There's a kettle of hot water on the fire there. You could use my bath.'

Alasdhair hadn't noticed the blood. He didn't like having Donald's blood on him either, but right now it was the least of his worries. He was finding it almost impossible not to look at the way her sark clung to the sweet curves of her body. He was finding the notion of sharing her bath water horribly appealing. His mind was conjuring up distracting images of her standing naked in the tub, with water streaming down her body, the valley between her breasts, the soft mounds of her bottom, droplets clinging to the damp curls between her legs. Under his plaid, his erection hardened.

'Alasdhair?'

He opened his eyes. She was standing right next to him. Close. Not close enough. Too close. 'I should…'

She wanted to tell him. The words fought for expression, clogging her throat, tingling on her lips. She wanted to tell him. She was taken aback at how much. She wanted to kiss him. She wanted him to hold her in his arms. He was looking at her so strangely. He must be so weary. She would not tell him, but she could tend to him.

Without giving herself time to think about

how bold she was about to be, Ailsa nudged Alasdhair towards the tub. 'Let me.' She started to undo the strings of his waistcoat.

'What are you doing? I can manage fine myself.'

'It's in a knot. I have smaller fingers.' She loosened the fastenings and pulled the heavy leather garment down over Alasdhair's arms, dropping it to the floor.

Alasdhair clenched his hands rigidly at his sides. If only she would move away, he would be able to regain control of himself. But instead of leaving him, she dropped down to her knees. 'Ailsa, what on earth...'

'I want to do something for you, that's all.' She undid the laces of his boots, her tongue peeking out between her lips as she concentrated on the task, tugging first one, then the other from his foot. Then she unlaced the ties on his stockings, rolling them carefully down his calves.

Rising to her feet again, she teetered, clutching at Alasdhair for balance. He closed his eyes.

He could feel the movement of her hair tickle his chest.

She picked up the huge iron kettle from the hearth and topped up the bath water. 'Get in,' she said to Alasdhair, pushing him to the rim of the tub and picking up the flannel.

'What are you doing?'

He looked dazed. He must be very tired. 'Get in,' Ailsa said with renewed determination. 'Let me wash you. It is my fault that you are in such a state.'

She wanted to wash him. Dear God, he wanted to let her. Alasdhair summoned up his last ounce of resistance. 'I can manage.'

'Please.' She looked up at him, all big violet eyes and pink lips and curling gold hair. 'Please. There is so little I can do, and you have done so much, let me do this one thing for you.'

Alasdhair took a deep breath. It just required him to take the flannel from her. To tell her to turn her back. He opened his mouth to say the words and instead found himself stepping into the water. It was what she wanted. For some reason, she seemed intent on it. Who was he to deny her? He would endure it. He could endure it. He gritted his teeth as she stooped to fill a cup with water and stood on her tiptoes to empty it over him. Who was he fooling?

He was beautiful, Ailsa thought, as she stooped for another cupful of water. She had not expected to find a man beautiful, but Alasdhair was. His entire upper body was tanned. Naked save for his plaid, he seemed much bigger, broader. A bruise was purpling on his shoulder, another on his ribs. She trickled water down over his shoulders, watching mesmerised as the droplets clung to the hair on his chest, into the hollow of his stomach, dipping into his navel, forging their tantalising way down beneath his belt. She trickled it down his back next, over the strange faint white ridges she had noticed earlier. 'Where did you get these marks?' She traced the pale lines with her finger tips.

'I told you, my first job was on a slave plantation. Let us just say they terminated my employment in a somewhat physical manner.'

Ailsa stared at the scars in horror. 'Do you mean they whipped you?' Tears started into her eyes. 'What did you do to deserve such barbaric punishment?'

'The overseer was very cruel to the workers, especially the slaves. I stood up to him, so they decided to make an example of me. It made a lasting impression, in more ways than one. Since that day I have always ensured that my workers are treated well and work in the best conditions possible. Here, give me the soap, let me do this.'

She snatched her hand away. 'No.'

'Ailsa, I really don't think…'

'Don't think, then. And don't talk,' she said, placing a finger over his mouth to shush him.

He ought to think. He ought to get his thoughts straight now, before it was too late, but his thoughts refused to be marshalled. Still reeling from the shock of her abduction, staggered by the fierce wave of protectiveness that engulfed him at the very notion of harm coming to her, Alasdhair was frightened by the strength of his own feelings. He did not know what to do with them, nor what to make of them, for they made everything else seem insignificant in comparison, and he could no longer fool himself into believing they were the remnant of anything from the past. This painful, tugging, wrenching thing inside him, which seemed to say *mine* with increasing conviction every time he looked at her or thought of her, had nothing to do with anything so insipid as calf love. He had never felt anything like it. He wasn't sure he wanted to. The only thing he was sure of was that he had to excise it, for it was painful, and he didn't want to have to endure it any longer.

He ought to think. He really ought to think. But how could he, when there was Ailsa standing so close, smelling so sweet, looking so incredibly lovely and horribly vulnerable and achingly desirable. The voice picked up volume again. *Mine*, it said, like a fierce growl. *Mine*.

He had never felt anything so sensual as the slow, sweeping motion of the flannel on his skin, the delicate touch of her fingers as she swept his hair back from his brow, leant against his back, his chest, his shoulders, to steady herself as she worked. Her breasts brushed against him through the damp cotton of her sark. He had never experienced anything so erotic as the rhythm of her stooping and pouring, stooping and pouring. Never known anything like the gentle intimacy of the scene, the scent of her damp skin against his, the sharing of the water, and the flannel.

She washed his hands and his arms. Standing on tiptoe, she worked her way across his chest, his shoulders. Down his arms. He stood perfectly still. The corded sinews on his forearms stood out like ship's rope. The muscles on his calves, too, braced. As she reached his stomach, he knew he could not resist much longer. The poor lass had just escaped from one seduction; the last thing on her mind was another, he was sure. She was doing this out of kindness and obligation, she had no idea of the effect she was having on him. None. And he would not allow her to see.

'That's enough.' Gently, reluctantly, determinedly, he wrested the flannel and soap from her. 'Thank you, but I can manage on my own now. You look exhausted. You should go to bed. I'll leave you in peace in a minute.'

Ailsa nodded and did as she was bid, sitting on top of the bed, a blush stealing over her cheek as wanting warred with belated embarrassment at how bold she had been. Not that she for a moment regretted it. Every inch of him that she had touched was recorded for ever in her mind. It was a worshipping, an adoration, and like to be her only chance to do so. She would never regret it. How could she when she loved him?

She loved him. She loved him. She loved him. The words filled her with delight. She closed her eyes, a smile guarding her precious secret.

Chapter Eight

When she opened them again, Alasdhair was standing before her, his body still damp, his hair sleekly brushed back on his forehead. He wore only his plaid, that was also damp. 'Alasdhair,' she said, just for the pleasure of saying his name.

He sat down beside her. He smelled of soap and damp wool. 'Do you think you will sleep now?'

'Not yet. I want to know how you found me.'

Alasdhair hesitated. 'Maybe in the morning, when…'

'No. I want to know now. It's all right, I assume my mother had some part in it.'

'Lady Munro seems very eager for you to marry Donald.'

Ailsa's mouth trembled. 'Enough to connive at my abduction. What a care she has for me.' She rubbed the back of her hand over her eyes. 'You know, the irony of it is that just before Donald broke into my room I was thinking I had been too hard on her. She said to me last night—I can't believe it was just last night—she said to me that despite how it looked, she cared for me. I thought, she's my mother, perhaps she deserves one final last chance. I should have known better. When Donald burst in I knew he would not have dared such a thing without my mother's knowledge.'

'Twisted as her logic was, I really do think she believed she was acting in your best interests in trying to speed your marriage to Donald.'

'How can you say that? She knows—I made it plain—that I do not want to marry him. How can she imagine that making me unhappy is in my best interests?'

'I'm sorry, Ailsa, I don't know the answer to that. I do know that she loves you though, for she told me so.'

'She actually said those words?'

Ailsa's big violet eyes looked eagerly at him. Such a simple, obvious thing for a mother to say, yet she obviously had not. Ever. 'Yes.'

'Do you think she meant it?'

Alasdhair felt as if his heart was being squeezed. He couldn't bear her to be disappointed, but he couldn't bear to lie to her, either. In his own mind, Lady Munro had behaved unforgivably towards her daughter. Whatever her motives, she had connived at Ailsa's kidnap and would have allowed her to be forcibly wed too, knowing full well how Ailsa felt about Donald. It was not just a selfish action, nor even just a thoughtless one, but a cruel one, and he despised her for it. But to say so, to make his feelings plain, would only hurt Ailsa, and she had suffered enough. Lady Munro had shown some contrition, but it was too little and too late; besides, he had pretty much had to force it from her.

'I think she meant it in her own way,' he said cautiously.

Ailsa ran her fingers through her hair, pushing the curls back from her face. 'Aye, perhaps.

But those sentiments will be short-lived, once she finds out that she's been thwarted, thanks to you.'

Alasdhair sighed heavily. 'I think she'll just be relieved that you're safe. Truly, Ailsa, I don't think she means to make you miserable. It's more that she's so set on having her own way that she can't see beyond it.'

'It's good of you, and I know you mean to make me feel better, but honestly, Alasdhair, you've no need.'

'Have you thought of what you will do next?' he asked.

Ailsa shook her head. 'I don't know. I don't want to think about it right now, if you don't mind. Stay with me a minute, tell me your own plans.' She didn't really want to know, for the implications were bound to be painful, but if she did not know then she would hope. And that would be even more unbearable. 'My mother let fall that she has known all along where your own is living. She told me you were heading off in search of her.'

'I was. I am. I intended to travel to Inveraray,

where she is, after saying farewell to you, but when I got to the castle and found you gone I changed my plans.'

'Inveraray is not so far from here, I haven't taken you too much out of your way after all. You must have so many things you want to ask her.'

Alasdhair frowned. 'Maybe. I mean of course, yes, I've questions for her. I just don't know if her answers matter any more.'

'Why not?'

'She left my father for another man and abandoned me in the process. She made no attempt to get in touch with me. She must have had her reasons, I'm sure she does, but what difference does it make now?'

Ailsa could not resist taking his hand. 'Alasdhair, you must not be putting off this business on account of me, if that is what you're worrying about. You're worn out and it's my fault. Tomorrow you will have regained your perspective. I can make my own way back to Errin Mhor quite easily, you know, I would not like—'

'No! Absolutely not.'

'I am perfectly capable—'

'No. You're not going anywhere on your own.' *Or anywhere without him, until he knew what was going on.*

'You can't possibly be worrying that my mother would engineer another abduction? Even if she wanted to, Donald is hardly in a fit state to be thinking of matrimony.'

Alasdhair smiled. 'No, McNair will not be capable of going down on bended knee any time soon, that will come as welcome relief to the womenfolk of Argyll.'

'You mustn't worry about me, Alasdhair.'

'But I do.'

The fire crackled. Alasdhair turned to tend to it, laying two dried peats on top of the embers. How well the plaid suited him, Ailsa thought, watching him. Some men had such spindly legs, but Alasdhair's were shapely. She hadn't really noticed before, how well the plaid showed a man's body—when he had the right body. Not many men looked as well as Alasdhair in Highland dress. None, really, now that she thought about it. She was willing to bet no man looked as good as Alasdhair.

He left the fire and came back to stand before her. 'I should leave you to get some sleep. Will you be all right?'

'I'll be fine.' But her voice wavered. She didn't want to be alone. She didn't want to think about what had so nearly happened to her, but mostly she didn't want Alasdhair to go.

'Ailsa, come here.' Alasdhair stooped to wrap his arms around her, hugging her tight against his chest. 'You're safe now, I promise. No harm will ever come to you when you are with me. Please don't cry. I can't bear it when you cry.'

'I'm not crying.' Her voice was muffled, for her face was pressed against his chest. He smelled so achingly familiar, so painfully perfect that if she could have found a way of bottling it, she would wear it as a perfume.

Alasdhair stroked her hair. She smelled of soap and sunshine. She felt soft and pliant and very disturbingly right nestling there.

Ailsa snuggled into Alasdhair's bare chest.

'I'm sorry to have put you to so much trouble,' she whispered, her voice muffled by his skin.

'I'd endure anything to keep you safe.' As he said the words he knew he meant it, meant it with all his heart. Her hair was dry now, tumbling in a river of gold down her back. Alasdhair laced his fingers through it, stroking the curls down the length of her spine, and the atmosphere between them shifted, so suddenly that they both tensed. Awareness.

He let her go. He stood back. 'I should go.'

'Don't.'

'You should sleep.' But he made no move. Her bare feet dangled down from the bed. He remembered then, that feeling of them on top of his, on the boat. The most erotic thing he'd ever felt. Before he could stop himself he knelt down to clasp one of them. It was high-arched, the ankles shapely. Her little toes looked unbearably delicate in the palm of his hand. Sadness, piercingly sweet, and longing, achingly painful, gripped him so fiercely that he could scarcely breathe. It was like seeing a picture of a dream he had not known he'd had, so clear, yet even as he looked he knew he would not remember it again, not exactly like this, not so clearly as this.

He kissed the pulse that fluttered above her heel before gently releasing her foot. Then he reached for her, meaning only to kiss her forehead. A consoling kiss, a comforting kiss, a keep-safe-and-goodnight kiss, that was all. But she smiled at him so sweetly, her violet eyes wide with anticipation, her skin softly tinged with the flickering firelight, and he was convinced in that moment that if he kissed her everything would be put right, and he would understand why his mind was in such a turmoil. And she would be healed, too, of all the hurt that had been inflicted on her today. His kiss would take her hurt away and keep her safe, if only he would kiss her.

He took her face gently in his hands, and held her there, gazing into those violet eyes of hers. The way she looked at him, he had the uncanny feeling that she saw right inside him, that she could reach in and show him himself, his real self that only she knew. He had never felt such tenderness, nor such a rush of longing to please, to ease, to pleasure. 'Ailsa.' He said her name just for the sake of tasting it. 'Beautiful Ailsa.' Then he kissed her.

Her mouth was even sweeter than he remembered, like a delicate flower, dewy and plump with nectar. He kissed her gently, the softest of kisses, running his fingers through her hair, twining its golden coils around his fingers. He kissed his way along the line of her jaw and suckled on the delicate shell of her ear. He felt her shiver and felt an answering shiver in his belly, that pierced like an arrow and connected directly to his groin. With a soft moan, he wrapped his arms around her.

Ailsa made no protest. She could not have; even if she'd thought about it, she would not have. It was right. She knew this with a certainty that would have astonished her former self. In this moment there was no past and no future, no barriers, no whys and wherefores. It was right. She had not the will or the energy to resist, but she would not have, anyway. He needed her. She could feel it in the way he touched her, see it in the way he looked at her. He needed her and she would give him anything, everything he asked, because she loved him unequivocally.

His kisses were soft, caresses rather than kisses, soothing, reassuring kisses that asked, but did not take. Like sinking into the downiest of beds, cushioned in satin, cosseted in silk. She felt as if she were melting, slowly, like the snow from the mountains in spring. His skin heated her. She clung closer, her fingers tangling in his hair, stroking the breadth of his shoulders, exalting in the rippling of sinew beneath her fingertips.

Still his kisses feathered and skimmed, making her feel light as air, floating gently on a breeze that caressed so deliciously she wanted it to go on and on and on. Kisses, kisses, kisses. On her brow, her eyelids, her throat, back to her mouth. She was lost, first in the wonder of it, then in the urgent need for more. She barely even registered the change to something darker and infinitely more delightful.

Alasdhair eased her down on to the mattress. She lay there, her eyes wide, looking like some fantasy goddess thrown to earth by a generous deity. He wanted to worship her. It was what she deserved, to be adored, venerated, to be shown how beautiful she was, top to toe, outside and in. 'Beautiful,' he whispered to her, 'lovely, lovely Ailsa.'

It felt like a dream. A perfectly lovely dream. 'Lovely,' she repeated, pulling him towards her.

The strings of her sark seemed to untie themselves. When he took her nipple into his mouth she moaned, such a sweet sound that he felt the blood rush to his groin.

His touch was making her ripple with pleasure, shiver with delight as he sucked and licked and nipped and stroked. His mouth was on her breast. His tongue on her nipple, first one, then the other, coaxing and tugging sensations from her she had not dreamed were possible. She felt weightless but taut. She felt hot and icy cold. She felt utterly safe, yet at the same time she was being led, tugged, straining towards some edge or precipice.

Alasdhair's hand was on her thigh now, stroking the soft flesh there. His mouth on her lips again, kissing, stroking her bottom lip with his tongue, stroking her thigh with his fingers so that everything seemed to meld, his touch, the feelings he conjured, linking and sparking between them so she could no longer tell what he did nor how he did it; did not want to know save to want more, so that she crossed the line between mere pleasure and craving without noticing.

Alasdhair kissed the valley between her breasts. He stroked the curve of her waist, the soft roundness of her belly through her sark. He shifted, moving down her body to kiss her ankle, her calf, the back of her knee, the inside of her thighs. He reached the soft nest of curls between her legs, kissing his way through to the slick warmth at its centre, kissing and licking, stroking, until he felt the damp heat of her, and felt an answering surge of blood to his already engorged shaft.

Ailsa was a rosy-pink kernel now, buried deep in the dark earth. Teasing fingers urged her upwards. There were red-hot tips of feeling inside her as his fingers stroked her, unfurling her like fern fronds in the damp heat. Alasdhair's mouth fed her growth, blushing petals crimsoned inside her as he touched her.

She felt suspended in mid-air. Jagged. And still Alasdhair fed the flames. She could hear panting and realised vaguely it was coming from her. Her nipples tingled and ached. The flower inside her thrust towards the light. Colours streaked pink and crimson beneath her lids. He licked into her, his hands held her safe, tight, and everything settled suddenly, focusing like a beam of sunlight on a piece of glass. Even the blood in her veins seemed to rush like the tide, draining the heat from the rest of her body. He licked again, and her body arched up of its own accord. Her mind registered shock and pleasure so intense it was almost painful, and release came like a shivering surge of all-encompassing, drenching delight.

He had never tasted anything so sweet. Never felt such a heady pleasure in giving, never felt such a deep tug of satisfaction. The pulsing and quivering of her climax on his mouth was heavenly. The need to be inside her, burrowed deep in the sweetly welcoming wet of her was a need like nothing he had ever felt. He craved her.

Alasdhair pressed a lingering kiss to the still-throbbing mound of her sex. Breathing heavily now, heart thumping like the pounding of the drums on the plantations, he kissed the delightful crease at the top of each leg, letting his tongue trace the curve of it. He made himself sit up. His shaft was so hard it was aching.

She opened her eyes to a hazy, pleasure-drenched world. There was a dark flush on Alasdhair's cheekbones. His eyes were peat-smoked, his chest rising and falling rapidly, as if he had been running. He leaned over to kiss her brow. He stroked her hair. 'Beautiful.'

'Lovely,' she murmured.

Longing replaced desire, a different, more unsettling kind of wanting. It frightened him with its persistence and its intensity, for he had no experience of it, nor any remedy. 'Go to sleep, Ailsa.'

'Alasdhair.'

'What?'

A delicious lethargy was creeping over her. She was floating, yet weighted. Anchored down, yet free as a bird. She snuggled into the warm lovely smell of him, as she had done that night in the inn. 'Goodnight,' she said. *I love you,* she thought, twining her arms around him.

Alasdhair tried to ease away from her, but she murmured a protest and he needed little persuading. This way he could be sure she was safe. This way, if she woke in the night he would be here for her. He pulled the rough wool blankets around them. Ailsa nestled against him. He pulled her closer, his arm around her shoulders, watching her, the halo of golden curls on her forehead, the pout of her lips, puffed with their kisses, as she breathed. Despite his own lack of release, he felt somehow sated.

He held her like that for a long time, watching the moon track its orbit across the sky. In all his years he had not once spent the night with a woman, not sleeping, any road. Not holding her safe. Not feeling this mixture of tenderness and protectiveness. Not wanting anything from her.

* * *

He slept, but woke early, rested and immediately restless as he came to consciousness and Ailsa immediately took possession of his thoughts, making him hot and hard.

Last night.

Oh God, last night.

Carefully disentangling himself from the delicious bundle beside him, Alasdhair threw on his clothes and made his way outside. The morning mist hung just above Loch Awe, eerily reflected in the still water. The hills that rolled gently down to the banks on the other side were still brown from the long winter, though the snow caps had melted and glimmers of golden gorse could be glimpsed nearer the shore. Breathing in deep, Alasdhair felt the sharp spike of cold, a warning to those who knew that the Highlands were not quite done with winter yet. He'd forgotten how pure the air here was and how sharp compared to the mellowness of Virginia.

Making his way down to the loch, he picked up a flat flint stone and skimmed it across the waters of the loch. It skipped five, six, seven times before it sank. He hadn't lost his touch. He and Calumn used to spend hours doing this, when they were lads. Momentarily distracted, Alasdhair skimmed another stone. Ailsa never could get the hang of it. Her stones always sank without trace after one hop.

Ailsa. Scuffing his way along the sandy shore, it all began finally to take shape in his head. He had come here, to his homeland, to make sense of the past in order to find peace in the future. To rid himself of the ghosts of his calf love. To call Lord and Lady Munro to account, and his mother too. To end his banishment in order to be content in his exile. To find answers.

He had found answers, but none of them, not a single one, were what he had expected. He sat down on an overturned tree trunk that, judging from its smooth surface, was a popular spot. Part of the problem was that the picture he had hoped to clarify had turned out to be a different landscape completely. His past, which he thought defined him, turned out not to be his past at all. He had hoped to return to Virginia at peace with himself. Instead he would be returning a different person.

Alasdhair stared, unseeing, out over the loch. It was one thing to recognise how much he had changed, quite another to face up to the consequences of those changes. He was so used to denial, so inured to the protective wall of his isolation, that he feared once breached, it would be irrecoverable. He would be exposed, and such exposure he had always thought weakening. But last night, had not it been the opposite? He had glimpsed something so blazingly bright it was awesome. A different quality of light, a different level of contentment.

Happiness?

Love?

'Love.' He said the word out loud and it sounded odd. New. Unfamiliar.

Love. It had been growing since the moment he saw her again. A tiny seed that flourished so vigorously in the sunshine of Ailsa's presence that he had been determined to weed it out for fear it would take root. But it had taken root all the same. He loved her.

He loved her. That is what it meant, this voice in his head that shouted *mine* every time he looked at her. Such an obvious explanation, yet the last one he had expected. And what was astonishing, astounding, was the relief of it; as if he had shed a suit of armour and discovered the war long won. He felt not exposed, but liberated. The shiny future Ailsa had once described to him glittered like a real thing in front of him.

He loved her and she loved him, too. She must. She must, for it was the only explanation for her giving herself to him last night. She would not have kissed him after that first time, or found the courage to be rid of McNair, or done any of the things he had been too much of a blind fool to see and understand. Surely there could be no other explanation?

Alasdhair leapt to his feet. He had waited far too long already to claim her; he could not bear to wait any longer. She was his, she could only be his. She *must* be his. This is what the last six years had been for. This is what the last few days had been for, the growing and reshaping. The timing before had not been right, but now it was. It must be, for without her the world would never make any sense, no matter which way he looked at it.

In Errin Mhor castle, Lady Munro paced back and forward across the space of her book room. She had not slept, save a few fitful dozes, since Donald had taken Ailsa away. Or, more accurately, since she had allowed her daughter to be abducted. Since Alasdhair Ross had confronted her with the evidence of her abject failure as a mother.

Donald McNair had arrived back in Ardkinglass, though the journey had taken so much out of him that at first it was feared he would die of his wounds. Even if he lived, the laird would be maimed for life. There were those who thought death was preferable for such a proud, lusty man as McNair. Lady Munro was not among them. She had no reason to care one way or the other. He would not be her son-in-law now.

She had been furious at first. It had cost her a great deal, knowing how Ailsa had come to feel about the match, to continue to support it, but the balm of saving Ailsa from herself had reconciled her to the necessity of such an action. Until Alasdhair Ross made her see that she was not saving her from herself. She was making her unhappy.

Alasdhair Ross. How she wished he had never set foot back in Errin Mhor. If it had not been for him, Ailsa would have been safe. Married or not, she would have been here, where she belonged, and they could have made a fresh start. They would have. It was not true, what Ailsa said. Alasdhair Ross had not forced her into action. She had been biding her time, merely. Waiting for the right moment. And now it might never come.

Christina Munro rarely cried. Only three times had she done so in the long duration of her second marriage. The first was when Rory was torn from her on her wedding day. A salutary lesson, her new lord had informed her, for she must love him, and only him. And she had, God help her, she had tried to love him as dutifully as she had promised to, faithful through all his cruelty and his own multitudinous indiscretions—that of course were not indiscretions in his eyes, for he owned everything and everyone within his jurisdiction.

She had loved him, but it had only the appearance of exclusivity that he demanded. Her love for her children she kept so secret none saw it, least of all them, but it was there. Three stones, weighted in her heart and encased in ice to protect them. Even now that she was widowed, the hard-learned habit of an indifferent front was proving almost impossible to break. But she would have done it, had not Alasdhair Ross come on the scene again. She would have.

The second time she had cried was when Ailsa was born, and the third time was not so long after that: the day Lord Munro put an end to her hopes of being reunited with her eldest son once and for all. It had been the last time she'd allowed herself that indulgence, until now. Now, as she looked back over the arid years of her marriage and peered forwards to the desiccated years that seemed certain to be her future, the tears flowed unchecked.

Despite all her efforts to prevent it, Ailsa was gone, off with Alasdhair Ross. They would sail for Virginia and never come back to Errin Mhor. Except…

Christina froze. Except before they went to Virginia, they would go to Inveraray. To Morna. Who would tell them the truth. Or what she thought was the truth. Dear God! Ailsa would think—Oh God, Ailsa would think exactly what *she* had wished Ross to think. And it was her fault. She had sent him. Sent *them* there! *Oh, dear God!*

'What have I done?' Lady Munro stared in anguish up at the portrait of the laird. 'You!' she exclaimed with loathing. 'This is your fault.'

Nigh on thirty years, Christina had suffered her husband. Nigh on thirty years of duty and loyalty and this is what she was rewarded with. She had lost the love of Rory, her first born. Calumn, her second son, tolerated her, but was like a stranger to her. And Ailsa, the daughter she had sacrificed so much to have, whom she had done everything possible to keep close, would soon be lost to her for ever. All she had done, especially what she had done with Donald McNair, had been to bind Ailsa to her, and it had taken Alasdhair Ross, of all people, to show her that what she had actually done was drive her away.

Damn him, Alasdhair Ross, he had been in the right of it! She hadn't taken any account of what Ailsa wanted, or what would make her daughter happy, blinded as she was by the vision of her own hopes coming to pass after all this time. And Ailsa had been right, too—what point in denying it now? She should have had the strength of mind to build bridges a long time ago, when the laird became too ill and too dependent upon her to hold any sway. She had not, and regretted it bitterly. Rory's wedding, Calumn's wedding, her granddaughter Kirsty's birth, all had come and gone, blighted by her cowardice, for that is what it was. One thing, she discovered, to dream of a time when she could finally play the maternal role, quite another to face the consequences of all the years of having failed to play it. She was afraid of rejection, so she continued to reject.

Christina's conscience, an embryonic creature with new-formed loyalties, was proving to have a very sharp bite. Procrastination was no longer an option. If she did not act now to make her peace with Ailsa, she never would. If she did not act now to tell her the real truth, to counter Morna's flawed version, Ailsa's life would be forever blighted by the belief that she had committed a terrible sin.

Lady Munro eyed the laird's image. He gazed down at her with a malevolent eye. 'I will go to her,' she told him defiantly, 'and I will tell her, and there is nothing you can do to stop me.' From her desk she took the little Macleod knife. 'Not even you suspected, did you?' she said with a vicious smile. 'Not even you.'

In one assured stroke, Christina Munro slashed diagonally through the canvas, severing the laird's head from his body. 'Goodbye, Iain,' she said, dropping the knife on to the desk, turning her back on the tattered portrait and heading off in search of her groom.

Ailsa had slept late, and was still abed when Alasdhair burst into the room after a perfunctory knock on the door. Startled, she sat up, clutching the sheet, her hair in wild disarray. 'Alasdhair! What's wrong?' Even as she spoke, she remembered last night and a flush crept over her cheeks.

Alasdhair, too, was flushed. There was a look on his face she had not seen before; his eyes glittered, his clothes were in some disarray, as if he had flung them on anyhow. 'Has something happened?'

'No. I mean yes. I mean…' Now he was here, he realised he hadn't thought it through. Never having declared himself before, he had no idea how to go about it. What's more, in the short space of time it had taken him to get here, some of the certainty about Ailsa's feelings for him had dissipated. What if she did not love him? Or worse, what if she had been on the verge of loving him again and he had warned her off too effectively? Why had he been so against marriage? So set against love? He couldn't remember now.

'Ailsa.' As a youth he had been impulsive, but success had come to him through deliberation and careful planning. Now he stood before her, about to make the most important declaration of his life, completely tongue-tied as what had seemed so simple a few moments ago now seemed impossible to articulate. It was like trying to catch feathers in a maelstrom. 'Ailsa.'

Her smile was uncertain. 'What is it?'

Alasdhair took a deep breath. 'Ailsa. Ailsa. Ailsa, I love you!'

She stared in astonishment, wholly unable to believe what she'd heard, unwilling to allow herself to believe it. Alasdhair, too, seemed dumbstruck. Then he made a strange sound, like a croaky laugh, realised he was still hovering in the doorway, closed the door and strode over to the bed. 'Sorry.'

'You didn't mean it?'

'No. Yes. Of course I meant it. I'm just sorry it came out like that.' He took her hand and rubbed it against his cheek before letting it go again. 'I've never done this before. I don't know how to.'

'Do what?'

'Asked someone to marry me.'

'Oh.' Ailsa's eyes widened in shock. Her hand went to her breast, as if to quell the jumping of her heart.

Alasdhair took another deep breath and sat down beside her on the bed, capturing her hand and holding it tight between his own. 'I love you, Ailsa. You must think me a fool, for I think myself a fool for not recognising I loved you earlier. I kept thinking it would pass, whatever it was. I suppose I didn't want it to be that. I thought it a weakness, you see, falling in love, and I've never had any problem avoiding it before. I thought I didn't need anyone, didn't want anyone to share my life. I thought I was stronger on my own. Safer. I thought—och, I thought all sorts of nonsense because the one thing I didn't want to acknowledge was the truth. I love you, pure and simple.'

'Oh, Alasdhair.' She could not speak for the emotion clogging her throat. It was the most perfect, wonderful moment of her life, and she could not find any words for it. And then she did, and what is more they sprang unbidden to her lips.

'Oh, Alasdhair, I love you so much.'

His smile wrapped itself around her heart. 'Ailsa. Oh God, Ailsa, if you knew how much—'

'But I do, I do, I do.' She threw herself into his arms. There was no need for words now, for they spoke with their lips and their hands and their bodies. Feverish kisses, burning kisses, kisses so different from all their other kisses. Passion ignited like a fork of lightning across the sky, its crackling, sparkling edges reaching into their blood so that they really did feel as if they were on fire. They tore feverishly at buttons and fastenings to touch skin, soft skin, heated skin, stretched-too-tight skin, their lips never once parting, fastened so close they could not tell who was kissing whom.

Alasdhair threw his waistcoat on to the floor. The shirt he had begged from the innkeeper quickly joined it. Ailsa sighed her pleasure as the long-pent-up craving to touch him was finally fulfilled: her hands spreading across the ridge of scars on his back, fanning out over the taut muscles of his shoulders, down, round to the crisp spread of hair on his chest, the dip of his ribcage, the flat washboard of his stomach.

Last night she had floated on a cloud of delight towards ecstasy. This morning she was like to ignite with desire, so brightly, fiercely did she burn with need, so desperately did she crave their joining that she would have clawed her way inside his skin if she could.

Her passion was feral. She would not have believed such elemental feeling was possible, never mind that she be capable of it. She wanted to prostrate herself and be taken, to be claimed, to be owned, and to be joined, united. His. She wanted to lick and bite and nip and kiss. She moaned at the constraints of her sark, the only clothing she wore, wanting only to be completely naked, flesh and skin and bone, for him to ravish and mark as his own.

Alasdhair, too, seemed caught in a maelstrom of white-hot desire. He cast off his boots and hose without lifting his lips from hers. He tugged at the lacing that tied her sark, cursing when it became a knot, resorting to brute strength to tear it open enough to free her breasts. He cupped them in his hands, tugging her nipples, making her moan, and when he stopped, it made her moan again. He dipped his head to kiss first one, then the other, rolling his tongue over and round, making her gasp with pleasure.

He pushed her back on the bed and spread her legs. He ran his hands up her thighs, kneading the tender flesh at the top. Her hair was a wild tangle round her face. Flushed cheeks. Frayed, ravaged mouth. Violet eyes heavy-lidded with passion. Breasts heavy and flushed, too, white and pink. Creamy white thighs and pink sex. His manhood pulsed. Blood surged. A tightening in his belly, at the base, made him want to enter her now. Instead he plunged with his tongue. His mouth enveloped her, the soft and wet of her between her legs. Her thighs tightened around him. The essence of her, vanilla and spice and heat and female, went straight to his head. He licked, unerringly finding the swollen bud, waiting for his touch, ready to pulse and burst. He licked and she moaned, and he licked again.

Ailsa's back arched as the throbbing pulse inside her erupted at his touch without warning. No flickering and floating, none of the slow languor of last night, just a sheet of flame, so hot it was cold, and a deep, elemental clenching inside her. She moaned his name. She clutched at his hair, and pleaded with him, though she didn't know what for.

Alasdhair loosened the belt on his plaid and dropped his last piece of clothing to the floor. He knelt between her legs, naked, his shaft curving upwards. He wanted her to touch him. He could see her looking, her eyes widening, felt a surge of purely male satisfaction in knowing that he pleased her. He wanted her to touch him, but not now, there would be time enough later. Right now he needed to be inside her. He had waited too long. He could not wait any longer.

Tender now, though the waiting cost him dear, he kissed her, parting her legs further. 'Ailsa,' he whispered, tilting her to him, feeling the tip of his shaft touch the hot wet of her sex, his breath thrust out of him as if he were winded.

'Ailsa,' he whispered again, then slowly, slowly, began the journey to completion.

She clutched at his shoulders. She watched his face as he entered her, wide-eyed with the wonder of it, the rightness of it, the quivering delight of it. Slowly, he pushed into her, slowly and carefully, she could feel the tension of it in his arms, see it in his eyes, could feel herself opening for him, then a tightness and a pain, brief and ragged, then gone.

'I'm sorry.' Alasdhair forced himself to wait, though it was like clinging on to the edge of the world. He kissed her, his tongue plunging and sliding, and he felt her relaxing, opening, and he crossed the threshold into a different reality. It was a place too hot, too dark, too tight and wet and all-encompassing to allow him to do anything but plunge and thrust deeper into it, then to slide out and plunge again.

The pain was like an echo. With each thrust of the silken sword that was Alasdhair inside her, she felt a *frisson* of shivering, followed by a ragged ripple. Her eyes drifted shut, the more to feel. Behind her lids, in her head, deep inside her, everything ran red. The red of blood and of pleasure. She was like a rock pool, jagged edges catching at the inrush of water, deep centre sucking greedily. Empty. Filled. Empty. Filled. With every inrush filled deeper. With every outrush the ragged pain receding. Clinging. Jolting under the shock of each thrust. Afraid again, but bolder. Something in the distance that she must reach. Something to make the pain worthwhile. She was afraid she was breaking. He was too big. Too much. But still she wanted more.

The clinging hotness of her was unbearable. The unfolding wetness of her, the mind-blowing perfection of her, too much. He wanted to feel her tight around his engorged shaft so that they could both feel the blood pulsing between them. He thrust hard, felt her jolting response. He wanted to come. He wanted her to come with him. 'Now,' he said through clenched teeth, thrusting high, and was rewarded with the indescribable, agonisingly sweet lurch of her muscles that made his own gut-wrenching climax unstoppable.

Ailsa whispered in his ear, just his name, but no one had said his name like that before, and he thrust again urgently, hard and high, kissing her hard on the mouth. His tongue thrust, his shaft thrust, she shuddered, he cried out and came, exploding inside her, and she welcomed him, clutching and crying. They were one, and the world felt as if it were in the right place, the only possible place, for the first time ever.

'Ailsa,' he said, with the tenderness of new ownership, stroking the heavy fall of hair from her heated brow. 'Ailsa Munro. I love you.'

Ailsa clung to him. Tears of release and surrender sparkled on her lashes, and she made no attempt to stop them falling. This is what she was intended for. This man, this joining, something so far beyond pleasure she could not name it. 'I love you, too,' she whispered, planting a sated kiss to his lips.

Chapter Nine

'Much as I would love to stay here all day, I fear we must make a move,' Alasdhair whispered sometime later.

His breath tickled her ear. She could feel the heavy weight of his erection pressing against her thigh. Heat trickled like warm honey through her blood in response. Ailsa sighed with contentment. 'Must we?' she asked, lifting her head from the crook of his shoulder to meet his gaze.

Peat-smoked eyes. A warm smile, but an anxious look that was somehow reassuring. 'We must.' His smile had a softness to it that she recognised as tenderness. 'You don't regret this, do you, Ailsa?'

'What do you think?'

'I think there is only one thing that can make me even happier than I am right now.'

'What is that?'

'Marry me. Marry me, Ailsa, and I swear there will not be a happier man in this world. Say yes.'

Ailsa's tears dropped unheeded from her lashes on to her cheeks. 'Yes.'

'Say it again.'

She threw her arms around his neck. 'Yes. Yes, yes, yes.'

Alasdhair kissed her lingeringly. Still kissing her, already hard, he rolled back on to the bed and pulled Ailsa on top of him. She could feel the solid length of his shaft pressing against her and felt the answering thrum of her own arousal kicking in, low in her belly. Alasdhair lifted her by the waist, and lowered her on to his engorged shaft. 'Mr Ross, I am shocked. If I did not know you better, I would think you insatiable.'

'Miss Munro,' he said, his breath fast and shallow, his face flushed with desire, as he settled her carefully and his fingers stroked into her slick heat, 'I think you will find that when it comes to you I am.'

By the time they dressed, the morning was well advanced. The mist had cleared, making way for a glorious spring day; the pale blue sky was dotted with puffy clouds like new-washed sheep skipping skittishly over the buttermilk sun.

'I've decided it would be best for you to come with me to Inveraray,' Alasdhair said. 'Though it doesn't seem anything like as important as it was before, I do need to see my mother, close that chapter of my life before we write a whole new book of our own.'

'I'm so glad to hear you say that. If you didn't go, you'd regret it.'

'Afterwards, we need to go back to Errin Mhor.'

Ailsa's smile faded. 'Must we?'

'You know we must. We can't just sail off to Virginia without facing your mother.'

'Why not, Alasdhair? She's made her views

plain enough—why give her the chance to air them again?'

'It wouldn't be right and proper.'

'Right and proper! Was it right that she lied to us both six years ago? Was it proper that she encouraged Donald McNair to abduct me when she knew I did not want to marry him?'

'Don't you want to be married in Errin Mhor castle?'

She gazed up at him, her lips trembling. 'Of course I want to, but not if it means more battles with my mother. Please, Alasdhair, I don't want to talk about this right now. I don't even want to think about it.'

Alasdhair's mouth firmed. 'Errin Mhor is your home and it is still my homeland, too. I have only just ended my banishment, I won't have your mother's presence preventing us from going there if we choose.'

'Virginia will be our home.'

'Our home, but never our homeland. Trust me on this, Ailsa, I know.'

'Alasdhair, I really don't want to talk about this now.'

'Very well, but I know I'm right. You'll regret it, Ailsa. I don't want you having regrets when you're too far away to do anything about them.'

'I won't.'

'I want you to think very carefully about that. We'll talk about it later.'

They crossed Loch Awe on the little ferry with their mounts swimming behind them and rode south along the well-established drover's track towards Inveraray, lingering for the sake of lingering together, sharing moments of laughter and *do you remember* interspersed with silences in which they simply gazed at each other, then kissed and murmured their *I love you's* over and over.

In the late afternoon, they came across a boatman who offered to take them, for a small fee, to a famous local beauty spot on a little islet on the loch. 'What do you think?' Alasdhair asked. Ailsa nodded her eager approval. Laughing, he tossed the boatman a few coins. 'There's no need to take us. We can manage fine ourselves. We'll bring your boat back safe, don't worry.'

Ailsa was sitting in the prow, her hair glinting in the sunshine. Looking at her, Alasdhair felt an ache in his heart, so painful was this love he felt for her, he could not believe it had taken him so long to recognise it.

Though he was loathe to spoil the mood, he forced himself to raise the subject of her mother again. 'You know I want you to be happy, Ailsa, more than anything?'

Alerted by the serious note in his voice, she sat up. 'What is it?'

'Whether we like it or not, our parents are the lifeblood we are formed from. No matter what she has done, Lady Munro is still your mother. No matter how much you deny it, I know that what she thinks matters to you. If you want to, we'll find a way of mending your fences with her.'

'I can't imagine how.'

'It doesn't matter how. If you want to, we'll find a way. Your happiness means everything to me.'

'I couldn't be happier, Alasdhair.' Balancing carefully so as not to rock the boat, she joined him on the plank that served for a seat across the middle and snuggled into his side. 'Don't let us talk about it now.'

Alasdhair kissed her brow. 'You can't keep putting it off. Virginia is a long way away, you might not see her again for some years—would you really be happy leaving here without even saying goodbye? Come, Ailsa, you're forgetting that I've been there myself. I know how these things can eat away at you.'

She was concentrating on nuzzling the delightful bit of Alasdhair's chest exposed at the opening of his shirt. He tasted salty. His throat was tanned.

'Ailsa.' His fingers forced her chin upwards. 'Stop avoiding the issue. You're worried she'll manage to taint what we have together, but you're wrong. What we have together is perfect. We are unshakeable, there is nothing she can do to harm us. I love you. You love me. Your mother cannot change that, can she?'

'No, of course not.'

'So what harm can it do to try to make your peace? Why have the fact that you didn't at least try hanging over you? We are headed for a new life, a fresh start—is it not worth making the effort to wipe the slate clean before we go?'

'What a long road you've travelled in such a short distance, Alasdhair Ross.'

'It's because I have done so that I know I'm right.'

Ailsa sighed. 'I know you're right too, but that doesn't mean I have to look forward to it.'

'Look forward to what will follow, then. Our wedding.'

'Our wedding.' Ailsa smiled hazily.

'So that's settled. We'll return to Errin Mhor and see Lady Munro after I've tracked down my own mother. We can then discuss preparations for our wedding with Calumn. Do you think he'll be surprised?'

'He'll be astonished! Somehow I don't think Maddie will be, though.'

'What do you mean?'

'You wouldn't understand. Call it female in-tuition.'

'I may have to leave you for a week or so before the wedding. I have important matters to attend to in Glasgow that are vital to my business. I can't neglect them any longer. There is a merchant there named Cunninghame whom I am eager to negotiate a partnership with.'

'Cunninghame? That is Jessica's name. My brother Rory's wife. Her family are merchants. They disowned her when she married Rory, so I have not met any of them, but I think her father's name is George. Do you think it can be the same family?'

'It sounds very much like it. George Cunninghame is one of Glasgow's biggest tobacco merchants, they have warehouses all along Chesapeake—that's the main bay where Virginia and Maryland have their ports.'

'I didn't realise. Jessica rarely talks of them. You're going into business with her father?'

'Perhaps. If the terms are right. He's also one of the few merchants who doesn't employ slaves to work the farms attached to his warehouses in America.'

'I'm looking forward to learning all about it.'

Alasdhair laughed. 'I'm glad to hear it, but you may not find it as exciting as you imagine.'

'I mean it. I don't want to be one of those wives who know nothing of their husband's business.'

'And I don't want to be one of those husbands who spends all his time on business and has no time for his wife. In fact, I suspect I'm going to be one of those husbands who is so besotted with his wife that he has no time for business at all.'

He kissed her then. His lips were salty. He kissed her slowly, lingeringly, savouring the sweetness of her mouth, relishing the way she melded into him, how her lips moulded themselves into the perfect shape for his and her tongue tangled with his, tantalisingly teasing. And relishing the way that passion ignited them at the same time, so that they clutched each other, as if afraid it would hurl them into another universe.

The boat rocked as they moved on the narrow seat, trying to get closer, their bodies eager for skin on skin, for heat on heat, matching touch for touch, kiss for kiss, need for need, as if they had always been like this, achingly familiar, because only this person and this body and these hands and this mouth would do.

Ailsa sighed with pleasure as Alasdhair stroked her breasts through her clothes, the ache of her nipples as they strained at her clothing adding a little *frisson* of frustrated pleasure. She tugged his shirt out of his belt to run her hands up his sides, over his ribs, into the dip of his belly, relishing the clenching of the muscles, the little moan he made, the way she could feel his breathing fast and shallow, feel his heart pounding in his chest, her own excitement heightened by the knowledge that she had caused this.

The boat rocked more violently. Ailsa giggled. 'We'll sink, if we're not careful. The boatman would take a very dim view of that. I don't think we can…'

'Oh, I think you'll find we can,' Alasdhair said, slipping his hand under her petticoats, making her gasp as he stroked her sex, at the same time as he thrust his tongue into her mouth in a deep kiss that made her head spin.

'Please don't stop,' she said frantically when

he lifted his mouth from hers, and his finger stilled its rhythmic caress.

'I don't intend to,' he muttered, his voice hoarse, his chest heaving. He dropped to his knees on to the bottom of the boat and pulled her with him, tilting her forward on to the narrow wooden seat before easing into her from behind with one slow, long, delicious thrust. They rocked back and forth in perfect, intoxicating harmony, at one with the movement of the boat. The pulsing sensation built within her, each pulse making her tighter, making him harder, swelling, until finally he heard that sweet little cry of hers and he thrust once, hard and high inside her and he spent himself, saying her name over and over and over as the little boat rocked and bobbed on the silent waters of the loch; the only sound audible was the gentle slap of the waves on the hull and the far-off cry of an osprey as it soared and circled overhead.

As they covered the last few miles to Inveraray the next day, Alasdhair grew increasingly silent and withdrawn. He drew his horse to a halt as the village came into view. He was nervous. It did not mean as much as he had thought, but it still mattered. Ailsa had been right. She had a way of always being right when it came to him.

Nigh on twenty years since he had seen his mother. Twenty years in which he had grown from boy to man, abandoned by one parent, deprived by circumstances of the other. Unwanted and unloved. He thought he had grown accustomed to that, and indifferent too, settled in his new life across the sea. Coming back to his homeland, he had been forced to face up to the fact that he was very far from accustomed to it. He didn't like it, any more than Ailsa liked to acknowledge Lady Munro's continued ability to hurt her. They had both practised self-delusion, he and Ailsa.

Laying his ghosts was proving an emotional experience. He had not expected to be so altered by it. The barriers he had erected around himself, that he had thought as impenetrable as the fortifications of the Duke of Argyll's original castle, a sturdy stone edifice just visible up ahead, hidden behind the excavations for the new castle being built to replace it, were eroded. He cared about this meeting. He cared about what his mother would say and cared about what she felt for him. The knots of his past were all but unravelled. He had not thought their unravelling would be so rewarding, had not dreamed he would be returning to Virginia with Ailsa by his side. His love for her made him confident he could deal with whatever version of his past his mother was about to disclose to him, but it was that same love that meant that he was exposed, raw to whatever emotions the truth would rouse in him.

He had a momentary impulse to turn around and head away from this place. He was happy now. Blissfully happy for the first time ever. Nothing could puncture or taint that, but maybe he should not tempt fate by testing it?

Beside him, Ailsa was pushing a long strand of her golden hair back from her cheek. As usual it had escaped its pins. The long days in the open air had given her face a rosy glow and a scattering of freckles across the bridge of her nose. The vitality that had been her essence, which he had thought lost forever, had returned in these last two days, though at this precise moment she was frowning.

'Are you sure you're ready for this?' she asked.

'As I'll ever be.'

'If you're having second thoughts, Alasdhair, it is only natural. Even after all this time, she is still your mother. What she says matters, no matter how much you tell yourself it does not.'

'Spoken from the heart,' Alasdhair said, reaching over to squeeze her hand. 'You are right, it matters. Matters more than she deserves, perhaps.'

The little fishing village of Inveraray was perched on the shores of Loch Fyne. The large sea loch sparkled as the noon sun played on its waters. The village was a mixture of long-houses, where the animals shared their living quarters with the occupants, and smaller cottages, some with separate barns, all with thatched roofs. Every house had its own kale yard. A few fishing boats lay above the water line on the narrow strip of sand that formed the shore. The small kirk stood on a high point at the far end of the settlement, with the howf, whose purpose was obvious from its lack of windows, at the opposite end.

Behind the village, on a small rise, the foundations of the Duke of Argyll's new castle were being laid out. Already it had a chequered history, for the design had first been made nearly thirty years earlier for the previous duke by Mr Vanbrugh, who had been responsible for the magnificent palaces of Castle Howard and Blenheim. It was Mr Adam who now had charge, though all that could be seen were the deep gouges in the landscape marking the site of the four towers, the new tracks formed from the banks of the loch to the building site for the transporting of the materials, and the bustling activity of the stonemasons and carpenters, most of them incomers brought in by the architect.

Two women were standing together on the shoreline. They were both knitting, the wool hidden in the panniers formed by the folds of their *arisaidhs*, but though their fingers flew, their eyes remained fixed firmly on the loch, where they were obviously awaiting the safe return of a fishing boat. A cow lowed from a byre built on to the side of a cotter's cottage. In a kale yard, some scrawny chookies could be seen scratching the bare earth. On the front step of a newly thatched longhouse a middle-aged woman was sitting with a piece of sewing, the dog at her feet enjoying the afternoon sunshine. She looked up at the sound of the horses and her sewing dropped unheeded to the ground. Ailsa looked at Alasdhair. The expression on his face told her all she needed to know.

'My mother,' he said, his voice stripped of emotion.

Morna Ross had black hair. The blue-black of raven's wings, with barely a trace of grey, though she was older than Lady Munro by five years. Brown eyes the colour of bitter chocolate. Strong features. The resemblance was remarkable, Ailsa thought, as she hitched her horse's reins to a post, her hands shaking. She was nervous, not for herself, but for Alasdhair. She could sense by the way he held himself how tense he was. She wanted to take his hand. She wanted to run up to Morna Ross and beg her to have a care for him. If there was a way of enduring this ordeal for him, Ailsa would have gladly taken it. But there was not a way and she knew how proud he was. He would hate her drawing attention to his nerves. Her own nervousness increased. She felt almost sick with anticipation.

Morna Ross was standing still as a statue. She was a striking woman and had obviously been quite beautiful in her youth. For a long moment, mother and son stood facing one another. 'Alasdhair?' Her voice was so faint it would have been lost on the breeze if there had been one. 'Alasdhair, can it really be you?' She took a step towards him. A faltering step. She held out her hands, as if in supplication. 'Alasdhair?' Her voice cracked.

'Mother.'

'It is you.' Morna Ross shook her head, as if she could not believe what she was seeing. 'Twenty years, but I would know you anywhere.'

'And I you.' His voice was harsh. Now that he was finally face to face with her, he could think of nothing to say. He felt nothing either, only cold indifference.

'They told me you were gone.' Morna was looking at him as if he were an apparition. 'They told me you'd run off. To America, is what I heard.'

'Virginia.'

'Virginia.' The word sounded so strange on her tongue. Morna shook her head. 'And has it treated you well?'

'Well enough.'

'Aye. You look well. I…' Morna shook her head again, and dashed her hand across her eyes. 'I'm sorry, I didn't expect—the shock. It's the shock. I didn't think to see you again. Ever. I can't believe—after all this time, I can't believe…' Her voice wavered, and she tottered back towards the step.

Alasdhair took her arm. 'Don't go fainting on me.'

'No. Just give me a second.' Morna took a couple of deep breaths. 'I'll be all right. Here, let me get a proper look at you.' Trying desperately to compose herself, she wiped her eyes with the corner of her apron and took a step back to gaze up at Alasdhair's handsome countenance. 'How tall you are, and so dark—you get your colouring from me.' She made as if to touch his hair, but Alasdhair flinched and Morna shrank back. 'Why have you come here after all this time, Alasdhair? Why now?'

'I need to know the truth.'

'The truth,' Morna exclaimed. 'I doubt there is such a thing any more. What is the point in raking over old ashes? I have done it often enough myself, and it does no good, believe me. Look at you, you've grown into a fine man; and you've made a life for yourself far away. It has done my heart more good than I deserve to see you. It's all I ever wanted, Alasdhair, to know that you are well. There is nothing to be gained by harping back to the past. Please, don't let us talk of it.'

'It is to talk of it that I came here,' Alasdhair said impatiently.

'What you don't understand, Alasdhair, is that

there are many versions of the truth, and none of them anything other than shameful. Please.'

'I want to know.'

Morna sighed heavily. 'Very well. If you must have it, then I must tell you. You'd better come in.'

She stood aside to usher him to the door of the cottage. Alasdhair beckoned to Ailsa, who had been standing to one side, partially hidden by the horses. 'Mother, this is…'

Morna, who was already pale, now turned a greyish shade, and put her hands to her breast. 'Merciful God.'

'What on earth is the matter?' Alasdhair asked.

'What's she doing here?'

'This is Ailsa Munro, Mother.'

Ailsa took a step forwards and dropped a light curtsy. Morna peered at her, her face rigid with horror.

'Merciful God,' Morna said again. 'It must have been you she was expecting.'

'Who?'

'Your mother. At least, I assume it was your

mother. Lady Munro. You're the living spit of her,' Morna said. 'What are you doing here?'

Ailsa looked helplessly at Alasdhair. 'I think maybe it would be best if I let the two of you talk. I'll take the horses to the stables at the howf.'

Alasdhair shook his head. 'No, you'll stay here with me. I want you to hear what she has to say.' He turned back to his mother. 'Ailsa has an interest in this. I'll explain later.' Until he heard her side of the story and could judge for himself its impact, he had no intention of sharing his love for Ailsa with his mother. It was too precious.

'On your head be it,' Morna said in a resigned voice. 'Any road, I suppose I might as well put to bed any lies that mother of yours has put about.'

Ailsa looked confused. 'What do you mean? What has my mother to do with this?'

He remembered then, the look on Lady Munro's face when she had called Morna the *root cause of it all*. A premonition of something malevolent made Alasdhair take Ailsa to one side. 'Perhaps it would be best if you—'

'No. If your mother's story has some bearing on me, I want to hear it. Come, Alasdhair, you can see how upset she is by all this; let us get it over with.'

Reluctantly, he allowed her to precede him into the cottage. This was not working out at all as he had anticipated. He had expected to find this meeting upsetting, but he was struggling to feel anything other than a wish to have done with it, added to that there was now an impending sense of doom. His mother seemed strangely reluctant to talk. He had thought she would be anxious to explain herself and couldn't understand why she was not.

Inside, the longhouse was partitioned in two, with the living quarters for the animals at the back where a second floor formed an attic. A peat fire burned in the middle of the floor, the smoke curling lazily towards the hole in the thatch that served as a chimney. A bed with a straw mattress took up one corner. There was a table upon which was the makings of a stew and, on the fire, a pot of broth set on a trivet simmered appetisingly. Four wooden chairs were set around the table. An aumrie, a low wooden linen chest, sat under the single unglazed window, whose shutters were open. A rag rug, a patchwork cover on the bed, a knitted blanket folded neatly on top of the aumrie and Morna's woollen shawl, spread across the back of one of the chairs, were the only signs of comfort in the clean but spartan cottage.

Thinking of the simple but elegant furnishings of his own plantation house, remembering the domestic comforts of his childhood home, Alasdhair was shocked.

'It is not much, I know,' Morna said, looking embarrassed as she pulled out chairs and ushered her guests towards them. They sat side by side. Morna took the seat opposite to her son, her hands clasped tightly together under the cover of her apron. 'I don't know where to start,' she said, pulling one hand out to rub her eyes, then put it back again. 'Maybe if you could tell me what you know it would help me to understand what it is you want from me.'

'They told me you ran off with another man. I've never understood how you could leave my father in such a cruel way, knowing what it would do to him. You never made any attempt to get in touch, not even when he died. And you abandoned me, too. I thought it didn't matter any more why; I've had twenty years to grow used to it, but now I need to know.'

'You came back all the way from America to see me?'

'No. Not at first. But since I got here, so much of what I thought was the truth has turned out to be such a different kettle of fish that I realised I owed it to you and to myself to hear your side of things. For better or for worse.'

Morna pursed her lips and nodded silently. She seemed to have regained her composure, though the effort it cost her was writ large in the rigid way she held herself. She did not seem able to look directly at Alasdhair, but rather snatched frequent glances at him, as if afraid that anything more prolonged would result in his disappearance.

Ailsa watched her from under her lashes. She

herself felt on edge, as if she were sitting on the sinner's stool outside the kirk, bracing herself for a dousing. Her nails were forming painful crescents on her palms, so tightly was she clenching her fists in an effort to stop herself from shaking. She was afraid of what was to come. Not for herself—she could not believe any of the ancient history Morna was about to divulge could have much to do with her—but for Alasdhair. She prayed that whatever Morna's secrets were, they were not any more shameful than those he had already imagined.

Morna gazed off to a spot over Alasdhair's shoulder. 'I came to Errin Mhor as a chambermaid, part payment for a debt my father owed. It was not long before the Munro married Christina MacLeod, and I married your father, his factor—a match the laird organised, as was the way, but we were happy enough.'

She paused to untangle her knitting wool, that had fallen from her pocket and twisted itself around the leg of the chair. When she sat up again, her colour was heightened. 'It was the laird's birthday. Lady Munro was big with child, and they were short-handed for the ceilidh, so Alec sent me to help at the castle. I was fetching a bottle of the special whisky for Lord Munro; he wanted it brought to his library. I knocked on the door and he bade me enter. He was alone. I never thought—I didn't mean to—I wouldn't have gone to the room alone if I had known.'

Morna's eyes were large with unshed tears. Watching her, Ailsa was suddenly afraid of what she was about to say. Looking over at Alasdhair, she saw the same fear on his face. Her impulse was to flee the room, the cottage, the village, with her hands over her ears, but if she did, then Alasdhair would blame himself for upsetting her. She must endure it, for his sake.

Morna's hands were shaking; she was obviously struggling for control. She spoke more quickly now, eager to have it done with. 'He forced himself on me. I didn't have chance to stop him, he was on me before I could escape.'

'The despicable bastard! He raped you.'

Morna turned scarlet. 'He was the laird. You don't understand how it was in those days, Alasdhair, most people would say he had the right to me. I should have kept out of his way. I should have had more of a care.'

'For God's sake, you talk as if it were your fault.'

'It was, in a way. I should have known better.'

'He took you against your will. You, a married woman.'

'Aye, but that was not the way he saw it, or the world. I could scream or I could just close my eyes and let him get it over with. I chose the latter. I thought if I made a fuss it would be worse for Alec, so I let him get on with it and, dear God, I wish I had not, for she walked in on us.'

Ailsa could hardly bear to speak, but she knew she must. 'My mother?'

'Lady Munro. She turned white as a sheet. I thought she would faint away. I actually felt sorry for her, though God knows it was misplaced. She has no entitlement to anyone feeling anything for her. She turned on me. She must have known how things had been, but I suppose she couldn't very well vent her temper on the laird, so she blamed me and he, God rot him, was happy enough to allow her. Until she started demanding retribution, that is. That he was having none of; he just laughed at her when she demanded I be sent away, but the more he denied her what she wanted the more upset she got, falling into hysterics and claiming it was damaging the child. Well, that swung everything in her favour, as you can imagine. She wanted me banished. He agreed, eventually, though only to my going. Alec was too good a factor for him to lose over a bit of skirt, and of course there was no way on earth he'd let me take you with me, Alasdhair. Thrawn old bastard that he was, the more I begged to be allowed to take you with me, the more he dug his heels in.'

'So you left.'

'I was banished.'

'The laird had a fondness for that particular punishment,' Alasdhair said sardonically.

'It is his right, and no matter what you might think, Alasdhair, it was partly my fault. If I had not tried to blame him as I did, if I had not tried to excuse myself, if I had just kept quiet, maybe Lady Munro would have allowed it to be forgotten and none of this would have happened. Your father might still have been alive. I would not have lost you. For years, when I first came here, it was all I could think about, finding ways to undo what had been done, ways to change what I couldn't change. It eats away at you, Alasdhair. The only way to deal with it is not to think about it.'

'And what of my father? What had he to say to all of this?' Alasdhair's voice was devoid of emotion, but his fists were clenched on the arms of the chair in which he sat.

'Alec had no more choice than I did. The deed was done before he knew of it. I was not allowed to say goodbye. Those are the rules for those banished and I didn't dare break them for fear of the retribution that would be wrought on the two of you.'

'I know all about the Munro rules of banishment,' Alasdhair said bitterly. 'So there never was another man?'

Morna laughed scornfully. 'No. There was only ever the one.'

'Why didn't you try to see me? Why didn't you try to tell me the truth?'

'That word again. I've told you, Alasdhair, there's no such thing as the truth. I didn't try to see you because I didn't think I had the right, especially not after your father died and the blame was laid fair and square at my door. Guilt and shame are terrible things. Seeing you today is more than I've ever hoped for. It's enough. If you can find it in your heart to forgive me, I will die happy.'

'There is nothing to forgive.' But the words did not sound forgiving, and though he meant them, Alasdhair did not feel them. He wanted to, but he could not rid himself of the conviction that Morna was allowing him only to see a part of the picture. 'None of this is your fault,' he said, though it was himself he was attempting to reassure.

Morna shook her head. 'It's nice of you to say it, but it isn't true. I always loved you though, Alasdhair. I've carried you in my heart these twenty years; there's not a day's gone by without me thinking of you.'

Now, surely, he had what he wanted, Ailsa thought, watching Alasdhair closely. Now he knew that he had always been loved, surely he could find it in his heart to make the first move? But Alasdhair remained in his chair, a frown drawing his brows firmly together. 'When my father died, why did you not come back for me then? If you cared about me as you claim, surely you must have worried about what would become of me? I had no other kin on Errin Mhor.'

Morna shifted uncomfortably in her seat. 'I knew the laird would take care of you.'

'How could you have known that? I was the son of his factor, nothing more. You said yourself that Lady Munro had made it plain she was determined to see the back of you. Why would you assume she'd be willing to take me in under those circumstances?'

'I knew the laird would do his duty by you.'

'What duty?' The feeling of impending doom he'd had earlier was closing in over him like the chilly black waters of the deepest loch. Morna was refusing to look at him now. 'Mother? What duty was it that impelled Lord Munro to make me his ward, when the obvious thing to do was to send me to you? He knew where you were.'

'Alasdhair, believe me, there are some things that it is best to leave buried.'

Alasdhair hesitated. Maybe she was right. But though part of him urged caution, the larger part of him, the part that had fought its way into the light with the aid of Ailsa's love, was stronger. 'What are you not telling me?'

Morna's eyes darted from Alasdhair to Ailsa and back again to her son. 'Maybe if you could ask the lass to wait outside,' she said hesitantly.

Alasdhair shook his head and reached for Ailsa's hand. 'Whatever you're about to say, she has the right to know. Ailsa and I are to be married.'

The effect of those words on his mother were astonishing. Morna rose out of her seat, her hands clutching at her breast. Her face turned from white to grey. 'No! Oh, dear God in heaven, no.' She clutched at the edge of the table to support herself. 'You mustn't marry the Munro's daughter.'

Alasdhair pushed back his chair so violently that it fell to the floor. 'Enough! Unless you wish our estrangement to be for ever, you will think very carefully before you say another word. I love Ailsa with all my heart. Whatever prejudices you have about her family—and Lord knows they have given you just cause—you will keep them to yourself.'

'Alasdhair, please don't,' Ailsa interrupted, completely bewildered by the turn the conversation had taken. 'It is perfectly understandable that—'

'No.' He pulled her to her feet and put his arm around her shoulder, anchoring her firmly to his side. 'You are to be my wife. If my mother cannot treat you with the respect you are entitled to, then she does not deserve to be my mother.'

Morna's knees gave way under her. She tottered back into her seat, waving away Ailsa's attempts to come to her aide. 'It's not you, lass,' she said, her voice made harsh by her laboured breathing. 'I swear to you, Alasdhair, it's not

Miss Munro's heritage that is the problem.' She took a deep breath. 'It's your own.'

'What do you mean?'

'Your father.'

'What about him?'

'Alec isn't your real father. He couldn't sire bairns; it was one of the reasons he consented to the match, so he could have a child to call his own.' Morna licked her dry lips and forced herself to meet her son's accusing gaze. It broke her heart to see the shadow of pain lurking there.

'So there was another man all along. You did run off with him, didn't you? Is he my father?'

'There is, there never was, another man.'

Alasdhair looked bewildered. 'Then who on earth *is* my father?'

The answer, when it came, was so quiet as to be barely audible. 'Lord Munro.'

'*What!*'

'Lord Munro is your father.'

Chapter Ten

'No!'

'Yes. I'm so sorry, but it's true. That night of the ceilidh,' Morna said, head bowed, 'was not the first time the laird had his way with me. When I first came to the castle he—he—it was his way of making his mark, you see.'

'No!' Alasdhair's roar was like a wounded lion. 'No! It can't be true.'

'I'm sorry, but you wanted the truth.'

'You're saying that I am Lord Munro's bastard? But that means…' Out of the corner of his eye Alasdhair saw Ailsa's face drain of colour, so quickly it was as if the blood had been let. He wanted to go to her. He wanted to gather her close to him and to run and run and run away from here.

She got to her feet and reached for him. 'Alasdhair?' Her voice was thread-thin. She looked bewildered. Lost. Her eyes like bruises, beseeching him.

It broke his heart to see her like this. 'Ailsa.' He pulled her to him, felt the achingly familiar shape of her nestling into him, bending to him, fitting so perfectly that it was meant for him. He turned to his mother again. 'You lie,' he said with conviction.

'I'm sorry,' Morna said wretchedly, seeing now in the way the girl cleaved to her son what she had not noticed earlier. It was too late. The ultimate sin had been committed, and it was her fault for keeping the truth secret. 'I'm so sorry,' she said again, for there was nothing else to say. 'You cannot believe how much I wish I could change things, Alasdhair, but I cannot. Why else do you think the laird so readily took you in under his own roof?'

Ailsa was shaking uncontrollably against him now. 'Alasdhair?' She tried to catch his eye, but he looked away, and it was that, the sliding away of his peat-smoked eyes, eyes that had looked so truthfully and so lovingly into hers only a few short hours ago, that made her realise the full, horrible implication of Morna's bombshell. Only a few hours ago the world had seemed to have been made for them. It was she who had insisted they come here. If she had not. If they had gone back to Errin Mhor instead of coming here to Inveraray. If she could just unravel the last few hours. If she could unpick them back to the flaw like a tweed still on the loom, if she could tie the threads anew in a different way so that the pattern they weaved would be different. If she could only…

Alasdhair, too, was beginning to shake, for it felt like the whole world was rocking under his feet. 'Why did you not say? Why did no one tell me? Why…?'

'I thought it for the best,' Morna said. 'No one else knew, save Alec, not even Lady Munro. Why land you with the label of bastard when Alec was willing to keep you as his own? And then when he died I was so ashamed, so guilty, knowing I had hastened his death—it seemed so—and I never thought, you see. I thought you were in America.'

Alasdhair put Ailsa from him. Bereft, she stood, swaying, her mind frozen on that one thought. If only they could turn back the world, just a few short hours. But she knew only too well that 'if only' never worked. It seemed to her as if she and Alasdhair were destined after all to live their lives in the land of 'if only'. The full horror of the implications had not yet sunk in. She did not think of her crime or of their sin. She could only think of 'if only' and 'if only' and 'if only'. And Alasdhair. 'Alasdhair.' She said his name, like a plea from a death bed. She turned to him. She reached for him. But he flinched and that was it. The end. Their ending. And she wished with all her heart in that moment of agonising revelation that it would be hers, too. Now and for ever.

'I'm sorry,' Morna said again, 'It never crossed my mind that you and she—the laird's daughter—it never crossed my mind that you would look at each other in that way. He would never have allowed it.'

'He didn't. "Ailsa's the very last girl you should be thinking of that in that way." That's what he said to me six years ago. That's what he meant.'

'Six years ago?'

'When Ailsa and I first…our feelings for each other are of—were of long standing.' Alasdhair's voice cracked. He felt as if he were dissolving. An ominous silence filled the cottage. Outside, the sun still shone. The birds still sang. The fishermen fished and the workmen continued to labour on the Duke of Argyll's new castle. Outside, the world went about its business oblivious. Inside, blackness brewed.

Morna, run out even of apologies, buried her head in her apron and wept, silent acrid tears.

Alasdhair stood motionless, his eyes glazed, his mind struggling to reassemble the facts into a logical order that made sense. That did not slay and flay. That did not destroy utterly.

Ailsa's heart beat faster and faster. Her breathing was ragged. Her mind darted first one way, then the other. She could not think of facts, but only of colours. The shining silver of the future she and Alasdhair had planned. The deep crimson of their love-making. The burning gold of her love for him. She tried to clutch them to her heart, to keep them safe from the marauding black that threatened to cloak them all in its vileness. The sins of the father. The sins of her father. Alasdhair's father.

'*No!*' Desperately, she tried to reach him. Only a few inches of floor separated them, but it felt like a vast void. The floor was moving under her feet, shuddering and tilting like a brewing storm. If she could just reach him, it would be all right. If he would just look at her, if she could just see the love he had for her in his eyes, it would be all right. None of this was true. It couldn't be. 'No.' She reached for him, but he stepped back. A roaring in her ears made her stagger. 'Alasdhair, say it's not true.'

The room tilted. Ailsa felt her knees give way, but just before she fell, Alasdhair caught her, holding her tight against his chest, his grip painful, a pain she welcomed, for at least she could feel it. 'Alasdhair.' She burrowed her head into his chest. She drank in the achingly familiar smell of him. Her mind reeled, a swirling mass of turgid colours. Then blessed unconsciousness claimed her as she fainted clean away in his arms.

Alasdhair deposited her carefully on the bed. Leaning over, he stroked her hair from her face and kissed her icy cheek. 'Look after her,' he said tersely to Morna, standing beside him like a spectre.

'Where are you going?'

'To hell,' Alasdhair barked and strode out of the longhouse.

He walked. He did not know where he walked, nor did he care. Along the banks of Loch Fyne he went, to the edge of the trees and then into the forest, where the gloomy ambiance suited his state of mind. He stumbled over the roots of the Caledonian pines that spread like the gnarled fossilised joints of ancient crones over the sparse earth. He splashed, indifferent to both wet and cold, through the burbling streams, swollen with the run-off from the mountain snow. He tramped over clumps of ferns unfurling from silver spores, over the sharp green shoots of bluebells and the soft browning velvet leaves of dying primroses. He tripped when his toe caught in a rabbit's burrow, causing a startled roe deer to leap with balletic grace from a clearing. The low-hanging branches of the trees caught in his hair as it flew out behind him. Gorse clutched at the pleats of his plaid. Alasdhair strode on and on, away and away, falling into a kind of trance somewhere between consciousness and unconsciousness, almost numb in a grey twilight world where his unwitting sin lurked like an evil kelpie in the deepest cavern of his mind.

Eventually, he stopped. Eventually, he came to the realisation that running away was futile. The fate that awaited them, a life for ever apart, must be confronted. He could not, nor would he, wrench Ailsa from his heart, but he must cut her completely from his life.

Garnering all his resolution, with a leaden heart that would, he knew for certain, grow heavier as each year passed, Alasdhair turned around. Slowly, like a man facing the gallows, he walked back the way he had come, instinctively taking the same paths he had not even noticed himself choosing, a man on a tumbrel of his own making, heading inexorably towards destruction.

Back in the cottage, the pale creature who had once been Ailsa fought her way back to consciousness. She looked like a wraith. She felt like a will-o'-the-wisp, the fabled marsh creature made of smoke whose destiny it was to cast fatal spells over men. She had no words with which to express how she felt, not even to herself. She wanted nothing so much as to bury herself deep in a dark place like a wounded deer, to endure the lonely vigil that would be her life from now on. If she could not have Alasdhair—and she could not, she could not, she could not—then she would have nothing and no one.

Though she could see that Morna, too, was suffering greatly, Ailsa had nothing to offer that would give her comfort. She pitied Morna in a way that she did not pity herself. Her pain was

too great for pity, the crime she had so inno-
cently committed too all-encompassing for her
to think beyond its existence. The full horror
of it would no doubt dawn on her, and with it,
perhaps, repentance and shame. But for now,
Ailsa's only way of dealing with the truth was
to reject it by simply refusing to take it in.

Every part of her was frozen, save her love
for Alasdhair. That continued to burn, feverish
and defiant, a straining of her heart. She knew
it was wrong, but she could not bring herself to
slay it.

Not yet.

Not yet.

Ailsa struggled to her feet, brushing aside
Morna's outstretched arm, shaking her head at
the offer of sustenance, for her throat felt as if
it were closed. Gathering her *arisaidh* around
her, she opened the door of the cottage and took
a deep breath of fresh air. She must find him.
When she knew he was safe, then she would
leave him. But first she must find him.

She was stepping down from the path to the

beach when a hand stayed her. A familiar hand. An achingly familiar body. 'Alasdhair.'

'Ailsa.'

They stared at each other for long moments. The world had changed utterly, yet it seemed utterly unchanged.

'I thought you were gone,' she whispered, her voice thin and parched.

'I will be. Soon.' His own sounded tortured.

'Alasdhair, I…'

'Don't!'

'If I had known, I would not have…'

'Ailsa,' he said, gentler now, 'it wouldn't have changed the truth.'

'Your mother was right,' she replied bitterly, 'there is no such thing as the truth.'

'No, you are wrong. The truth is what you feel in your heart. I love you. You are a part of me. You were made for me, and without you I won't ever be complete. That love is not wrong, Ailsa—I won't ever believe it is. I love you, and though it is a profanation, and I can never tell the world of it, I will always love you. If that is a sin, then it is one I will continue to commit, in thought if not in deed. This parting which must be is not an ending. I have you tucked in my heart. Though it feels as if I am slain, knowing I must never again feel your lips on mine, your hand in mine, my love is strong enough to transcend even that.'

'Oh, Alasdhair,' Ailsa said brokenly, 'I have you in my heart, too, I promise. Always.'

'I know you do. I know you do, Ailsa, and it is enough,' he said fiercely, fighting with all his might the urge to take her in his arms. 'It is enough,' he repeated, determined to make it so. 'It will be.'

They were too wrapped up in their own tragedy to notice her presence until she was upon them, too caught up in contemplating the pain and agony that awaited them. The terrible journey they knew they must undertake, from blissful togetherness to desolate separation, lay ahead.

She had left her horse at the howf, and come on foot. She was dressed entirely in black, her golden hair, which the years had not faded, concealed under a widow's cap.

It was Ailsa who saw her first, startled by the motionless figure whose attention was focused on her in a way that reminded Ailsa of the Errin Mhor village women when the fleet was overdue. They would stand on the end of the pier just like this, still as statues, frozen between joy and grief until each boat landed and each man was accounted for.

'Mother,' Ailsa said numbly. 'I don't understand, what on earth are you doing here?'

'Ailsa.' Faced with her daughter and disconcerted by the bereft expression that was written over her beloved countenance, the extent of her task overwhelmed Christina Munro. Frozen by fear of failure or, worse, outright rejection, she took a faltering step towards Ailsa, then stopped. Any normal mother would envelop her daughter in a hug, but Lady Munro knew, having had ample time to reflect on the journey here, that she was about as far from being a normal mother as it was possible to be. 'Ailsa, I had hoped I might find you here. I need to talk to you, explain. It is very important.'

'Whatever you have to say, it is too late now,' Ailsa said flatly.

Gazing helplessly into her daughter's eyes, the same violet shade as her own, Lady Munro felt despair wash over her. 'You don't understand. I wanted to see you—to tell you—I want to put things right.' She tried to smile encouragingly.

'Put things right! Nobody can put things right. Nothing will be right ever again.'

Looking closely at her daughter, Christina Munro noticed for the first time the tightly drawn look of her, her eyes huge in the chalk-white face. 'You look as if you have seen a ghost.'

'I have,' Ailsa replied. 'And it is a spectre that will haunt me to the end of my days.'

Christina felt as if the little blood she had was icing over. 'Morna. You have spoken—she has told you.' She clutched at her daughter's arm. 'It's not what you think. What your father did—it's not the whole story. If you would let me explain, Ailsa…'

'How can you? What can you possibly say to change the fact that my father is also Alasdhair's?' Ailsa said hysterically. 'I presume you knew that, Mother? I presume that is what was at the bottom of your hating Alasdhair so much? My father's exercising of his feudal rights!'

'Ailsa, it's not—'

'To hell with the laird and his sins,' Alasdhair snapped. 'I'm sick of hearing about him. What about the sins of omission?' he said furiously, turning on Lady Munro. 'Why didn't you tell me? I don't understand why you just didn't— before we.... Dear God, woman, have you any idea what this has done to us? To your own daughter?'

Lady Munro clasped her hands together to stop them shaking. She cleared her throat and forced herself to look at her daughter. Her Ailsa. Her lovely Ailsa. 'It doesn't mean what you think it means.'

'What? What the hell else do you think it could mean?' Alasdhair said disgustedly. 'Unless you are saying that my mother somehow got it wrong and mistook the man who planted his seed in her...'

'No, I'm not saying that.'

'Then what, Mother? What are you saying?' Lady Munro threw back her head, meeting her daughter's gaze full on. 'Alasdhair might be Lord Munro's child, Ailsa, but you are not.'

It seemed for a moment as if the world stopped. The air resonated with tension. Alasdhair and Ailsa were incapable of speech, too terrified to believe, too scared to even move in case the spell was broken and it proved another devilish twist in the nightmare that had befallen them.

'It's true.' Lady Munro broke the silence, her voice shaking.

'But why? Who? How?' Ailsa's voice shook pathetically. 'I don't understand. Why did you not tell me? Why, all these years, did you lead me to believe—why?'

'Oh, Ailsa, why would I? There were all the reasons in the world not to tell you.'

'But...' Ailsa clutched at her head, that was reeling.

With an immense effort of will, Alasdhair

took charge. 'Not here. We need to—not here. We'll go back to my mother's cottage.'

'Morna Ross won't want me in her house.'

'If what you say is true, she will welcome you with open arms.'

'I promise you,' Lady Munro said fervently, 'I promise you it is true. You are no kin of my daughter.'

The look that passed between Ailsa and Alasdhair contained a tiny flicker of hope, like a candle flame trying valiantly to burn in a draught. They looked and they hoped and then they looked away, for fear of tempting fate. As the three of them made their way to the cottage, the white clouds of the morning, which seemed now so very long ago, gave way to a watery blue sky bearing a weak sun.

Morna Ross was waiting for them on the doorstep, her arms folded tight across her chest. 'Well, well, as I live and breathe. To what do I owe this dubious pleasure?'

'Mother,' Alasdhair said, ushering Morna into the cottage, 'Lady Munro has some extraordi-

nary news which may put all to rights. Let us
go inside.'

They did so. Morna and Christina Munro
took stock of each other across the table, like
old adversaries trying to ready themselves for
a battle neither relished, but would die rather
than default from.

Ailsa and Alasdhair sat side by side so that
every nuance of expression was felt rather than
seen. Though they did not touch, their bodies
harkened towards one another, pulled by some
unseen force, like a magnet pulls the point of a
compass north. They waited with bated breath
for Lady Munro's explanation to release them,
still fearing that by some chance her words had
been misinterpreted, condemning them utterly.

Lady Munro sat ramrod straight in her seat,
her long thin fingers plucking at the lace of her
delicately embroidered handkerchief. 'I never
wanted anything else but your happiness,' she
said suddenly, turning towards her daughter. 'I
know you don't believe that, but it's true. It's all
I ever wanted.'

'Then help me now, Mother, please,' Ailsa

begged her, 'because the only thing that will make me happy is being with Alasdhair.'

Christina Munro nodded. A piece of lace came away from the fine lawn cotton handkerchief with a little tearing sound. 'Yes. Yes, I see that now. I'm only sorry it took me so long.' She nodded again. Silence stretched taut as a sail in a head wind. She closed her eyes as the past, a country from which self-preservation had prevented her setting foot, beckoned like a forgotten continent, the contours of the landscape familiar, the surroundings changed. Christina took a deep breath and opened her eyes. 'I loved my first husband,' she said, her gaze focused only on Ailsa. 'I was devastated when he died,' she continued in a harsh tone. 'We had not been long married, and I was young, not even eighteen, with my first-born bairn, Rory, still in swaddling.' She began to rock in her chair, backwards and forwards, backwards and forwards. 'You see, Ailsa, I can say his name well enough. I just find it—experience has taught me it is better not to. When you cannot heal a wound, it is better not to pick at it.'

She hesitated briefly before continuing. 'I was a widow just a few months before the clan married me on to the Munro. My boy was not a year when they tore him from my arms. I didn't know, you see. They didn't tell me that it was part of the nuptial agreement. Rory was the heir to Heronsay, the Macleods wanted him under their wing, and my new husband did not want a Macleod cuckoo in the Munro nest. But I didn't know any of that.'

Rocking. Rocking. Rocking. Ailsa stared at her mother as if she had never seen her before. She seemed to have aged these last few days, not in her looks, but in her carriage. The straight-backed rigidity in which she had been sitting was gone. She was curled into herself now, struggling to hold herself together. She looked pitiable. She had never looked pitiable before.

The rocking slowed, but did not quite stop. Lady Munro's fingers ripped at the lace. 'It broke my heart to leave Rory in Heronsay. On our wedding night the laird promised me that when I gave him his own son he would let me have my first born to live with us. I thought he meant it.' Her lip curled. 'But when I gave him Calumn he just laughed at me. *When I'd had a second child,* he said, *one more than I'd given the Macleod.* So I let him back into my bed and endured his attentions though I knew him for a liar, because what else could I do?'

Lady Munro turned briefly to Morna. 'When it is our children's well-being at stake, we will endure much.'

Morna gave a half-shrug of assent, but said nothing.

'I tried, but to no avail,' Lady Munro continued, 'and after four years I was nigh on giving up hope. I did not really believe he would grant me Rory anyway. You won't believe me—why should you after the way I've treated you?—' she said to Ailsa, 'but what I really wanted was a daughter of my own.'

She paused again, and Ailsa was astonished to see a blush steal over her mother's cheek. 'Go on,' she said, wondering what on earth was coming next.

'I wouldn't have thought of it had not circumstances conspired,' Lady Munro said, her words coming out in a rush now, anxious as she was to have the shameful part of the tale over with. 'The laird was away from Errin Mhor on clan business. He'd been gone nearly two months, visiting cousins in the Hebrides. Neil Murray was an old flame of mine. When Rory's father died, he asked for my hand, but though he was of good family and I liked him very well, he had not the wealth nor the lands of the Laird of Errin Mhor, so his offer was rejected.'

This confession was so far from what Ailsa had expected that her mouth fell open in astonishment. She made to speak, but Alasdhair's hand on her arm stopped her. 'Wait,' he mouthed, afraid that were Lady Munro interrupted she would falter.

'He called at Errin Mhor with a message for my husband,' Lady Munro said, her blush now apparent to all. 'He stayed seven days and nights, and we—I—he came to my bed on every one of them. I was lonely, and I was desperate, and Neil showed me kindness, which my husband had never done, and he reminded me of better times. I know that is no excuse. By the time he left Errin Mhor I suspected I might be carrying his child. By the time my husband returned, three weeks later, my suspicions had been confirmed. I know it was wrong to deceive him, no matter that he had deceived me, but that is what I did. I made sure he had no reason to doubt me, and I was lucky, for no one questioned you being supposedly a few weeks early, Ailsa, for Calumn was an early baby, too. I was lucky, and I was careful. No one knew, not even Neil. Until today, this has been my secret.'

'Are you sure?' Ailsa asked urgently, leaning forwards in her seat. 'Are you absolutely positive, there can be no doubt of my true father?'

'No doubt at all, I promise you. I am quite certain of my dates, but there is something else, if you need further proof. Look at your hands.'

Ailsa spread her fingers on the table in front of her. 'What am I looking for?'

'See.' Lady Munro did the same. 'The middle finger and the fourth—in most people they are different sizes, but yours are the same length.

It is a quirk Neil told me of, all his family have it.'

Frowning, Ailsa examined her hands, surprised to find that her mother spoke the truth, more surprised to find that she herself had never noticed it before. 'Is it really so unusual?'

Lady Munro nodded. Alasdhair and Morna, both examining their own hands now, nodded too. 'It's true,' Morna said, looking at Ailsa's hands now with interest, 'I've never seen that before.'

'So I am definitely not a Munro,' Ailsa said slowly.

'No,' Lady Munro answered, her voice tight.

Morna spoke for the first time, her voice tinged with something akin to admiration. 'You cuckolded the laird in his own nest.'

'Aye, I did.' Lady Munro said, meeting Morna's gaze firmly, still as stone, even her fingers at peace. Each word seemed drawn from her like a sharp stone, so painfully that there could be no doubting the truth of them. 'When I found him with you that night, I was furious that he could do so easily and thoughtlessly what had cost me dear. It was not your fault, I know that, but I did not see it that way at the time. If it is any consolation at all, you should know that he punished me, too, for the shame of having discovered him. What I did to you was done to me in return and your son took my son's place at the castle.'

'It is hardly the same,' Morna said heavily.

'I do not make any claim that it is,' Christina agreed. 'Nor do I claim that I committed no sin. I only want to explain. And it is not your forgiveness I came here to seek anyway but my daughter's.' She looked over at Ailsa again, her eyes now clearly damp with unshed tears. 'I loved you all the more for who you were, Ailsa, and who you were not, but the laird must always come first, you see, so I took care never to allow him to see what I felt for you. But you were right. There has been time, more than enough time since, for me to change things between us, and I have not. I've been afraid to, for the damage I've inflicted has been too terrible to contemplate. I've always loved you, Ailsa, even though I've never shown it. I came here to tell you that whatever you want from your life, it has my blessing. Can you find it in your heart to forgive me?'

'Màthair!' Careless of her tears, Ailsa got to her feet and knelt at her mother's feet, wrapping her arms around her knees and putting her head on her lap. 'I have never been so happy in my life to hear that the man I thought my father is not. For it means I can have what my heart desires above all, which is to be with Alasdhair. I can forgive you anything for that.'

Hesitantly, Christina touched her daughter's soft curls. 'All I ever wanted to do was to keep you safe. I thought no one else could do that but me. I was wrong and I'm sorry. If marriage to Alasdhair Ross is what you want, then it's what I want, too.'

Alasdhair lifted Ailsa to her feet and hugged her so close she could not breathe, though for neither was it close enough. 'Do you swear that what you have told us is the truth?' he said, looking sternly at Lady Munro.

'I swear.'

That it should be the one woman in the world

who had done the most to keep them apart who now demolished what had seemed an insurmountable barrier to their happiness was an irony, but, like Ailsa at present, he did not much care about anything other than the fact that it meant they could be together. 'Thank you,' he said to Lady Munro. 'I take it, then, that your daughter has your blessing?'

'With all my heart,' Lady Munro said.

Morna, too, got to her feet now. 'Well,' she said, fixing Lady Munro with a stern stare, 'I don't pretend to forgive you, but I do feel sorry for you, Christina Munro, and since it looks like we are to be kin through marriage, I will do my best to overlook the worst of your sins.'

Lady Munro got to her feet 'It's late, you'll be wanting some time alone, and I'm suddenly very tired so, if you'll excuse me, I'll return to the inn and rest.'

Ailsa slipped out from under Alasdhair's arm to give her mother a tentative kiss on the cheek, and was rewarded with a painfully fierce embrace before her mother dashed her hand over her eyes and fled the room.

'I'd better go after her,' Morna said, 'make sure she's all right. It's been quite a day for all of us. Quite a day and no mistake.'

Alone at last, Alasdhair put his hand around Ailsa's shoulders and guided her out of the cottage towards the shores of the loch. It was almost dark, but there was a full moon, glowing hazy through the remnants of the grey mizzle cloud. He turned her towards him, his hands cupping her face, drinking deep of her beloved countenance. For long moments they gazed at each other, violet eyes on bitter chocolate, the horror of the last few hours easing gradually away as the glowing light of their love suffused their bodies.

'I love you,' Alasdhair said huskily, his lips so close that they brushed hers. 'I love you. I love you. I love you. I will never, ever tire of saying it, nor will I ever cease to be grateful that I can.'

'I love you too, Alasdhair,' Ailsa whispered, 'more every moment that passes.'

He pulled her closer. Her soft curves pressed and moulded themselves into his hard form. She smelled of sunshine and sea and Ailsa.

Alasdhair closed his eyes and drank her in, relief giving way to desire as the horrors of the day began to fade.

He kissed her then, finally, a kiss that emptied his heart into her, wrapping her tight in the balm of his love, binding them together in a way that left them in no doubt that they were two halves of one. It was a kiss that seemed they had been waiting a lifetime for. A proclamation and a promise.

'I love you, Alasdhair, I love you so much.' Ailsa took his hand and rubbed it against her cheek. 'This is our clean slate, isn't it? You don't mind that I'm not who you thought I was?'

He laughed. 'No. You're exactly who I thought you were. I'm only worried that you'll mind the same about me.'

'You're you, exactly who I thought you were. Isn't it funny—you came all the way from Virginia to find answers and you weren't even asking the right questions.'

'There's only one question in my mind, and that's how soon can we be married?'

'Soon. As soon as we can call the banns.'

Ailsa sighed with contentment and nestled closer into Alasdhair's comforting embrace. 'I can't believe it's really happening.'

'And you promise me you've no regrets, Ailsa? You mean it when you say that leaving here, returning with me to Virginia, is what you really want?'

'You are what I really want. If I can have you, nothing else matters.' She stood on tiptoe to kiss him. 'I want a new world, not this old one.'

'Then the New World you shall have. What of your name?'

Ailsa frowned. 'I don't know. Calumn must be told the truth, it would not be fair to hide it from him, but I doubt very much that he'll want it known. As far as I am concerned, my name will be Ross and that's all that matters to me.'

Alasdhair kissed her again, lingeringly this time, and sweetly, savouring the fullness of her lips, his hands caressing the sweet contours of her body. 'Then if my mother is happy to keep her secret, and yours is too, there is no need to proclaim the truth to the world—are we agreed?'

'Yes,' Ailsa said, pulling his head back towards her. 'And now can we stop talking about mothers, please?'

He pulled her closer. 'Let's stop talking all together,' he whispered. Then he kissed her. And he kissed her again. And he did not stop kissing her until she lay glowing and sated beneath him.

Chapter Eleven

They were to be married under their baptised names. After much heart-searching, both Morna and Christina had agreed that the truth should be kept under wraps, provided Calumn was also in agreement.

Alasdhair had insisted on telling him himself, rightly judging that Calumn would prefer to hear the unvarnished facts rather than to have to listen to the competing emotional reactions of two women.

Calumn listened with a growing look of astonishment on his face, but when the tale was finally told, he shook his head in resignation. 'My father took the precaution of unburdening himself of much of his wrongdoing before he died,' he said with a grimace. 'His religion does not require confession, but he chose to burden me, his eldest son, with the worst of his sins, just in case the question of reparation came up. Canny to the end, the old goat. You've no idea,' he said with a wry grin, 'the cess pit of a black soul he was carrying around inside him, but I did not think even he capable of this. I expect he thought forcing himself on your mother and fathering you were duties rather than sins. I'm sorry, Alasdhair.'

'It's not your fault.'

'No, but it is my dishonour to inherit.'

'Not as far as I am concerned. You do realise this means you and I are brothers?'

Calumn's brow cleared. 'By all that's sacred, so it does!' He clasped Alasdhair's hand. 'I know I'm twenty-odd years too late, but welcome to the family, brother.'

Alasdhair laughed. 'Better late than never.'

Ailsa awoke on the morning of her wedding to find that fate had provided them with a beautiful day. She would still have thought it beautiful even if the skies had opened and the rain pelted off the ground, for the sun seemed to shine straight out from her heart these days. Though under strict orders to keep to her room this morning, she was far too excited to stay in bed, so she wrapped a blanket around herself and perched on the window seat.

Outside, she could see the fishing fleet strung out on the seas beyond the Necklace like one giant fishing net. The shoals of herring had come to Errin Mhor's waters. The silver darlings ran here for only a few weeks of the year, but when they came they were plentiful. Within the hour almost every woman from the surrounding villages would be down at Errin Mhor harbour, her fingers bound with strips of cotton, ready to gut and salt the catch as soon as it was landed. The precious harvest would then be packed in careful layers in wooden barrels, providing vital sustenance throughout next year's long winter.

Out on the moors, the back-breaking task of peat cutting had already begun. In the big enclosed kitchen garden on the far side of the castle, they were getting ready to plant out the summer vegetables. Madeleine had been experimenting with some strange specimens she'd had sent over from her father's farm in France, with no encouragement at all from Lady Munro, of course. The new orangery that Calumn had had built for her was filled with boxes of unfamiliar seedlings. Lambing was over and calving had begun, and soon enough the rush of early summer bairns would also be born. Another harvest, this time the product of the long autumn's nights. It was a pattern so familiar that Ailsa thought of it as a huge round tapestry, like a wheel. The seasons, and Errin Mhor life with it, revolving slowly and inexorably.

'And very, very soon, I'm going to a new world with a whole new round of seasons I know nothing of,' she said to herself as she stared, unseeing now, out of the window. 'Far across the ocean, a whole new beginning. With my husband, Alasdhair.' A now familiar heat spread out from her belly at the thought of him. 'My husband,' she whispered again experimentally.

Her face softened into tenderness. Though the

last six weeks had passed in a blur of activity, from preparing her trousseau and her bottom drawer, the all-important collection of things a bride must bring with her to the marriage, to organising the wedding feast and taking her leave of all her special places, the man in question had been forced to spend much of his time in Glasgow on business, though he had been to the kirk, as required, on the three Sundays when their banns had been called. 'It makes it easier to keep my hands off you before the wedding,' Alasdhair had whispered the last time he'd set off for the south, but Ailsa found it a poor consolation. She ached for his touch. Much as she longed for the ceremony and looked forward to the celebrations, she could think of little else but this, their first lovemaking as man and wife.

A knock on the door heralded the arrival of Ailsa's breakfast. Madeleine and Lady Munro, now formed into a most unlikely alliance, were conspiring to keep her appearance secret until the moment she left for church. Guests had been arriving from near and far for days now. Morna Ross had graciously accepted the invitation to attend her son's nuptials, but had declined the offer of a room at the castle, preferring instead to stay with the Sinclairs where she and her old friend Mhairi spent many happy hours reminiscing about the old days and catching up on the latest gossip. The castle was overflowing with visitors, including friends and acquaintances of Lady Munro from her childhood, of whom neither Calumn nor Ailsa had even been aware. Her daughter's wedding, a long-overdue visit to a frankly astonished Rory and his family on Heronsay, and the imminent arrival of her second son's first-born had given Christina Munro a new lease of life. It would be something of an exaggeration to say that she had become light-hearted, but a smile had been sighted on at least five occasions, and once she had laughed, quite startling all those present. She was softening, mellowing, Ailsa thought in astonishment, as she realised that her mother was not about to fidget with her hair, but was actually kissing her cheek. She was blurring at the edges, like an icicle caught in the first rays of the spring sunshine.

* * *

As the morning progressed, Ailsa bathed and washed her hair and tried to relax. But the clatter of a constant stream of people going up and down the stairs, doors banging, the scraping of heavy furniture being moved about, and over it all the continual muffled noise of people talking and laughing, made her desperate for the ceremony to begin. The clock seemed to tick more and more slowly, seconds becoming minutes, minutes stretching into hours. As she finally began to dress, she felt as if she'd been waiting a lifetime in her room for this moment. Her wedding to the man she loved.

Madeleine and her mother helped her with the final preparations. Her dress was silver and blue, the colours of constancy, a striped open robe worn over a sky-blue silk petticoat. Her stockings were tied with silver ribbons, her hair dressed with silver pins, and a silver coin placed in her left shoe, after she carefully put her right shoe on first. Though she was not usually superstitious or one for following tradition so slavishly, she wanted nothing to go wrong, nothing to be left to chance, even allowing her mother to drape the mirror in her room, lest she catch sight of her own reflection. Pearls were for tears, and so were considered unlucky, but as she was preparing to leave, her mother produced the most delicate gold locket and fastened it around her neck.

'It belonged to my own mother,' she explained. 'I wore it myself on my first wedding day, to Rory's father, but not on my second.' She gave Ailsa another unprecedented peck on the cheek and went so far as to hug her. 'My first marriage was a happy one. I know yours is going to be, too.'

'Thank you, Mother.' Ailsa fingered the gift, touched beyond words.

'And this is from Calumn and me,' Madeleine said, fastening a bracelet around her wrist. 'The sapphires are for the sea, and the little diamonds are for the sand, so you never forget Errin Mhor and your family here.'

'I'm going to miss you, all of you.'

'You'll be far too busy with your exciting new life to be worrying about us. Anyway, I've got plenty to occupy me here. There's Rory and his family to get to know and Maddie here is about to provide me with a new grandchild.' She smiled benignly at her daughter-in-law. 'Now, no crying on your wedding day,' Lady Munro said, hurriedly dabbing at Ailsa's eyes. 'Stand there now, let us look at you. Aye, you'll do well,' she said, nodding crisply, but Ailsa could not help noticing her mother dabbing surreptitiously at her own eyes too.

The two women left her to descend the staircase on her own. She paused at the top, looking down into the great hall that had been transformed by swathes of bunting and spring flowers. Calumn awaited her at the foot of the stairs, in full ceremonial Highland dress, ready for the short walk to the kirk where everyone else awaited them. She took his arm, grateful for his solid presence, for her legs were beginning to feel decidedly shaky, her heart was a-flutter and she could think of nothing except that in a few short moments she would be there. Alasdhair would be there, too, and they would be joined for ever as man and wife. A new entity made of two separate people.

Later, she would have no recollection of the walk, a journey she had made thousands of times. The doors of the kirk were open wide. Those who arrived too late for a seat inside clustered round the gate, lining the path, crowded around the entranceway, smiling and shouting good luck wishes, but their faces were a blur.

'Are you sure you want to go through with this?' Calumn said to her gently. She smiled with such certainty that he laughed and kissed her cheek. 'I'm duty-bound to ask, but I recognise that look. You're sure,' he said and gave her his arm.

'How do I look?' Ailsa asked nervously.

'You look radiant, Sister, and I am the proudest man in Scotland to be giving you away. Alasdhair is the luckiest man alive.' He squeezed her hand reassuringly. 'Come, now, let's get you wed.' With that, they walked slowly into the church.

Ailsa had eyes only for one person. It was

always the same, as far as she was concerned, if Alasdhair was there, he was the only one present. And he was there, waiting for her exactly as he had promised he would be. He wore a touchingly anxious expression. She took a deep breath and walked with graceful confidence towards him, her eyes locked on his, her mouth hovering on the cusp of a smile—for it would not do to smile too openly on such a solemn occasion.

Like Calumn, Alasdhair wore full formal Highland dress. His plaid had been woven especially by Mhairi Sinclair. The buckle at his waist bore the Ross arms, made for him by Hamish. His coat was of dark blue cloth, short and fitting tightly across the breadth of his chest, the width of his shoulders. His *filleadh mòr* was fastened with an ornate pin made of silver topped with a large sapphire, a tiny version of which was nestled in his necktie. His hair was neatly tied back.

His face, his beloved face, softened into the most tender of expressions as she made this, her final journey as Ailsa Munro. Alasdhair took her hand when she arrived at his side, pressing a tiny kiss to her palm, pulling her as close into the solid shelter of his side as decency would allow.

They said their vows not to the minister, but to each other. In truth, he almost felt superfluous to the occasion, and in truth he was rather shocked at the kiss that followed the conclusion of the ceremony. A simple peck on the check was the custom. A touching of the lips was just about permissible. But what he witnessed— well, he could only be relieved that the cheering and stamping of the congregation finally reminded the two of them of where they were.

Later, it would be said that no one had ever said their vows so earnestly, though there were some who felt that Ailsa should have shown more maidenly hesitation. Later, it would be said that never had such a bonny couple graced the kirk at Errin Mhor—a statement much disputed by those who had attended the wedding of Calumn and Madeleine. Later, it was rumoured that Lady Munro shed a tear, though that was never proved conclusively. But none disagreed on the touching charm of the occasion, and all agreed vehemently there was no doubting the radiant love that seemed to emanate from the happy couple.

The formal ceremony over, everyone save the happy couple were very much focused on beginning the festivities back at Errin Mhor castle as soon as decorum would allow. Calumn threw the shoe, symbolising the passing of responsibility from himself to the groom. Everyone cheered and clapped, and Ailsa and Alasdhair led a long and extremely noisy procession back to the castle where they presided at the top table over endless toasts to their health, wealth and happiness, holding hands under the table and feeling guilty for wishing to be left alone.

'I recognise that look,' Jessica McLeod, Rory's wife, whispered to Madeleine, nodding in Ailsa's direction.

Madeleine giggled. 'Me, too. Guilt at wanting to escape from your own wedding party.

I remember. How long do you think it will be before they sneak away?'

'As you did,' Jessica teased.

Madeleine blushed. 'I thought no one noticed.'

'Don't worry about it, Rory and I did the same thing ourselves.' She nodded at Lady Munro, keeping an eagle eye on her daughter. 'If we could just distract our dear mother-in-law, we'd be doing Ailsa a very big favour.'

'Teenie!' A rasping voice was heard above the mêlée.

'*Mon Dieu!* That is Angus McAngus,' Madeleine exclaimed, spotting the distinctive tangle of faded red hair across the room. 'I have not seen him since before I was married. I remember now, he told me he used to have a *tendre* for Lady Munro before she married Calumn's father.'

The two women inched forwards, eager to see what their stiff-necked mother-in-law would make of the man being presented to her. Angus McAngus was a typical Gael, short and lean, the top of his head falling some inches short of Lady Munro's height. His hair was a rusty colour, streaked with grey, but it was obvious to Madeleine that he had made an effort on Lady Munro's behalf, for though it still resembled a bird's nest, it was a combed one, and his straggly beard had been trimmed. With a claymore by the look of it, but trimmed none the less.

'Christina,' he was saying with a roguish smile, 'you've no' changed a bit. Still as bonny a lass as I've seen in many a year, you're a sight for sore eyes.'

Lady Munro bowed stiffly. 'Laird.'

'Away now, it was always Gussie to you, as you were aye Teenie to me.'

Madeleine and Jessica exchanged looks, their eyes dancing.

'I have not been referred to as Teenie for many years,' Lady Munro said in her best cut-glass voice.

Anyone else would have dropped her hand and made his excuses, but McAngus, it would seem, was made of sterner stuff. 'That's because you've no' met anyone else to replace my special place in your heart,' he chortled. 'Aye, Teenie, 'tis a long road we've travelled apart, but destiny has brought you to me, widowed and free at last. I'll no' mince my words. I'm a lonely man with a cold bed for you to warm. What do you say?'

'If that is a proposal, Angus McAngus,' Lady Munro said, her voice now as chill as the January gales, 'the answer is categorically no.'

'Come now, Teenie, ye've no' thought it through. That laddie of yours is going to be filling the place wi' weans soon enough, and before you know it, ye'll be turned into an old crone of a grandmother wi' no life of your own. I ken for a fact that man o' yours was a cold bugger—God rest his soul. What you need is a bit of a life of your own.'

'Nonsense. I am far too old to be thinking of marriage. As you are, Angus.'

McAngus chortled. 'You're in the prime of life, Teenie, and as for me—well, you know the old saying.' The old laird patted his sporran with a leer. 'The older the stag, the harder the horn.'

Jessica managed to stifle the shocked laugh that rose in her throat, but Madeleine did not, though she made a paltry attempt to turn her giggles into a fit of coughing. Her husband muffled her mouth with his hand, and the familiar warmth of his palm on her lips had the effect of distracting her completely from the tableau playing out before them. In fact, she would have happily taken advantage of Lady Munro's preoccupation to drag her husband up to their rooms, for she never could resist him in his plaid, and they had not been alone for what seemed like days, what with the wedding preparations and…

But Calumn resisted her tugging at his sleeve. 'Later. We can't all disappear, and much as I would love to, my sweet, I think it's only fair that we let Alasdhair and Ailsa have first call. It is their wedding day, after all.'

Even as he spoke, Madeleine noticed that the couple were making good their escape, heading through a side door unnoticed by their celebrating guests. 'Remember our own wedding night,' she whispered, standing on tiptoe to reach her husband's ear.

His arm curled around her, and he rested his

hand on the swell of her belly. 'I love you, Madeleine Munro.'

'I love you too, my lord,' Madeleine replied with an answering gleam.

'Maybe we could just...'

But at that moment, the resounding slap of Lady Munro's open palm making contact with Angus McAngus's cheek made them look round. There was a shocked silence, then McAngus laughed. 'I've a mind to take your mother off your hands,' he shouted over at Calumn with a lascivious wink, 'auld leather makes a fine saddle.'

They had opted to spend their wedding night in the relative privacy of a cottage out by the stables that Calumn was having refurbished for Madeleine's new French head gardener, not yet arrived from her native Brittany. It was a simple affair, two rooms separated by a wooden partition, but Calumn had had a fireplace installed, and the two small windows glazed. The fire was lit when they arrived, and an oil lamp was burning in one of the windows. Madeleine's work, Ailsa guessed. She had caught her sister-in-law's conspiratorial wink as she and Alasdhair left the great hall.

Ailsa was nervous. Turning to her husband for reassurance she was suddenly lifted off her feet, and carried, laughing, over the threshold. Alasdhair kicked the door shut and headed straight for the bedroom. The lamp and the firelight cast a warm glow. Flowers were everywhere. Madeleine must have scoured the entire reaches of Errin Mhor to find such quantities. Even the covers of the bed where Alasdhair set her down were strewn with petals. She had no doubt that underneath would be a twig of willow, traditionally used to bestow fertility. She had already been presented with the pot of salt and the moppet doll by the women of the village, Shona MacBrayne at their head, that signified the same thing.

She watched from the bed as Alasdhair unfastened the pin that held his *filleadh mòr* in place and divested himself of his boots and hose. Such domestic actions, but so incredibly intimate. He was her husband. She was his wife.

She couldn't quite believe it. He looked over at her and smiled, the smile that made his eyes turn smoky and made her insides turn to jelly.

'I love you, Ailsa Ross,' he said, joining her on the bed.

'And I love you,' Ailsa whispered, 'with all my heart.'

'The last few weeks have felt like years,' Alasdhair said, slowly and deliberately extracting the many pins that by a miracle had held her hair in place throughout the day. 'You have no idea how much I've longed for this moment.'

'Oh, but I do,' she said, with a shy smile. 'I do.'

He ran his fingers through her hair to spread it out over her back. He cupped her face in his palm. She tilted her head up, then he kissed her. Warmth spread through her blood like a flood of sunshine. With a sigh, she kissed him back and melted into his arms. Such strong arms. Such familiar arms. Arms that would keep her safe and hold her close for the rest of their lives.

'Make love to me, Alasdhair,' she said, wrapping her own arms around his neck and pulling him back on to the bed with her.

'I intend to,' he said.

And he proceeded to do just that, slowly divesting her of her wedding finery, lavishing kisses on every bit of flesh he exposed in the tantalising process, until she was alight with his touch. Her stockings were the last thing to go. She lay completely naked, excited, exalted by the way his eyes feasted on her, damp with anticipation at the thought of his possession of her.

'You're so lovely,' Alasdhair said, 'I can't believe you're really mine.'

He was lying on his side, running his hand over her breasts, down her stomach, to the top her thighs, dipping into the heat there, then running his fingers back up again, tantalising and teasing, stroking and stoking her into a tingling mass of clamouring nerves and throbbing heat. She could not believe she had ever hated her body. She could not believe she had ever wished her curves away, not when he looked at her so. Not when he touched her so. They were made for him to enjoy. For him to pleasure. For her pleasure. Ailsa moaned as he dipped his hand once more between her thighs. She grabbed his wrist. 'Take off your clothes. I want to see you,' she said.

He grinned and obliged far more quickly than her own fumbling fingers could have managed. When he stood before her, completely naked, she sat up, catching her breath at his stark male beauty. Her head was on a level with his stomach. She wanted to touch him as he had touched her. She wanted to learn his body as he was learning hers. She wanted to share. She stood up and reached for him, daringly fluttering her fingers over his buttocks to his flanks, round to the softer skin between his thighs, then up, to the proud length of his manhood.

Alasdhair moaned.

'Show me,' she whispered.

'You're torturing me, wife,' he said with a twisted grin, but he could not resist when she already had her fingers loosely, tantalisingly tentative, on him, and all he could think about was doing what she bid him.

Taking her by surprise, he lifted her by the waist, pulling her with him back on to the bed, so that she lay on top of him, her breasts soft mounds of delight on his chest, her nipples grazing his skin, streaking sensual pleasure. He moaned again, half-sitting up, in order to kiss her mouth, to twine his fingers into the fall of her beautiful hair, before pulling her to him and kissing her deeply, lingeringly, rousing them both to an intoxicating heat that was nigh on unbearable. They had the rest of their lives for slow pleasure; he wanted to be inside her now. Alasdhair tried to roll her over on to her back again, but Ailsa had other ideas.

She slipped from his grasp, slithering down his body, skin on skin, to kneel between his legs and drink in the shape of him. The length of him. The curve and weight of him. Awed, she touched, running her fingers over him intimately, lightly stroking, then enclosing, then cupping, and with every touch more blood surged to engorge him further, so that he wondered if he could endure without exploding. She leaned over and her nipple grazed the tip of his shaft. She gasped with the pleasure it gave her and repeated the action so that she did it again.

She wrapped her fingers around his shaft and stroked him. Alasdhair moaned, thrusting his hips upwards. She remembered that feeling when he touched her, too, and did it again, enjoying the answering surge in herself at seeing the pleasure she could etch on him, feeling him throb and pulse in her hand. She stroked again, then leaned forwards to touch her tongue to the tip of him. He tasted exactly as she felt inside. Hot and delightful. She could feel herself tightening between her legs. She wanted him there. But she wanted to touch him more. She wanted both.

Watching the pleasure and concentration on her face, seeing how her touch touched her, despite the wholly untutored nature of her caress, Alasdhair had never felt anything so deeply arousing. But he needed to be inside her urgently, now. He pulled her forwards so that his shaft nestled against her curls.

Ailsa writhed with pleasure. Below her, Alasdhair's face was flushed. His hands held her thighs. His chest rose and fell rapidly. Her own, too. She leaned forwards to kiss him and he gripped her bottom and tilted her and the tip of him nudged and slipped inside her and she kissed him as he filled her, and almost immediately he did, the pulsing, tightening coiling inside her started.

He kissed her swiftly, hard. Then he pushed her back upright, so that his erection surged up inside her, and when she moved, the twisting tantalised and teased the burgeoning bud between her folds. With his encouragement she lifted herself, then dropped back on to him, closing her eyes briefly at the whoosh of his release and plunge. Again, bracing herself, tilting forwards, and as she did, crying out with the pleasure of it. Alasdhair reached to stroke the swollen, swelling pulsing roundness and just one touch and she was lost, lost, swirling and moaning his name, but still he gripped her, and even as she pulsed around his shaft she felt it swell and surge and explode high, impossibly high inside her, and heard his answering moan, heard him say her name, and she collapsed on to the damp of his chest, just holding on to him, clinging on to him, and knowing, really knowing, what it meant to be one.

It was rude, it was ungrateful, but they were reluctant to return to the wedding feast. Wrapped in one another's arms, they wanted only to stay there for ever. It was Alasdhair who finally moved first, kissing the top of Ailsa's head and gently forcing her into an upright position.

'We have the rest of our lives,' he told her when she protested. 'We really should get back.'

They dressed slowly, with much kissing and touching and whispering of tender endearments. While she struggled with the laces of her robe, Alasdhair leaned over to pin a brooch just above her breast. A luckenbooth made of gold, two hearts entwined, with a thistle and a crown. 'A present to mark our wedding day,' he said, kissing the irresistible curve of her neck. 'I love you, Mrs Ross. I told you that we were naïve six years ago, that love changes nothing, in the real world. Well, I was wrong because love changes everything. It's certainly changed me.'

'And me,' Ailsa concurred. She smiled. 'Mrs Ross. I like that, it just sounds so right.'

'I like it, too.' Alasdhair wrapped his arms around her and kissed her deeply. 'Ailsa Ross, you have made me the happiest man in the world.'

'Then we are a well-matched pair,' Ailsa said, rubbing her cheek against his chest and drinking in the delightful essence of him, which seemed to linger at that precise spot, 'for I am most definitely the happiest woman in the world.'

'I think, then, that we'd best return to our wedding and spread that happiness among our guests.'

So that is what they did. Eventually.

One day and for always. A solemn vow. And today was that day.

* * * * *

HISTORICAL

Large Print

RAVISHED BY THE RAKE
Louise Allen

The dashing man Lady Perdita Brooke once knew is now a hardened rake, who does *not* remember their passionate night together… though Dita's determined to remind him! She's holding all the cards—until Alistair reveals the ace up his sleeve!

THE RAKE OF HOLLOWHURST CASTLE
Elizabeth Beacon

Sir Charles Afforde has purchased Hollowhurst Castle; all that's left to possess is its determined and beautiful chatelaine. Roxanne Courland would rather stay a spinster than enter a loveless marriage… But Charles' sensual onslaught is hard to resist!

BOUGHT FOR THE HAREM
Anne Herries

After her capture by corsairs, Lady Harriet Sefton-Jones thinks help has arrived in the form of Lord Kasim. But he has come to purchase Harriet for his master the Caliph! Must Harriet face a life of enslavement, or does Kasim have a plan of his own?

SLAVE PRINCESS
Juliet Landon

For ex-cavalry officer Quintus Tiberius duty *always* comes first. His task to escort the Roman emperor's latest captive should be easy. But one look at Princess Brighid and Quintus wants to put his own desires before everything else…

HIST1211 LP

HISTORICAL

Large Print

SEDUCED BY THE SCOUNDREL
Louise Allen

Rescued from a shipwreck by the mysterious Captain Luc d'Aunay, Averil Heydon is introduced to passion in his arms. Now she must return to Society and convention—except Luc has a shockingly tempting proposition for her…

UNMASKING THE DUKE'S MISTRESS
Margaret McPhee

At Mrs Silver's House of Pleasures, Dominic Furneaux is stunned to see Arabella, the woman who shattered his heart, reduced to donning the mask of Miss Noir. He offers her a way out—by making her his mistress!

TO CATCH A HUSBAND…
Sarah Mallory

Impoverished Kitty Wythenshawe knows she must marry a wealthy gentleman to save her mother from a life of drudgery. Landowner Daniel Blackwood knows Kitty cares only for his fortune—but her kisses are irresistible …

THE HIGHLANDER'S REDEMPTION
Marguerite Kaye

Calumn Munro doesn't know why he agreed to take Madeleine Lafayette under his protection, but finds that her innocence and bravery soothe his tortured soul—he might be her reluctant saviour, but he'll be her willing seducer…

MILLS & BOON

HISTORICAL

Large Print

MARRIED TO A STRANGER
Louise Allen

When Sophia Langley learns of her estranged fiancé's death, the last thing she expects is a shock proposal from his twin brother! A marriage of convenience it may be, but Sophie cannot fight the desire she feels for her reluctant husband…

A DARK AND BROODING GENTLEMAN
Margaret McPhee

Sebastian Hunter's nights, once spent carousing, are now spent in the shadows of Blackloch Hall—that is until Phoebe Allardyce interrupts his brooding. After catching her thieving, Sebastian resolves to keep an eye on this provocative little temptress!

SEDUCING MISS LOCKWOOD
Helen Dickson

Against all advice, Juliet Lockwood begins working for the notorious Lord Dominic Lansdowne. Juliet's addition to his staff is pure temptation for Dominic, but honour binds him from seduction…*unless, of course, he makes her his wife!*

THE HIGHLANDER'S RETURN
Marguerite Kaye

Alasdhair Ross was banished for courting the laird's daughter, Ailsa. Six years later, toils and troubles have shaped him into a man set on returning to claim what's rightfully his. When Ailsa sees him, she knows a reckoning is irresistibly inevitable…

HISTORICAL

Large Print

THE LADY GAMBLES
Carole Mortimer

Incognito at a fashionable gambling club, Lady Copeland is drawn to a rakish gentleman, whose burning gaze renders her quite distracted! She can't risk letting anyone close enough to expose her secret—though her body craves to give in…

LADY ROSABELLA'S RUSE
Ann Lethbridge

Lady Rosabella must pose as a widow to find the inheritance she and her sisters so desperately need! Baron Garth Evernden is known for his generosity and is so *very* handsome…surely becoming mistress to this rake would bring definite advantages?

THE VISCOUNT'S SCANDALOUS RETURN
Anne Ashley

Wrongly accused of murder, Viscount Blackwood left home disgraced. Now he has returned, and, along with the astute Miss Isabel Mortimer, he hunts the real culprit—while battling an ever-growing attraction to his beautiful companion …

THE VIKING'S TOUCH
Joanna Fulford

Courageous widow Lady Anwyn requires the protection of Wulfgar Ragnarsson, a legendary mercenary and Viking warrior. Anwyn learns from Wulfgar that not all men are monsters— but can they melt each other's frozen hearts?